THE
YOUNG WRECKER
ON THE
FLORIDA REEF

THE
YOUNG WRECKER
ON THE
FLORIDA REEF

OR, THE

Trials and Adventures of Fred Ransom.

BY   RICHARD MEADE BACHE

Introduction by Tom Corcoran

The Ketch & Yawl Press
~ Key West ~

Cover and Book Design © 1999 Tom Corcoran

Published by   The Ketch & Yawl Press
                PO Box 6891, Lakeland FL 33807
                and
                Key West Island Book Store
                531 Fleming Street, Key West FL 33040
                (888) 715-0723 / e-mail: kwbook@aol

International Standard Book Number: 0-9641735-2-2

Printed in the United States of America

INTRODUCTION.

You can't go far into this novel without asking how Richard Meade Bache could have known so many specifics of weather, lifestyle, commerce, survival, and geography in the Florida Keys of 1839 and 1840. Parts of *The Young Wrecker*'s content is history as fiction—the surprise August 7, 1840, Seminole attack on Indian Key is well documented. But Bache's descriptions of topography, backcountry channels and lakes, wave action in the Gulf Stream, native flora, and perils of the reef are so accurate, they must have been based on experience. No writer could have guessed such details, or absorbed them during a quick visit to the region.

To learn more about the author, we turned to a modern research tool—the Internet, specifically familysearch.org, the genealogical site of The Church of Jesus Christ of Latter-Day Saints, and NOAA's archives at history.noaa.gov. We also found information in *Patronage, Practice, and the Culture of American Science* by Hugh Richard Slotten (Cambridge University Press, 1994), and the University of Pennsylvania Archives and Records Center. We discovered much about Bache and those who shaped his life, and we recommend our sources for anyone desiring further information.

Born in Philadelphia, February 16, 1830, Richard Meade Bache was the son of Hartman Bache and Maria del Carmen Meade. Not incidentally, he was Benjamin Franklin's great-great-grandson, and part of an extended family of sailors, adventurers, scientists, soldiers, and intellectuals.

Benjamin Franklin's daughter Sarah, known as Sally, married Richard Bache, Jr. in Philadelphia in 1767. Bache, born in 1737, would become the third Postmaster General (Franklin was first, appointed by the Second Continental Congress). Richard and Sally's son, Benjamin Franklin

Bache, our author's grandfather (born in 1769), was the pub-
lisher of the Philadelphia-based *Aurora* who first defied the
Alien and Sedition Acts. Benjamin Franklin Bache's brother,
also Richard (born in 1784), was father of Alexander Dallas
Bache. More than any other figure in this lineage, Alexander
Bache would influence the lives and reputations of his rela-
tives throughout the nineteenth century.

Alexander Dallas Bache graduated first in his class from
the U.S. Military Academy in 1825, taught mathematics and
natural philosophy at that school, oversaw construction of
Fort Adams at Newport, Rhode Island, became a University
of Pennsylvania professor of Natural Philosophy and
Chemistry, the first president of Girard College, and eventually second Superintendent of the United States Coastal
Survey. He would become instrumental in launching such
respected organizations as the American Association for the
Advancement of Science, the Smithsonian Institution, and
the National Academy of Sciences. But it was his 1843
appointment to head the USCS that put Alexander Dallas
Bache at the forefront of United States scientific study.

At the USCS, A. D. Bache's philosophy concerning field
work was, "The life of anyone on the Coast Survey is essen-
tially and necessarily one of sacrifice for the public service,
and not of ease." His brothers, naval officers George Mifflin
Bache and (yet another) Richard Bache, had been attached
to the U.S. Coastal Survey beginning in 1838. George was
brother-in-law to naval officers David Dixon Porter and
Carlile Pollock Patterson, both of whom served on the Coast
Survey. Porter went on to head the Navy after the Civil War
while Patterson became the fourth Superintendent of the
Coast Survey. One of A. D.'s brothers-in-law was Major John
James Abert, head of the Army Topographical Engineers.
Another brother-in-law was Major W. H. Emory who became
head of the Mexican Boundary Survey and achieved distinction in the Civil War. Alexander also had a cousin in the
Army, Major Hartman Bache, the father of our author, who
was associated with coastal surveys and engineering and
lighthouse work for many years. Major Hartman Bache was

an accomplished hydrographer, topographer, and artist. During 1845-1847 he oversaw an extended topographical survey of the Dry Tortugas and the reefs of Florida. Richard Meade Bache then would have been in his mid-teens. It is quite possible that the young man accompanied his father at some point during this project.

One other relative, Army Second Lieutenant George Gordon Meade, Hartman Bache's brother-in-law (therefore our author's uncle), was in 1842 appointed to the Corps of Topological Engineers. A military engineer, he would work —often with Hartman Bache—in constructing lighthouses and breakwaters, and in coastal and geodetic work. During the Civil War he rose through the ranks to command the Army of the Potomac, fought alongside Ulysses S. Grant, and reached the grade of Major General.

One of Alexander Dallas Bache's primary USCS projects, the mapping and study of the Gulf Stream, was an extension of work begun by Postmaster General Benjamin Franklin. Franklin learned that the durations of trans-Atlantic crossings varied greatly, depending on ships' destinations and ports of departure. Once he had learned of the gulf current from Nantucket fishermen, he theorized the Stream track, put the term "Gulf Stream" into common use, and began to study the Stream's temperature, width, and speed.

In 1846, Alexander Bache sent his brother, Lieutenant Commanding George Mifflin Bache, U.S.N., in command of the United States Surveying Brig *Washington,* to study the Gulf Stream. It was not nepotism; George had commanded a Coast Survey vessel in 1839, before A. D. became his boss, had been instrumental in suggesting a standardized buoy system for United States waters, and had been a pioneer in marine geology. By the mid-1840s, George Bache was among the senior naval officers attached to the Survey. He was regarded an innovator and thinker.

After a summer's successful work in tracing Stream temperatures, the *Washington,* on September 8, 1846, was overtaken by a hurricane off the east coast. Lieutenant Bache and ten crew were swept overboard and lost. The vessel managed to reach port, and the captain's observations, made at such a cost in life, were preserved. Lieutenant Bache gave the name "Cold Wall" to the change in temperature usually found at what is supposed to be the inner edge of the Stream, and also confirmed that there were alternations of hot and cold water across the Stream. The surviving officers of the vessel praised Bache: "During the trying scenes which preceded his loss, his coolness and decision were remarkable: every thing that seamanlike skill could effect for the safety of the vessel he accomplished. He appeared never to think of himself, but, with his characteristic solicitude for the performance of his duty, only of preserving what related to that upon which he had been engaged during the cruise."

A monument in the form of a broken mast, in the Congressional Cemetery in Washington, D.C., is inscribed with the names of Lieutenant Commanding Bache and the crew members who died. These men were among the first in the United States to lose their lives in the pursuit of scientific knowledge. Another of Alexander's brothers, Lieutenant Richard Bache, later would drown after volunteering for a Navy reconnaissance survey near Point St. George, California. A footnote: it was the *Washington* that, on August 29, 1839, under temporary command of Lieutenant Richard W. Meade (possibly Richard Meade Bache's cousin, or maternal grandfather), seized the renegade "Black Schooner" *Amistad* (a/k/a *La Armistead*). Listed among officers then aboard the *Washington* was another relative, R. W. Bache.

Having enrolled in the University of Pennsylvania for the school years 1846-1847, and 1847-1848, our author left college to join the USCS. The death of George M. Bache must have occurred while young Richard Meade Bache was spending his first months at sea.

In the mid-1850s, R. M. Bache explored the Louisiana coast for the USCS. NOAA's records include this passage:

"Approaching the delta of the Mississippi River, the character of the country changed rapidly. Assistant R. M. Bache, in charge of the Coast Survey Schooner *G.M. Bache,* [named in honor of his father's deceased cousin] conducted a topographic survey of Lake Borgne in 1856. His report noted problems that exceeded those of working in Florida:

"'In the country which I have just surveyed the cane was in many places so high as to render necessary the use of a portable platform, and so dense as to greatly impede the movements of the party, requiring sometimes the forward signal to be carried ahead in an extra boat, and the back signal to be sent for in the same way; so that, instead of making from thirty to thirty-five stations in a day, which can readily be done on the outside shore-line, generally only ten could be made, and those with the greatest labor.'"

Richard Meade Bache remained with the Coast Survey for forty years. He wrote *The Young Wrecker* while in his mid-thirties. Published first in 1869, *The Young Wrecker* was reprinted four times in two years, and a fifth time in 1887. It is easy to understand that Bache's knowledge of the work of the famed scientist Louis Agassiz (sent by Alexander Dallas Bache to study the Keys in 1849; his voluminous 1851 report remains a scientific milestone), and the studies of his father, Hartman Bache, plus his own experiences (as noted in his original preface, included here), led to his mastery of Keys lore and lifestyle.

Bache wrote *Vulgarisms and Other Errors of Speech* (1869), *American Wonderland* (1871, on Native American folk tales) and *Under the Palmetto in Peace and War* (1880). In 1897, H.T. Coates, Philadelphia, published Bache's biography of his uncle, *Life of General George Gordon Meade, Commander of the Army of the Potomac*.

Richard Meade Bache had seven brothers and sisters, two of whom died in childhood, and none of whom lived beyond age thirty-three. He married twice, and died in 1907. He was survived by a son, Rene Bache, and a daughter, Edith Markoe Bache.

-Tom Corcoran, September, 1999

An artist for *Harper's New Monthly,* in 1858, sketched this Florida Keys wrecker at the helm of a salvage boat.

PREFACE.

The author has endeavored, in the following story, to deviate as little as possible from fact, so as to combine instruction with amusement. Personal familiarity with the scene of the tale has enabled him to make its descriptions strictly accurate. The incidents are natural, many of them having actually occurred. The original Dr. Cluzel was the well-known Dr. Perrine, whose amiable character, and great enthusiasm in the cause of science, caused his untimely death to be universally regretted. The warning received by the Indian Key settlement, as introduced in the story, is historically untrue. The attack by the Indians was a surprise.

-R.M.B.

CONTENTS.

xiv

xvi

THE
YOUNG WRECKER
ON THE
FLORIDA REEF

CHAPTER I

AN OLD BACHELOR INTRODUCES HIMSELF TO THE YOUNG READER—
DESCRIBES HIS PRESENT APPEARANCE AND FEELINGS—TELLS THE
STORY OF THE ADVENTURES OF HIS BOYHOOD.

I AM an old bachelor. I have reached that time of life at which we old fellows are generally supposed to be fat, and to wear gold spectacles and very easy shoes. If you will picture me thus, the result will be a sufficiently accurate portrait of my personal appearance and identity.

Although I am about to write some of my own adventures, I do not purpose writing about my present self, but of myself when I was very different from the sketch which I have made. Every old bachelor was once a young one, and every young one was once still younger, when, although a bachelor, he was known only as a boy. It is the story of the boy, who is now an old bachelor, that I am about to narrate.

As you may perchance wish to know something of the character and feelings of the person who addresses you, and how he came to do so, I will indulge your curiosity.

We old fellows have not all those cares of family which fill the hours of others with pleasurable duty, and time often hangs heavily on our hands. Many of us try to do our duty. Heaven forbid that we should be blind to the need that this world has of earnest workers! But, after all, a man may minister to the needs of others, and yet there come vacant hours, when he must return to himself, and require ministering to his own. If he lacks not plenty of the goods of this world, he may have heart yearnings that are quite as pitiable as hunger, thirst, and want of shelter. Would that every one could be spared the sharp pang that I have sometimes experienced

1

when fondling the joy and pride of some household,—the chubby boy who tossed his arms with glee, and twined his little hands in my shaggy beard!

Sometimes, especially at night, when I return to my lonely chambers, and feel the influence of a home where there is no presence of a life closely allied to mine, a vague, aching sense of void bends over my nature. But these are feelings which you are now too young to comprehend, and which I trust that you may never experience.

I read, walk, go where my services are needed, I force myself to accomplish set tasks; but yet, with all this, I am not contented. Of friends I am not destitute. One may possess friends, and still be very lonely; for one cannot live forever at their houses. So it happens that I generally dine at my club, but now and then I accept a friend's hospitality. But I am not sufficiently engaged, for regular employment is necessary to happiness. I will write, thought I. If I have no boys of my own to listen to the story of their father's life, the family of boys in the world is large enough to gratify my wish for hearers. I had often thought of writing it, but my intentions came to nought, until a trivial incident, occurring a few days ago, fixed my resolution to carry out the project.

I will now tell you the circumstance which determined me to write, to show you upon what trifles great undertakings sometimes hinge,—for it is no small undertaking to write a book,—and then I shall enter upon the story of my adventures.

The other day, I returned home after a lonely dinner, and throwing myself back in an easy chair, I went off into an after-dinner reverie. It was a warm afternoon,—one of those when the atmosphere seems to hum with heat. At such a time, one's senses to be peculiarly alive to the impression of sounds, the faintest murmur being articulate, and yet a part of one grand chorus. A big fly kept droning around the room, except when it inserted itself in a crevice, and extricated itself with a whiz and dash against the nearest obstruction. Lulled by the intense heat and the buzz of the insect, my mind rambled away to the places in which I had spent some of my earlier years. I vividly recalled the tropical scenes, among which I had passed my days. They came to me like a story of adventure, and passed in review as if a diorama unrolled before me. Suddenly the big fly struck violently against my face. I started, and made a switch at it with my pocket handkerchief.

"Too bad," I thought, "to miss the rest." I laughed aloud, as I exclaimed with delight,—"Why, it is my own story. If it could be so interesting as a reminiscence, why would it not prove interesting to those who have never heard it? My mind is made up. I will write it for the entertainment of others, and for my own."

CHAPTER II

OUR HERO, MOVED BY A SPIRIT OF ADVENTURE, BEGS HIS FATHER TO GRANT HIM PERMISSION TO MAKE A VOYAGE—HE IS REFUSED—REPINES AT WHAT HE CONSIDERS HIS HARD FATE—MAKES THE ACQUAINTANCE OF THE SON OF A SEA CAPTAIN—RENEWS HIS REQUEST TO HIS FATHER, AND IS AGAIN REFUSED—VISITS HIS FRIEND, AND RUNS AWAY BY ACCIDENT.

I WAS born not of "poor but respectable parents," as the phrase goes, but of respectable parents who were well-to-do in the world. At an early age, my father settled in New York. He was an Englishman, born in the town of Sheffield. Soon after his arrival in this country, he established himself in New York, in the business for which Sheffield is famed, and very soon afterwards he married the lady who was the mother of our hero—myself. Not many years after that event, my poor mother died. Not so early, however, that I have not a distinct recollection of her; but early enough for me to lose, at a tender age, the affection and cherished counsel which exercise so great an influence over the life of every one who has been so fortunate as to possess them.

My father intended me for his own business, but having a thorough appreciation of the value of a good education for everyone, no matter what course of life may be pursued, he placed me at an excellent school in the city, intending to keep me there until I should be at least seventeen years of age. Without having any distaste for business generally, or for my father's business in particular, I grew up with that indefinable longing that is common to many boys—a desire to roam. A vague feeling constantly beset me that I must ramble somewhere in the world. I persuaded myself that if my wish were gratified, my propensity might be overcome. It was not long before I imparted these feelings to my father, and begged him to let me go upon a voyage of some sort; but I found him opposed to it, and I thought him obdurate. He represented to me that my wish was nothing but a senseless craving for excitement, and that if it were manfully resisted, it could be subdued, and that it was my duty to conquer it. All this he said to me, talking as many a father has done to his son and will do fruitlessly to the end of time. My arguments were based, as I have intimated, upon the very reverse reasoning. I contended that the gratification of my wish would serve the purpose of allaying my desire, and that deprivation would only serve to increase it. We could come to no satisfactory conclusion, as we were so diametrically opposed, and time passed, and, after a while, the subject was not resumed between us. I saw that he was fixed in his determination not to give his consent to my wish, and when, after many unavailing attempts to shake his purpose, I came to this conclusion, I was silent in reference to the matter.

Meanwhile, I continued to go to school, and to fulfill my duties, but I also continued to brood over the hard fate, as I thought it, which prevented me from seeing something of the world, and which would probably sentence me to a life spent without ever visiting those scenes which I delighted to picture in my mind. Whether it was that I had a natural propensity for rambling, or whether the obstinacy of my nature had been aroused by the opposition with which the first expression of my wishes had been met, or whether both these causes conspired to render me impatient of control, and doubly desirous of escape from it, I do not know, but certain it is that my longing to travel somewhere became daily more intense. However, I pursued my studies with some relish, for books have always been to me sources of interest and enjoyment. But the undercurrent of my existence was the vain, ill-defined desire which I have expressed to you. Possessed with this constant longing, which seemed immeasurably removed from the possibility of gratification, it gradually became my habit to frequent a certain tier of wharves which were situated at a convenient distance from our house. In my uneasy condition of mind, I felt that if I could not travel, there was some solace in being near the instruments with which man has learned to conquer space, and transport the arts and treasures of other lands to his own door. These wharves of which I speak were chiefly frequented by a class of small vessels which brought fruit from the West Indies to the New York market. Laden with fragrant oranges, bananas, and other tropical fruit which, heaped up in fabulous profusion, seemed to me to have brought with them the very atmosphere of the sunny climes in which they grew, these tiny vessels possessed to my youthful eyes the beauty of gondolas. And yet they were sorry-looking vessels, the largest not more than a hundred tons burthen.

Of course, it was not long before I formed the acquaintance of some of the people who sailed in them, and naturally enough, too, I first made the acquaintance of a boy who was about my own age and who turned out to be the son of the captain of one of the largest of the vessels. From that time forward, my desire to go to sea became more uncontrollable than ever. I sometimes passed the whole of my leisure in the cabin of his schooner, and often diverted myself by imagining that we were at sea. Boy-like, I soon frankly confided to him my wishes, and the ill-success that they had met when I expressed them to my father. He consoled me by saying that the "old man would come around after awhile," but he observed that, for his part, he could not see why I was so anxious to go wandering about, especially to leave such a city as New York, where there were lots of fun going on all the time. He only wished that he could change with me for that then we would both be suited, for he would give me his place, and welcome.

"Where was the fun," said he, "in pitching around at sea, between New York and the West Indies, when a fellow could live all the time in a city, and go to the theatre, and have a regular jolly time."

6

I replied that it was all very well for him to talk in that way, when he, although so young, had seen something of the world, in touching along the coasts of Mexico, South America, and the West Indies, but I felt that I had, in comparison, seen nothing. My visits generally ended by our spending the evening together at some entertainment, which he declared to be better fun than going to sea, and joked me about asking our fathers whether they would not swap sons.

This acquaintance was not particularly congenial, except from his being associated with my chief desire. Soon after meeting him, his father's vessel made two or three voyages, and I saw him only at intervals of several months. During the absence of the vessel, I committed all sorts of vagaries. I used to go down to the wharf and take a look at the berth in which she usually lay, and everything connected with voyaging had now become so dear to me, that I kept in one of my pockets a piece of tarred rope, such as sailors call old junk, and this I would sometimes furtively withdraw and smell, as if it exhaled the most delicate perfume.

The vessel had been absent for three or four months, after I made the acquaintance of the captain's son, when she came into port about the middle of September. It was in the year 1839. As usual, many hours had not elapsed before I heard of her arrival, and paid a visit to the wharf. For several days, I made my customary visits to the place. One day as I parted from my friend, who was called Charley Edson, I mentioned that I should probably be unable to see him on the morrow, as it would be my fifteenth birthday, and my father had intimated that we would spend it together as a holiday. He answered that I must be sure to come on the following day, for that they had sold their cargo, and intended to sail as soon as some other business was transacted.

The next day my father proposed that we should make an excursion to a certain place—one of the numerous beautiful spots by which New York is surrounded. I eagerly acceded to his proposition, and we started off together.

It is not necessary to my story to enlarge upon the events of this trip, for I cannot even now recall my father's kindness, and his solicitude for my enjoyment, without pain at the recollection of the sequel. Perceiving that he was in an unusually pleasant mood, I judged that a favorable opportunity had arrived, to resume the subject upon which I had been so long silent. I therefore commenced by reminding him that I was now fifteen years of age, and represented to him that I had lately shown my discretion by not urging him to grant my wishes; but that now, as they were as strong as ever, and I had, for some time, zealously pursued my studies, I hoped that he would permit me to indulge in at least one voyage. At this discourse his countenance fell, and I saw, subsequently, that his pleasure for the day had gone. However, he replied, kindly, that he wished me, as he had already said, to continue my studies until I was at least seventeen years of age. He remarked, that he had hoped I had given up my whim, and seen how foolish it was. It was best, he continued, that I should remain at school for two or three years longer, and then settle down into a business man, and aid him in his affairs, the burden of which was daily increasing.

It was my turn now to be disappointed, and the rest of our holiday passed uncomfortably enough. I had not a thought that was not loving and filial, or else I would not have been so sad.

Late in the afternoon we returned to the city. My father parted from me kindly, saying, as I went towards my room, "You will think better of this, my son, and one of these days, you will know that I am right." I was sorrowful and vexed—sorrowful that my scheme had again miscarried, and vexed with myself because I had caused my dear father unhappiness on a day when he had sought to contribute to my pleasure.

In this uneasy frame of mind, I wandered out of the house, about dusk, and mechanically bent my steps towards the wharves which I frequented. The shades of evening deepened as I walked along, and lamp after lamp was lighted along the streets through which I passed. By the time that I had reached the river, night had fallen, and the badly illuminated docks looked gloomier than usual, owing to my emerging from the brilliant streets of the city. Here and there one could discern the tracery of rigging defined against the sky. An occasional glimmer of a smoky lamp, a hoarse voice, the fall of a plank, or something of the sort, now and then indicated that the vessels at the wharves were not wholly deserted. The night was very sultry, and I sauntered leisurely along, until I reached the place where the schooner lay.

The only person about seemed to be the cook, who was stirring around his galley, making preparations for his next day's duties. I hailed him, and asked where all the people were. He told me that the men had gone to town for a while, and that the captain and his son had gone there too, on business, as the schooner was to sail early in the morning, so as to take advantage of the first of the ebb, for the tide would turn to run out about daylight. I answered that I would wait, and seated myself on the taffrail, and watched the lights of the shipping which lay at anchor in the harbor. The tide was running out then, so there would be one intervening tide before the one which was to serve the schooner. As the stream flowed swiftly by the vessel, as she lay bow foremost in one of the wharf slips, the laving, gently plashing sound was most agreeable on an evening so hot. I became impatient of waiting, however, and after I had amused myself with seeing all that could be seen on deck, I resorted to the cabin, and took a seat on a cushioned locker.

I felt sure that my friend would not return before ten o'clock, but as I had determined to wait, I lay down on the locker and thought over my day's excursion, my father's disappointment and mine. At last I fell into a doze. When I awakened, I thought, from my feelings, that I must have been sleeping soundly. I awoke giddy; everything seemed to reel around me. With a strong effort, I fully aroused myself, jumped up, and staggered across to the other side of the cabin. Sick at the stomach, I clambered with difficulty up the companionway, and plunged into the arms of a man at the helm.

I was at sea!

CHAPTER III

THE MYSTERY OF THE PRECEDING CHAPTER EXPLAINED—OUR HERO'S PAINFUL REFLECTIONS—HIS POSITION ON THE SCHOONER—FLYING FISH, PORPOISES, DOLPHINS, WHALES—DIVERSIONS OF THE CREW—SOUTHERN CROSS—GULF STREAM—WATERSPOUTS—ARRIVAL OFF THE PORT OF HAVANA—GLOOMY FOREBODINGS AGAIN OVERWHELM OUR HERO—HIS LETTER HOME—CAPTAIN EDSON'S SYMPATHY AND ADVICE.

I PLUNGED, as I said, on deck, and into the arms of the steersman, who staggered against the wheel as I lurched over to leeward, and, steadying myself by a strong effort, glanced around just in time to see the captain and my friend rushing aft with blank amazement written on their faces. Blank as they looked, my expression must have out-rivaled theirs, as I stood supporting myself by the rail of the vessel, and swaying to and fro with every roll of the sea—sea-sickness and dismay blended in my countenance.

"How did you get here?" breathlessly ejaculated the captain, as soon as he and his son reached my side. My friend uttered not a word. I saw, at a glance, that he thought I was a regular stowaway.

At this point, the poetical unities of time, place, and action, suggest that I should introduce a thrilling passage consisting of a pathetic appeal to be put ashore. The soberness of truth, however, induces me to tell the fact, that, at the moment when the captain greeted me with the words, "How did you got here?" a spasmodic effort contracted my body, I turned from him, and falling heavily on the rail, and hanging over it like a limp bolster, I poured forth those libations which man offers alike to Bacchus and to Neptune.

11

I dwell not upon the ensuing scene, in which I made a fruitless attempt to explain the fact of my presence. I was assisted to the cabin, and induced to lie down until a more favorable opportunity for talking should arise. They would have left me on deck, for the benefit of fresh air, had not the sea been running so high, that the schooner was constantly wet from stem to stern by spray, and occasionally shipped some water.

Although I was not in a condition to explain matters, I was not so far overcome that I could not think; and the misery of the ensuing hours, during which, perfectly realizing my situation, I turned over in my mind the occurrences of the preceding day, was almost intolerable. The thought of what my father must imagine made me wretched, when, in addition, I recollected that I was absolutely powerless to control the course of events.

Two days elapsed before I was able to crawl from the berth which my boy-friend kindly relinquished for my benefit. But long before that, mutual explanations had been made of the occurrence which appeared so extraordinary; and which, nevertheless, happened in so simple a manner, that that is the point which is really extraordinary.

It seems that the cook of the vessel had correctly informed me, when he told me that the captain and his son had gone to the city on business, and that the men were also off on leave, in anticipation of sailing in the morning. It happened that the captain and his son, when on their return, came across the sailors, who were engaged in carousing, and making a disturbance in one of the streets adjacent to the vessel. Perceiving, at a glance, that if he was to carry out his purpose of sailing in the morning, he must ensure the presence of his crew, who might be commencing one of those sprees which sailors sometimes prolong for two or three days, the captain halted, and, after a long altercation, in which promises and threats were mingled in about equal proportions, he managed to prevail upon his men to accompany him to the schooner, where they arrived in a very lurching and sea-men's last-day-on-shore fashion.

After getting them aboard and below, the captain was puzzled to know what to do next, for the men were in that rickety condition of moral perception, when they would have readily made the most solemn promise not to go ashore again, and would have broken it the next minute without the slightest compunction. In this dilemma, he chanced to look at the river, and perceived that the tide was still ebb. In a moment, he made up his mind to secure his crew, by taking advantage of the last of that ebb, instead of waiting for six hours, and then taking the first of the morning's ebb. No sooner said than done. A schooner does not require many men to handle her. The captain, his son, and the cook soon cast off the hawsers by which she was made fast to the wharf, and by putting her jib aback, forced her out of the slip. In a few minutes all sail was set, and we were underway, with a fair wind.

The cook, it appeared, had seen me sitting on the taffrail, where I had taken my station to await my friend's arrival; but soon missing me, he concluded that I had gone home. At that very moment, however, I was sleeping with a boy's heavy slumber, and with the lethargy entailed by a long and hot day's excursion, and a previously agitated condition of mind. The sea, at first, was comparatively smooth, and the motion had been violent only for a short period preceding the time when I arrived on deck. The men, having been ascertained to be incapable of duty, the sole remaining chance which I would have had of being discovered by the captain or his son, failed, as they, with the cook, were obliged to remain all night on deck, and navigate the vessel.

The affair is now explained. Morning dawned, and found us far out of sight of land, the men just returning to their duties, one having already been stationed at the wheel; and the captain and his son would, within a few minutes, have found me in the cabin, had I not at last awakened, owing to the violent rolling of the vessel, and rushing up on deck, discovered myself to their astonished eyes.

The question soon arose as to what was to be done. What could not be done was very plain—at least to the captain. If I had ever had the slightest notion that he would touch at some point on the coast and land me, I was soon disabused of that impression. Every sea captain, even the most amiable, has the idea that the laws of his vessel, be she never so small, are as immutable as those of the universe. Nothing renders the human mind so despotic, as the command of a few planks at the mercy of the elements.

It was clear that I could not land anywhere short of the place where it had been decided that the schooner was to make a port unless, indeed, we were to be shipwrecked, an event not likely to befall a vessel possessed of a captain accustomed to the coast along which we sailed.

After much debate, it was finally settled that, as the vessel was not to return to New York before three or four months, I should be left at Havana, at which place she was to stop for a few hours on her way to one or two ports in the islands to the southward of Cuba.

Idleness at sea is an abomination in the eyes of every good skipper, and I was soon set at work to earn my right to the passage which I was taking very much against my will. I was very anxious to do what I could, to render my title good to my board and lodging, and to ingratiate myself with the captain, who, all things considered, treated me very kindly. Not that I was really so much indebted to him, if I faithfully performed the tasks allotted to me, for there is always so much to do about a vessel, that any supernumerary can fairly earn his salt. But my introduction had been so unceremonious, that notwithstanding its being unintentional, the affair was very likely to try the patience of many a man. Here was I, neither officer nor common seaman,—a passenger without money or clothes, and, on account of many circumstances, to be got rid of at the first opportunity that offered, and yet to be got rid of with decency, and as the friend of the captain's son, although an uninvited guest, occupying a place in a cabin where there was little room to spare, even to one most welcome.

As to my own feelings, I had settled into a frame of mind in which, although still distressed at the late event, I had summoned up my fortitude, in order to make the best of everything and to be guided by circumstances. I resolved that I would write to my father the very moment we arrived at Havana. As for returning to his house before I received some intimation of his pleasure, reflection showed me that such would not be the most prudent course; for I now felt, to the full extent, how almost impossible it must be for him to credit the statement which I had to make, that the occurrence which followed the conversation on my birthday had no connection with it, but was a mere coincidence. I made up my mind to write to him, to explain everything, and to await his reply before going home. If he told me to return, I would return immediately. Whether he believed me or not, I resolved that my course should be equally obedient. I must wait, however, to learn his decision. I had no doubt that, in the meantime, I, a strong, healthy lad, could successfully measure myself with the world, and earn my own livelihood.

For a few days after sailing, the wind proved light and baffling, and we did not make much progress. My sea-sickness wore off, and I began, in a measure, to relish the novelty of the life and scenes by which I was surrounded. At last, a whole-sail breeze from the northwest set in. The vessel careened with every stitch of canvas set, and steered due south.

As we sailed farther and farther south, we began to find our clothes oppressive. I had no change, and my friend no change to spare, so I suffered at first from what, after all, was a very petty inconvenience.

The vessel's track often lay through water alive with schools of flying-fish. These, when alarmed at our approach, or at that of some voracious fish in search of prey, often leaped by hundreds from the water, and skimmed along just above the surface of the waves, on which they occasionally struck and with a ricochet prolonged their flight. They make no movement with their wings, which they merely extend

upon leaping from the water with the impetus of their previous speed through that medium. On rising above its surface, the wind propels them, and judging by the manner in
which they sometimes slant their wings, and diverge from
their original course, the probability is that they possess the
power adroitly to take advantage of the different currents of
wind; or, with the same current, to modify, in some measure,
the direction of their flight. The wings of this fish are its
long pectoral fins. They are slight, translucent, and supported by delicate spines. To show you that, beyond a very limited degree, the flying-fish cannot control the direction of its
flight, you only need be informed that it often flies over the
bulwarks of a vessel and falls on her deck. It frequently
comes aboard at night, and, in that way, we sometimes found
a mess of fish all ready for the pan.

Porpoises we saw by thousands. They disported themselves about the vessel, seemingly without the slightest fear.
They are much quicker than the fastest steamship underway.
They often indulge in queer freaks. As I watched them under
the bow of the schooner, I often saw one swim with its tail
almost grazing the cut-water. In that position it would adopt
the same course as that of the schooner, without deviating
so much as half a point, and swim thus for a minute or two,
then dart off, and return almost immediately to its station.

We once saw a school of whales; but they were too far
off to be distinctly visible. Of course, there were many other
fish which we saw, and many sea-birds were often in sight.
We were ceaselessly followed by the inevitable Mother
Carey's chickens.

I must not omit that wonder of wonders, the dolphin.
The men harpooned one of these fish, and all hands were
soon collected to see a sight which is always fascinating. My
satisfaction was marred by knowing that what gratified our
curiosity was agony to the poor creature.

If you expect, from my description, to receive anything
like an adequate idea of the beauty of the dolphin, you will
be astonished when you see one. No painter that ever lived,

could paint a dolphin, for he would have to paint fifty dolphins, in colors of a brilliancy which art of man has not yet produced. I can but give you a faint impression of what I saw.

Recall the colors of rich changeable silks, or all that ever charmed you in a soap bubble, and then imagine a great fish with these gorgeous hues covering the glossy surface of its body. On emerging from the water, it looks as if it had come from a bath of rainbow. The prismatic colors blend, dissolve, renew, and fade away. With convulsive throes the fish approaches its death agony, and then slowly the colors pass away and a cold, ashen, lead-like hue steals over the body. The dolphin is then dead.

The weather was so fine that no one spent much time below. As there was not much distinction between quarterdeck and forward, we boys generally found ourselves grouped with the sailors, under shelter of the bulwark to windward. There I was for the first time instructed in all those mysteries of tying intricate knots, splicing, plaiting, carving, sewing, and the thousand and one knickknackeries with which the sailor beguiles his moments of leisure. As the wind was now fair, there was scarcely anything to be done from morning till evening, except to wash the decks down at daylight, and to take an occasional turn at the wheel.

We had so much leisure that, at last, even the amusement of making knots began to fail, from sheer exhaustion of all the various devices; and symptoms of a desire to tattoo every body within reach took possession of one of the sailors, who was adept in that branch of the fine arts. As I had not the slightest mark upon my person, I was looked upon as a very desirable subject upon which to practice a little etching, but I resisted all overtures, and he was forced to content himself with adding a few dolphins to the waters which surrounded a ship under full sail that decorated the arm of one of the old salts. Although I have been a good deal at sea since that time, I have never changed my mind about this kind of ornamentation, which many a boy has been silly enough to adopt and heartily repented.

17

The Southern Cross was now visible. I must say that I was much disappointed in this constellation. Like most others, it has no very marked figure. It can be recognized as a cross, but it is a very misshapen and lopsided one.

Grand, mysterious, awful, I thought the waste of waters, but they were not blue. I could not distinguish blue, or else the sea was not blue, but a dull green in bright light, varying in shadow to a slaty tint. I found that the seamen did not trouble themselves much about such investigations. I inquired of Captain Edson, who briefly replied that the sea was blue in some places and green in others. This answer made me hope that we should come to one of the places where it was blue. As he had not volunteered to tell me more than I mention, I did not press him, for a captain of a small vessel is a very great dignitary, not to be approached when at sea, except with much awe and circumspection.

We soon stood in further to the westward. As we had been steering south, we had kept well away from the coast, to avoid the current of the Gulf Stream, which, you remember, leaves the Gulf of Mexico, and after running parallel with the coast of the United States for some distance, gradually recedes from it until off the Banks of Newfoundland, whence it is deflected in the direction of Europe. The weather was so clear, and the wind so favorable, that Captain Edson determined to run toward the westward until he neared the edge of the Gulf Stream, and then lay a new course for Havana. He altered the direction of the vessel by a few points, and we then felt as if we had almost reached our destination. The slightest incident at sea, looking to a prospective arrival, no matter how distant, gives zest to life aboard ship. We changed our course about daylight, and before eleven o'clock I saw plainly, by the great number of birds, that we must have greatly reduced our distance from land. Very far from the coast, even at the greatest distance at which we had sailed, sea-birds had followed in the wake of the vessel, but now they were ten times as numerous.

About 11 A.M. I was standing near the captain, when he

turned suddenly to me, and, pointing over the vessel's bow, said, "There, my boy, you said you wanted to see blue water. I hope you will find that blue enough for your taste. That is the Gulf Stream."

I looked ahead, and saw at about two or three cables' lengths off, that the color of the water was entirely different. But it looked dark; I could not detect the slightest bluish tint. I had barely time to say so timidly, when the vessel clove her way into the dark liquid, and, in the schooner's length, we passed from the faint green sea into the deepest indigo that you can conceive. I almost shouted with delight. The water in which we were sailing seemed to be a different medium from that which we had left. It was so dark that it looked as if it could not be so thin as the other—so watery. When the shadows of the clouds rested on it, it was as black as night, but when the sun shone out, it lighted up with every tint of blue, from dark indigo in the trough of the wave, to light, brilliant blue, just before the feathery crest broke into diamond spray. I could have stood for hours on deck, gazing at this phenomenon, had we continued in the stream; but the captain had no idea of stemming a strong current of several miles an hour, and he kept away by changing his direction to the southward and eastward, and, in a few minutes, during which we ran on the edge of the stream, we gradually left it, and in an hour or two shaped our course afresh for Havana.

The next day I saw another sight,—a water-spout, or, I should say, many water-spouts. The weather was extremely hot, and great clouds which, to my inexperienced eye, seemed to betoken immediate rain, gathered in huge masses, like mountains in the sky. As I was watching these form and dissolve, and change unceasingly, I suddenly observed a tiny cone protrude from one. I knew in a moment what it was. Then, a similarly shaped object arose from the sea. The upper cone gradually grew longer and longer, all the time approaching the other, and waving gently to and fro with the action of the wind.

Little is known of the cause of this phenomenon, which occurs on land as well as at sea. In the former place, there is not sufficient moisture to produce the lower cone. At sea, sometimes the upper cone is the first to form, and, at other times, the lower one precedes it. There are many variations, too numerous to describe in this place.

The water-spout is supposed to be similar in character to the dust-storms which prevail in portions of Asia, Africa, and in the interior of South America. The best authorities on the subject ascribe the phenomenon to the action of the wind, but confess that it is marked by a highly electrical condition. There are other theories, but I have told you enough of what relates to the scientific part of the phenomenon, and I now return to the description of the way in which it generally looks at sea.

There is no appearance to which the upper cone in motion can be so well compared, as to the gently waving, hesitating manner with which an elephant approaches its proboscis to an object on the ground. No sooner do the cones meet than an agitation seems to take place, and the column, reaching from sea to heaven, commences to reel and whirl rapidly off; until broken and dissipated in its frantic waltz. Sometimes I saw three or four water-spouts at the same time, either formed, or in various stages of formation. Occasionally, a cloud would let down its trunk for some distance, and then withdraw it, as if it had concluded not to take a drink at that place.

From certain indications, it is known that the column is not composed solely of vapor, but that a great body of water is actually suspended in the air. It is possible, therefore, that as the column is continuous, water from the sea may be carried up and enter the vapor of the clouds. We know that the clouds, by the reverse process, discharge their vapor in the form of water. Some observers state that the column in breaking invariably discharges fresh water.

On the morning of the day following the last of which I have spoken, the captain announced to us boys that we would probably arrive off Havana by evening, but that he was afraid he could not reach there before sundown, in which case, we would not be able to enter the port before daylight the next morning. A regulation of the port of Havana forbids vessels to enter after sundown. The reason assigned for this rule is, that the shipping is so crowded in the harbor, that vessels entering at night endanger those lying at anchor.

As the captain had surmised, we arrived too late,—just in time to see the first glimmer from the lighthouse which stands at the entrance of the harbor. However, we had known for an hour that we would not be able to get into the harbor that night. The captain, after some orthodox grumbling and knocking around everything within reach, steered away and got a good offing, still within sight of the light, and here we lay off and on, as they say at sea, all night. The captain and Charley soon turned in, after the former had given some directions as to the sailing of the vessel. They were soon sound asleep, and I was left alone with my meditations.

These were not of the most pleasant kind. In a few hours, I was to lose the only friends I had in those parts, and be put ashore in a country where I did not even speak the language of the people. However bravely youngsters may frequently talk,—and they do often indulge in that way,—when it comes to such a pinch, they are not apt to consider themselves more than a match for any difficulty, as they would lead people to suppose when the difficulty is imaginary. I confess that I felt my courage quite abated now, when I was in sight of the spot where my self-reliance was to be put to the test. As I sat at the cabin table, with my face buried in my hands, the better to exclude external objects, and bring my thoughts to a focus, I did not feel myself to be such an intellectual and physical giant as I had deemed myself when I purposed grappling with the world. I felt that I was a boy, and not a very big one either, nor a very wise one for his years, few as they were. In fact, I felt very miserable, and I,— the cabin was very dark, and the captain and Charley were fast asleep,—well I blubbered. You must not mention it. Of course, it was very babyish. You would have done very differently, you think. Pooh! That is just what I would have said, had I been told of such a scrape as the one in which I found myself, but,—I blubbered. How long I continued to cry I do not know, but I was suddenly startled by a gruff voice from the captain's berth.

"Hollo, my fine fellow," said the voice, as a tumbled-looking head protruded from the curtains. "Have you taken so much to the sea that you are brimming over with salt water?"

The head nodded at me in a kindly way, and I saw that it meant its words to cause me to cheer up.

"Captain," I stammered in reply, "if I had only known you took a little interest in me, this would not have happened; but I didn't like to speak to you, and ask your advice."

"Speak away," said he, bringing his legs outside of the berth, sitting bent forward on the edge of it. "You mustn't suppose because I'm not inclined to lay much out on words, that I haven't got some heart for other people's troubles. I knew you'd have to speak to me afore you went ashore, and I just waited till you raised a signal of distress."

Upon this I opened my heart freely, and, in the course of half an hour's talk, found that I had mistaken the captain's nature, as boys are very apt to do in the case of their elders. He told me that he would be obliged to land me,—that was certain,—but that he would do everything in his power to aid me in getting shipped aboard of some vessel. In reply, I mentioned my projected letter to my father, and my intention not to return to New York until I received news from him. After cogitating awhile, he approved of this; and added that, as I might tomorrow ship aboard of some vessel which might be on the eve of sailing, I had better write my letter at once. So he got out his ink bottle, and a few dilapidated pens, which looked as if they had been used for cleaning bedsteads; and I was once more left alone, as the captain rolled over into his berth with a last kind word and a cheery good night.

So, by the light of a miserable lamp, and with the aid of

a miserable pen, and my own thoughts, more miserable than both, I wrote to my father, and narrated all that the reader knows. And, meanwhile, we tacked to and fro, and the night waned, and day had almost broken before I threw myself exhausted and feverish into the berth by the side of Charley.

CHAPTER IV

SUNRISE OFF HAVANA—THE HARBOR—THE WRECKER FLYING
CLOUD—CAPTAIN EDSON'S PROMISE—HIS VISIT TO THE WRECKER—
MINGLED DESPONDENCY AND HOPE.

AINLY did I essay to sleep. The bustle and the swash of water overhead, as the crew sluiced the decks, the noise made by my companions while dressing, and the rapidly increasing light prevented my obtaining the rest which I courted. I dressed myself and joined the groups on deck. We were about three miles from land. As I looked towards shore, I could distinctly perceive the lighthouse and some of the dwellings near Havana. The wind was ahead, and we were beating towards the harbor. The only thing on the water was a schooner, which, by her evolutions, appeared to be making for the same destination.

There is something inexpressibly lovely in a fair weather sunrise at sea in a tropical climate. The air which, later in the day, becomes too fervid, is then tempered with a pleasant coolness. Gliding through the dark blue waters that encroach upon the very shores of Cuba, surrounded by the peaceful-looking sky, and inhaling the sea breeze, just scented with fragrance from the land, one may travel far without finding a lovelier scene than a clear sunrise off Havana.

The schooner which I had noticed was sailing on the opposite tack, and we rapidly increased our distance from each other. Just as we went about, I observed that the other vessel was also in stays. We then rapidly approached each other, and I could distinguish a long, low, fast-sailing vessel, flying at her peak what I took to be the American flag.

I ran forward to find the captain, who was seeing that

the chain was all clear, preparatory to letting the anchor go in the harbor. I pointed out the flag to him.

"Yes," said he, glancing up, and answering, as if he understood my thoughts. "If I don't mistake, you are in luck." After another look at her, he resumed, "If things can be arranged, as I guess we can manage, this vessel will suit you to a T. You see, according to your plan, as you didn't want to return immediately to the North, I was puzzled; for, said I to myself, of course, he cannot very well find employment in Havana, for he don't speak Spanish, and, likewise, if he ships, of course, he won't want to ship aboard of any but an English or American craft, where they speak his own language. Then I thought to myself, he don't want to go a long voyage to England, and perhaps some other cruise before he is free, nor yet to the North, until he hears from his father. The short of it is just this here. If that vessel turns out to be what I think she is,—a Florida wrecker,—and her captain is not a most uncommon obstinate man, you're suited at the first go off. You can ship aboard of her, and there you'll be until you can get word from New York. I don't believe there'll be a mite of trouble; for you see the wreckers take a crew on shares. If they get any salvage, every man has his portion; but if they are not lucky, the owners only lose the grub they provide."

While the captain was engaged in this unusually long speech, the two vessels were rapidly nearing each other upon opposite tacks, which seemed as if they would bring them into collision if they maintained the same course. But as we approached still closer to each other, I perceived that the other schooner, being a fast sailer, would cross athwart our hawse. Sure enough, a few minutes afterwards, she ran past us, cleaving the water as if she had been instinct with life, and triumphed in her speed.

As she weathered us, our captain shouted through his trumpet: "What schooner's that,—bound in?" Another trumpet answered from the stranger's deck, "Wrecker, *Flying Cloud;* Key West, for Havana; who are you?" Our captain bellowed in reply, "*Cygnet,* from New York." Then plash, plash,

plash, went the water from our bow, as the voices ceased, and the noise of the rush of the other vessel subsided, and we once more clove our way alone through the sea.

The captain's apparent certainty that I would find no difficulty in shipping aboard of the trim-looking wrecker, raised my spirits, and when, a few minutes afterwards, we were catering the harbor, I felt sufficiently relieved in mind to be able to enjoy the scene.

On the left of the entrance of the harbor stands a magnificent lighthouse, placed on the comparatively low rocks which form the base of some great hills on which Moro Castle is situated. The entrance itself is extremely narrow, and so uniform in breadth, before it expands into the harbor, that it seems almost like a canal. Moro Castle runs along the lofty hills, its walls dipping into the ravines, and so adapting themselves to the peculiarities of the surface, that they look as if they had become molten at their base, and had run into the slopes.

The tall, smooth shaft of the lighthouse, rising out of dark, rugged rocks, and contrasting with the undulating lines of Moro Castle, completes the outline on the left of the entrance. The reader must add to the masonry a tint of dark yellow, in vivid relief amidst tropical green. Under these southern skies, nature blends colors, and adds shades of her own. Man can scarcely devise anything so hideous, that, in time, she will not beautify it with vegetation, and paint it with a master hand.

On the right of the entrance, the ground is low, and there, houses are numerous, but the city does not fairly commence until just beyond the narrow gut which leads from the sea. As the wind was ahead and very light and the passage narrow, short as it was, we would have had to make many tacks before getting inside of the main harbor, had we not lowered our sails, put some men in the jolly-boat, and towed the schooner through.

The wrecker had preceded us by half an hour, and we could see her lying at anchor in the harbor.

When the men had pulled about four or five hundred yards, we came in plain view of Havana, which is situated on the right of the harbor,—a land-locked bay, whose only communication with the sea is through the narrow passage described. The unhealthiness of Havana can, in part, be properly attributed to its situation on the bay, which, filled with numerous shipping, from which filth of all kinds is constantly discharged, lies under a tropical sun that must breed disease from its almost stagnant waters. The tides in this portion of the Gulf of Mexico rise and fall only between one and two feet; so that in Havana there is no influx and reflux of vast quantities of water which would cleanse the harbor of its impurities.

We were soon swinging at anchor. Now that the excitement, caused by our arrival and the novel scenes which presented themselves, had ceased to distract my thoughts from the uneasy reflections which had beset me, I relapsed into the gloomy train of reflection which my unhappy situation engendered. I was looking disconsolately at the shore, and completely lost in my thoughts of home, when I started at being touched on the shoulder. Turning around, I saw the captain, who smiled pleasantly, and said:

"Now, my lad, cheer up. Don't be downhearted. All will come right. You have explained everything in your letter to your father. He'll believe you, I know. You see, I'm a father myself, and I how how one feels."

This was balm indeed to me, for my doubts of my ability to take care of myself weighed lightly in the balance, compared with the heartache which I experienced when I allowed myself, for an instant, to dwell upon the thought that my father might perchance refuse to believe my story, repudiate me, spurn my love, and, perhaps even declare that I should never have his forgiveness. Loving, I had always known him to be, but then I was about to call upon him to credit what appeared to be an impossibility.

"Captain," I said, turning towards my kind friend, "you have said the very word I needed. It isn't the thought of how

I'm to get along that distresses me, but just what you said."

"Well, then, cheer up," said the captain, in reply. "I tell you again, it will all come right—my word for it. For the present, I'll help you out of one part of your trouble. I didn't intend to stay very long in this port, but I'll settle your affairs before I sail, or else I'll never leave it. I'm bound for that wrecker now. You wait here. I can get along without you better than if you were with me. Keep up your courage. Hollo," he shouted, to the men in the jolly-boat, which was now lying alongside, "drop a little astern."

He threw his leg over the schooner's rail, caught hold of the man-ropes at the side, and, in a jiffy, he was steering for the schooner; I was left on deck wistfully looking after him, until Charley came up, and began to chaff me in regular boy-fashion, as to whether I hadn't had about enough adventure. At a certain age, boys are apt to possess so little sensibility, that they are often brutal without meaning to be. However, on this occasion, I was not hurt. The captain's certainty that with my father all would come right, coupled with my strong hope that I should be able to get a place aboard of the wrecker, had revived my spirits. I felt as if I had quaffed some subtle elixir that quickened my pulses and made my heart beat high with hope.

CHAPTER V

CAPTAIN EDSON'S MISSION CROWNED WITH SUCCESS—THE CAPTAIN
OF THE WRECKER AN OLD FRIEND—CAPTAIN EDSON OBTAINS A
SITUATION AS CABIN BOY FOR HIS PROTÉGÉ, WHO, IN MENTIONING
HIS NAME TO HIS EMPLOYER, NECESSARILY ANNOUNCES IT TO THE
READER.

AN hour passed before I saw the captain's boat quit the side of the wrecker and row for our vessel. The length of the captain's absence had created in my mind a misgiving that his mission had been unsuccessful. Now that I saw him leaving the wrecker, I rejoiced; for to know the worst was better than to be in suspense. As my gaze was directed towards the boat, I saw the captain rise up in the stern-sheets and wave his hat. I was instantly relieved—he had succeeded. In a few minutes he was aboard, and, shaking me by the shoulders, clapped me on the back, as he exclaimed, "I told you so. I felt in my bones that the vessel had arrived 'specially for you. Why, the captain turns out to be an old friend of mine, although I had not seen him for these fifteen years. That's what kept me so long. Meeting an old friend that way made me forget, for a few minutes, the business I went on. Then, when I came to talk of you, it took a few minutes longer. But there is no trouble about your shipping. He's glad enough to get a boy. He says he's wanted one for some time. The place is only a cabin boy's, mind you, but I don't see that you can better yourself, for you're not a sailor, and not even a man.

I professed myself delighted, as you can very well imagine. Then the captain told me that the wrecker would not sail for two or three days, and that his own vessel must leave early the next morning, but that I should stay with him until just before sailing, when he would put me aboard of the *Flying Cloud*. He then left me, as he had to go ashore on business, and, by his advice, I went down into the cabin, and added a long postscript to my letter to my father. I told him to address his reply to Key West, Florida. That is the port in which the wreckers "fit out," and receive letters, papers, and supplies of every kind.

The captain, his son, and I, spent the evening together, and I felt as if I was about to leave friends whom I had known all my life, so entirely do constant companionship, intercourse, and kindly offices disregard time as a measure of the length of friendship.

My letter had been posted, and it would probably leave Havana in the course of a day or two. At the time of which I am speaking, no regular line of steamships plied between New York and New Orleans, touching at Havana on both trips; so it might be a month before my letter to my father would reach him, and another month before a letter could reach Key West. And then, if I were off on a wrecking cruise, as I expected to be, it might be three months before I should hear from New York. This was supposing the most unfavorable case,—that each letter would be a month in reaching its destination; but, then, both vessels carrying the mails, in which the letters were to go, might make short passages, and, instead of each being a month on the voyage, the time consumed might be less than two weeks for each. This, on the other hand, was too favorable a supposition, so I concluded to take the mean,—to allow three weeks for each trip. That would bring a reply to Key West in the course of six weeks. Allowing three weeks more before my letter reached me, at the unfrequented point where we would probably be stationed, I concluded two months to be the time by which I might reasonably expect to hear from home. Before I turned in for the night, I had gone through my calculation many times, as people in such circumstances always do; and by dint of reasoning to myself, that, at the worst, it would not be very long before I should hear from my father, I felt more ease of mind than I had yet experienced.

Matters appeared to be taking a satisfactory turn, and the captain's view of my father's action in my regard had had so happy an effect, that I resolved to give way no longer to despondency.

When day dawned, our deck was at once astir with preparation for departure. The captain seemed grieved to be obliged to let me go, although he tried to be cheerful, and to give me courage. I was very loth to leave; so much so, that I verily believe, had the choice of going or staying been mine, I would not have had resolution to put in practice the plan which had been so well matured. I was scarcely able to eat a morsel at breakfast, and, after that meal, I silently followed the captain out of the cabin. While he was ordering the boat to be lowered, I bade good-bye to Charley, and then took my seat in the boat, by the captain's side. In six or seven minutes, we were alongside of the wrecker. I clambered up the side, after the captain, who gave me a shove by way of introduction to a jolly-looking person who was standing on the quarterdeck to receive us, and whom he accosted as Bowers. "Mind you do well by this boy, Bowers," he said, "or else we two'll fall out. He's my property. He's a sort of a sea-waif that I picked up." Capt. Bowers' appearance was so very good-natured, that I at once felt relieved of the only doubt that I had had about my change of commanders.

"And now," said Captain Edson, "I have not a moment to spare; I must take advantage of this wind. Good-bye, Bowers." He shook the captain's hand heartily, and then taking mine in both of his hands, he gave it a wring, and just as he released it, clasped it over a hard little package, which I mechanically clutched. "Good-bye, boy," he said, as he turned to go. "It will all come right. So far, so good." By the time that he had finished his last sentence, he was in the boat, and pulling rapidly away.

I made a faint attempt at twirling my hat around my head, in token of farewell, but I failed miserably. I felt that I had lost a dear friend; as in truth I had, for I never saw him again. A few months afterwards he died of yellow fever.

"What did Captain Edson say your name was?" inquired a voice at my ear.

"Fred Ransom, sir," I replied, starting and letting fall the paper which Captain Edson had left in my hand.

"You've dropped something," said Captain Bowers. "Your money, I reckon, by the ring."

"I haven't got any money, sir," I said, "unless"—I paused, stooped, and recovered the paper, and hastily tore it open. Out rolled fifteen dollars in gold coin.

CHAPTER VI

CAPTAIN BOWERS GIVES FRED RANSOM A VACANT BERTH IN THE
CABIN—FRED RANSOM PERFORMS HIS DUTIES ABOARD OF THE
SCHOONER—THE CAPTAIN GIVES HIM LEAVE TO GO ASHORE—THE
QUAYS, FISH-MARKET, HAVANA LOTTERY, VOLANTES, THE PASEO,
TOMB OF COLUMBUS, CAPTAIN-GENERAL OF CUBA.

THE object of the wrecker's visit to Havana was to procure a supply of sugar for some of the merchants of Key West. Happening to be at Key West, for the purpose of undergoing repairs, which were just finished when the merchants desired to replenish their stocks of sugar, the vessel was chartered for the voyage to Havana. Her business in Havana was not to detain her more than two or three days, at the end of which time she could in a few hours run over to Key West, which is about eighty-two miles distant.

Captain Bowers turned out to be as good-natured as his appearance indicated. As Captain Edson had predicted, I was certainly in luck; for, besides having a most desirable commander, I was accommodated aboard the vessel, as I believe cabin boy never was before. There was no bunk forward to spare, and this fact gave the captain a plausible excuse for granting me permission to occupy one of the vacant berths in the cabin. How Captain Bowers came to be guilty of this queer proceeding will be best explained by the following conversation which ensued between us, immediately after I had gathered up the fugitive coin which had dispersed in as many directions as there were pieces.

"Fred," said the captain, "my friend, Captain Edson, has told me all about your situation, and appealed to me to do the best I can for you. I intend to do that, if you deserve it.

33

Whether you do, or not, is yet to be tested. Meantime I'll take it for granted, and commence by doing the best I can for you. You've been carefully brought up, and wouldn't find it very pleasant to stay forward with the crew, who are good fellows enough, but rather rough, and not exactly the kind of people you've been used to living with. So, although I never heard of a cabin boy's shipping in the cabin, as it happens my friend takes an interest in you, and I'm disposed to do the same, now I know your story, why you can have a berth in the cabin, and live aboard the schooner until you can get word from your father. You'll have to serve the cabin, just like any other cabin boy, and lend a hand anywhere you're needed; but I think you're pretty well off for a chap who has got into such a scrape."

"Indeed, I am, captain," I replied, "and I am very much obliged to you for your kindness to me, and I'll do the best I can to deserve it."

(This promise, let me here say, I religiously observed.)

"Well, see that you do, and it'll be the best thanks that you can give me," rejoined the captain. "Now I've got through with what I had to say, and I'm going ashore on business. What are you going to do with yourself?"

I answered that I supposed I would begin my duties immediately.

"All right," said the captain, "I'm glad to see that you realize your position. But after you get things set to rights, suppose you go ashore, and buy some clothes, for Captain Edson told me you hadn't a stitch except what you've got on your back. Hold! I guess you'd better wait for that, until we arrive at Key West. This is an awfully dear place, and your money wouldn't go very far. However, if you're inclined, you can go ashore tomorrow, and see the sights. I guess it will take you pretty much all day today, to get things fixed about the cabin, as it hasn't been cleared up this long time."

A few minutes afterwards the captain was off for shore, and I spent the whole day in setting things to rights, cleaning out the lockers, throwing accumulated rubbish overboard, and washing and putting away that portion of the cabin crockery, which, not having been in daily use, was as dusty as it ever could have been when lying in the china shop. These operations, with sweeping, scrubbing paint, rehanging the curtains of the cabin windows and berths, occupied me during the whole day, and I had barely finished by evening, when the captain returned, and congratulated me upon the favorable change effected by my exertions.

The next morning, after I had served the captain's breakfast, there was nothing for me to do, so, as he was again going ashore to spend the day, he took me in his gig, and landed me, with full permission to devote my time to seeing Havana. Telling me that if I would return to the same place at six o'clock in the evening, he would then be going off to the vessel, he bade me good-morning, and left me standing on the quay.

The quay was not formed of a number of projecting wharves or piers, but consisted of a long line of wharf, following the outline of the shore of the harbor. Although small, it presented the same general appearance as the levees which, some years afterwards, I saw on the Mississippi, at New Orleans. This quay, at the time of which I speak, was planked wholly, or in great part, with huge timbers of mahogany. These have been since replaced by a less valuable wood; but you must not suppose that mahogany is as dear a wood in Cuba as it is in the United States, for it grows in the West Indies.

Besides the vessels lying at anchor in the harbor, among which were some Spanish men-of-war, numerous small craft lay alongside of the quay. These, from the limited amount of accommodations afforded by a single wharf-line, were chiefly moored "end-on" to the quay. Numerous little boats, with awnings over the stern, lay along shore, in quite a tier, awaiting their chance of a fare. Others, which had been so fortunate as to find one, plied busily about the harbor.

I saw the fish-market of Havana, which is one of the finest in the world. The sale of fish was a monopoly enjoyed by an individual who had matters pretty much his own way, as far as the fishermen were concerned; for he paid a stated price for fish of five pounds in weight, but if they were less than five pounds, he exacted four or five fish, and paid no more. Nevertheless, owing to the abundance of fish in those waters, catching them proved profitable enough to induce men to supply the market.

In so warm a climate, fishing is a somewhat precarious business; for a cargo is sometimes lost when a vessel is becalmed for many hours. That, however, is not of frequent occurrence. The cause of the loss of fish, at such a time, is that they then lack a fresh supply of water. When the fishing smacks roll and plunge in a seaway, the water is constantly changing. These vessels are built with a large compartment, which is called the well. The well is supplied with water, by means of holes bored through the vessel's bottom. When such a vessel is underway, or even when she is rocking at anchor, the water in the well is constantly changing; but when there is no motion, the supply ceases, and the fish sicken and die. Fish are extremely delicate in their nature, and the fishermen are obliged to watch and remove any which may show symptoms of being sick; otherwise, the whole cargo may become infected. The operation of removal is generally performed by boys, who dive into the well.

Some of the things which I have mentioned, and others which I still have to tell, I did not learn on shore, but gathered from Captain Bowers, or later experience of my own.

After I had rambled about the quay for some time, and seen everything there, I concluded to go into the city.

The first place that I visited was the tomb of Columbus, in the cathedral. The city seemed to me a most curious place. The houses are often painted blue or yellow; and they have bars at the windows, so that the first street into which I rambled reminded me for all the world of a menagerie. The houses generally had large *portes-cochère*, which are carriage ways passing through the face of a building. The houses are constructed around the sides of quadrangles, thus enclosing a courtyard in the centre. This is the usual mode of building in hot climates; for it ensures coolness, especially in the courtyards, which are often planted as gardens, and embellished with fountains.

By this time, the sun had got pretty high, and I stopped under the shade of a massive *porte-cochère*, and looked out upon the busy streets. The pavements are of stone, and so narrow that it is in vain for pedestrians to attempt to confine their steps to those walks. Had they existed in Europe at a period when men were apt to take the wall and make it a point of honor not to budge an inch, the adult male population would have been exterminated.

I had read Don Quixote, and some of the sights that I saw reminded me very much of the scenes described in the adventures of that renowned knight. I saw mules carrying water in casks suspended at their sides. Others carried loads of green fodder, which covered them so completely that nothing was visible except their tiny hoofs stepping daintily along. Others, again, bore panniers of oranges. I stopped the owner of one of these, and bought some of his fruit. I could not speak Spanish, but I held out ten cents that the captain had given me as part of the change for one of my gold pieces, and made a sign towards the oranges. I have since found that money is a language which is universally understood and which, more than any other, appeals to the human heart. I expected to get only a couple of oranges, but I received ten and had not pockets enough in which to stow them. So I disposed of seven about my person, deposited two on the ground of my shady nook, and commenced operations on another. Many as I received, I suppose that I must have paid the usual penalty of a foreigner—that of being cheated.

I sucked away very complacently at my oranges, and, at the same time, continued to take in all that was going on in the street. The volantes, or carriages, are very peculiar. They are like great gigs. They have no springs, but the absence of springs is compensated for by the position of the body of the vehicle, which, being placed forward of the axle-tree, and resting on the shafts, receives the benefit of their elasticity. These volantes are generally drawn by one horse, bestridden by a Negro in top-boots. They hold two persons comfortably, but they are often occupied by three. Private volantes sometimes have an extra horse attached by traces, which meet at a pintle that is inserted in an eye placed on the outside of one of the shafts. Even with two persons,—what with the big gig-top and the people inside of it, and the Negro on the horse,— the horse seems to be the smallest part of the turnout. He is constantly reminded of his duty by lashings, which his driver freely bestows. In truth, I never saw horses and mules so unmercifully treated as they were in Havana. Of course it is not among the horses belonging to private carriages that this maltreatment occurs.

Seeing so many of these vehicles pass, I came at last to examine one which stood in the corner, just in the rear of my sheltering *porte-cochère*. It was a very elaborate one, and seemed to be very much out of place, for it was carelessly backed up on a pile of rubbish, and the harness was thrown over the dasher, and trailed in the dust. I afterwards ascertained that those circumstances are not at all unusual in Havana, where, even in handsome establishments, there is generally manifest a thorough absence of what we call "keeping." I afterwards learned from Captain Bowers that many volantes were made in the United States, expressly for the Havana market. I confess that on hearing this, my interest in them was considerably lessened. People are so constituted, that remoteness strangely affects the imagination. In a foreign land, they gaze with deep interest at objects on which, at home, they might perhaps bestow a passing glance. I recollect that once when, years after the adventures that I am now recounting, I visited Table Rock, in South Carolina, I saw an old woman who lived at the foot of it, and marvelled in my presence why people came so far to clamber to its giddy height. From girlhood she had lived there, but never once thought of setting foot to its ascent.

It was dreadfully hot by the time that I left the shade of

the *porte-cochère,* having determined to see more of the city, as I had only a few hours left, and we were to sail on the following day. I wandered about, stopping every now and then to take shelter in some nook, and recruit my energies by partaking of another orange.

I was so lucky as to come across the drawing of the famous Havana lottery. This is an institution carried on by the government, and as fairly conducted as it is possible to be; but, like all lotteries, it does not benefit the buyers of tickets as much as it does the proprietors of the concern. Individuals occasionally draw large sums, but dearly do they pay for their success, by imbibing the spirit of gambling, which generally leads them to risk and lose all and more than all that they have gained.

The monthly drawing of the lottery was conducted with great ceremony. It is the event upon which the hopes of thousands are centred, and there is always a large crowd in attendance. All the saints in the calendar are dinned with applications for a lucky number. The amount of injury effected by this lottery is incalculable. The gambling it begets and encourages, the petty thefts suggested by a desire to buy tickets, the misdirection of thought and energy, in the hope of some lucky stroke, are all such evils as no good government would visit upon its people. And the government of Spain is not good. It is unscrupulous. If it can contribute to its coffers, what matters a little vice among its subjects!

As evening approached, I followed the current of people, which seemed to be tending in a certain direction from the quarter of the city in which I then happened to find myself, and I came to the Paseo, or drive, upon which there was a great concourse of carriages and pedestrians, and a fine military band playing. Here is the palace of the Governor of Cuba, who is called the Captain-General. His is a distinguished post, with large emoluments in salary and perquisites of office. In fact, the position is that of viceroy, and it is always held by Spain's most powerful nobleman.

This drive, promenade, and music are the everyday amusements of the Habanese. I did not remain very long to enjoy the display, for I observed that the sun was going down rapidly. I took my departure, and hurried back to the quay, following the streets which I imagined would lead me to the spot at which I had landed in the morning. I did not hit it exactly, but after a little search, I discovered it, and seated myself on a pile of boxes to await the captain's arrival. In a few minutes he appeared, and made a signal to the schooner to send the boat ashore. While the boat was pulling in, the captain inquired kindly of me how I had managed to worry through my long day ashore. I gave him a brief sketch of my doings, at which he laughed, and said,

"Who but a boy could have been contented to wander, for pleasure, about the streets of a city, so hot that the chief occupation of the inhabitants is to try to keep cool. And where did you get dinner, prey?"

I replied that I had bought so many oranges for ten cents, that I could not have eaten anything more, if I had tried. At this he laughed again. In a few minutes the boat reached the quay. The captain motioned me to get aboard. He jumped in after me, and we shoved off for the schooner.

CHAPTER VII

THE FLYING CLOUD SAILS FROM HAVANA—THE VESSEL—THE CREW—
THE COOK—THE NEWFOUNDLAND DOG, JACK.

UT into the waters of the deep blue Gulf we sailed, as the rising sun threw a golden pathway over the expanse of sea. The morning was beautiful, and as the schooner dipped merrily into the waves, and sped away on her course, the buoyant movement, balmy air, clear sky, and lovely scene, dissipated the last vestige of melancholy with which I had been oppressed. I felt that I had done all that lay in my power. The full consciousness of this renewed my determination of the previous evening, to cast away all vain misgivings, and put my trust in Providence. From that hour forward, I was myself again.

The shores near Havana are very abrupt; for within a few yards of the stagnant-looking water of the harbor, the schooner was dancing amid the deep blue waves.

I was not disappointed in the *Flying Cloud.* She was a trim-looking craft, rather long for her beam, and with quite low bulwarks. She had that easy movement which one accustomed to vessels can recognize as indicating a good sea-boat, as readily as an accomplished rider can judge, by the first few paces of his horse, whether it possesses the elasticity fitting it for the saddle, or the jolting gait that should consign it to the cart.

Our crew consisted of eight men. One was an Englishman, one an Irishman, and another a Norwegian. The five others were Conchs from Key West. In reference to the Conchs of Key West, I shall, hereafter, have something to say.

I must not forget to mention our black cook, Hannibal. A most important personage everywhere is a cook, white or

41

black, and in no place more important than on board ship. Even in the worst pro-slavery times, I never saw a black sea-cook that was not thought to have rights which white men were bound to respect, and, in truth, which they were very anxious to respect.

A cook at sea has it in his power to make the men very comfortable or very uncomfortable. In either case, whether too favorably disposed to them, for the interest of the ship's stores, or inclined to annoy them, by bad cookery or short allowance, he can safely follow his own devices in a thousand ways so covert as to escape detection, while the effect of the whole is clearly apparent. For instance, how can the fact be fixed that the "doctor" deliberately burned the coffee, instead of its condition being owing, as he states, to the men's calling him at an inopportune moment to lend a hand somewhere. Or, how can it be proved that the salty and nauseous flavor of the pea soup was not caused by someone's meddling with his bucket of fresh water, and leaving it filled with salt water when, while all hands were engaged, the "doctor" had secretly dipped the water out of the sea, and filled the soup kettle to the brim.

We had another blackey on board, but he belonged aft, although he did not confine himself to that portion of the vessel. He was a fine Newfoundland dog, the finest that I ever saw. He was not one of those unwieldy beasts which pass their existence in acquiring excessive fat, but a great rollicking fellow, all animation and playfulness. He was a noble brute—no, not a brute!

"------the poor dog, in life the firmest friend,
The first to welcome, foremost to defend,
Whose honest heart is still his master's own,
Who labors, fights, lives, breathes for him alone,
Unhonored falls, unnoticed all his worth,
Denied in heaven the soul he had on earth,
While man, vain insect! hopes to be forgiven,
And claims himself a sole, exclusive heaven."*

42

Although Jack, as I said, belonged aft, he was not allowed to make use of the cabin, unless in case of storm. So even at night he remained on deck, taking up his station by lying across the door which was at the head of the companionway, as it is called, the staircase leading to the cabin. The sagacious animal knew the occasion upon which he was not to be considered an intruder, and when it rained, he tumbled down the steep stairway, and ensconced himself in a corner, with an air of self-possession and of being quite at home.

The captain was as kind as possible to me, but his manner, after our first interview and my day's liberty on shore, was less demonstrative, as if he felt that the discipline of the vessel required me to know and keep my place. As I was not destitute of tact, I took the hint, and kept aloof. Boy as I was, I saw quite clearly that my position was a very strange one, and on observing the captain's manner to me, I determined to avoid all that might savor of presumption. I was therefore careful not to approach him unless he addressed me.

Of course, I did not eat with the captain, for, being the cabin boy, I was obliged to serve his meals. I was not required to wait, but to be within call, and after the captain had finished, I sat down at the same table. It was considerate in him not to send me forward to eat with the men, as well as to allow me to sleep elsewhere.

It was the 20th day of October when we left Havana. We had sailed from New York on the 26th of September, and although, during part of the voyage to Havana, we were favored with a fair wind, the light, baffling winds of the first few days had prevented our making much way, so that the voyage to Havana was not a quick one.

The wind was now ahead, but we had so short a trip to make, that unless we were becalmed, it could not, even with a headwind, consume more than two days.

---

*Byron's "Inscription on the monument of a Newfoundland dog." The dog, "Boatswain," died, and was buried at Newstead Abbey, at which place the monument may still be seen.

43

CHAPTER VIII

THE FLYING CLOUD ANCHORS OFF THE MARQUESAS—A PARTY FROM
THE SCHOONER GO ASHORE—THE SCENERY OF THE KEYS AND INNER
BAY—THE GRAINING—ONE OF THE PARTY DEVOURED BY A SHARK.

N the evening of the second day after sailing from Havana, we arrived off the Marquesas, and came to anchor for the night, intending to run into Key West on the following morning. The Marquesas Keys are a group of small islands lying to the westward of Key West. They are the westernmost group of Keys, except the Tortugas. The group consists of numerous islands, with only slight intervals between them, sweeping around in a gradual curve, thus enclosing a land-locked and shallow bay, studded with little tufts of islands rising out of its shallow waters. Beneath these waters, narrow and deep channels run in various directions, and connect with the straits separating the encircling land.

When day broke we found ourselves becalmed. We were only about fifteen miles from Key West, and lying in the Reef Channel. As the island of Key West was indistinctly visible, although the town of Key West could not be discerned, we felt as if we had almost arrived at our destination. Meanwhile, there were no signs of a breeze, and as it would not probably rise until the sun became considerably higher, three of the men, about an hour after daylight, came aft, and asked the captain for the use of the schooner's boat, for the purpose of going ashore and having some sport. The captain, after a glance around the horizon, gave the men permission to go, cautioning them to be on the lookout, and return the very moment that the breeze sprang up. Turning to me, he said, "How would you like to go? I shall not need you, now that I've had breakfast."

I was very glad to receive permission, and after request-ing and obtaining leave to take Jack, who had become very sociable with me, I started with the party, which was com-posed of the Englishman, the Norwegian, and one of the Conchs. When we came within fifty yards of the shore, Jack jumped overboard, despite our endeavors to hold him, and swam for the beach. The men were afraid that he might be devoured by the sharks, but he reached the shore in safety, and long before we had landed, he was tearing up and down the beach, thrusting his muzzle into the water along the edge, and rending the air with barks and howls of delight. The wildest thing in nature is a dog just released from ship-board, and landed on a long, smooth beach. Poor Jack was frantic with joy, and it was some minutes after we had land-ed before he sobered down into a mood of quiet enjoyment, in which he gambolled ponderously around us, while, with panting sides and protruding tongue, he regained his exhausted breath.

Near the mouth of one of the straits which divide the Keys, we fastened our boat, by its painter, to a stake of drift-wood thrust into the beach. We then strolled off along the outside shore to the end of the Key on which we had landed, and came back to our starting point.

Not a breath of air was stirring yet, as we distinctly per-ceived by a glance at the schooner's pennant, which trailed down the main mast, without the slightest flutter.

"What do you say, boys, to a trip inside of the Keys?" inquired the Conch, who formed one of the party. "We can see the schooner's top-masts over the trees, and if a breeze springs up, we'll be out and aboard in a jiffy. There's always lots of fish feeding inside, and I've brought the grains along, and we may come across something."

"I'm agreeable, for one," answered Bill Ruggles, the Englishman. "What do you expect to strike?"

"Oh! anything we come across, that's fit to eat," said the Conch, whose name was John Linden. "Hurry up, we may not have more than a few minutes longer on shore. The wind scarcely ever keeps down beyond nine o'clock. It's eight now."

As Ruggles disengaged the knot of the painter from the stake around which it passed, we jumped into the boat, which he shoved astern and, heading her bow towards the inlet, shot her fairly into it. Springing into the stern-sheets as she passed, he took the tiller, and the two other men put out the oars.

The channel leading into the bay between those two Keys was quite deep, and not more than fifty yards in width. The men had not rowed more than as many yards before the boat passed the slender line of Keys which enclosed the bay, and we found ourselves in the land-locked waters which I have described.

With the exception of the channels which traversed the bay in several directions, the water was evidently very shoal. Silence reigned supreme. Except for, at intervals, the discordant cry of some wild bird, and the noise made by our party, everything was still. These occasional noises only served to heighten the effect, as an indifferent light is said to render darkness visible. So completely shut in from the ocean was this little lake, that, even in a gale, its surface must have been all but unruffled.

"Hollo!" exclaimed John Linden, as he looked over his shoulder, while he tugged away at the bow-oar, "I see a rippling, way ahead; who's to get the grains ready and strike?"

"You, I suppose, you're the best hand at that," replied Ruggles. "Who ever heard of anybody's using the grains when there's a Conch aboard?"

"All right, but I can't strike and row too. What kind of a hand are you at an oar, Fred?" said he, addressing me. "Can you pull?"

"I never tried," I said, "but I'm willing to do my best."

"Never tried, but you think you can!" said Ruggles, grinning. "That's like the Irishman and the fiddle. He hadn't ever tried to play, so he didn't know but he could."

"It's lucky Brady is aboard the schooner, or you'd have a

spat with him about making jokes on Irishmen," observed Linden. "Don't waste any more time with your chaff. You come and take my oar, for we're gaining on those fish, whatever they are. You can let the youngster steer. You can steer, I suppose, can't you?" said he, again addressing me.

Being more confident of my steering powers than of my rowing ones, as green-hands about a boat usually are, I said that I could steer.

"Well," said Linden, "there's no help for it; we want a good strong oar, so you take mine, Bill, and let him take the helm. I don't intend to trust much to your steering, though, Fred. Jest recollect this, when I say 'starboard,—starboard,' keep putting your helm more and more down that way, to your right, and when I say 'port,—port,' keep putting it more and more t'other way."

Bill Ruggles stepped over a couple of thwarts, and took the oar which the Conch relinquished, and the latter pulled out his grains and adjusted them on the end of a pole. Meanwhile, I kept repeating to myself, 'starboard goes this way, port goes that way;' for although by the time I had reached Havana, I considered that I was able to steer pretty well, I felt somewhat doubtful when I found the duty suddenly devolve upon me, with doubts clearly expressed as to my ability.

The grains are of iron, consisting of a socket joining a two-pronged fork with barbed points. A stout line, about the size of that generally used for hanging out clothes to dry, is made fast at the junction of the socket and prongs. The end of a pole of about twelve feet in length is then placed in the socket. The line is led up along it, and kept taut, so as to hold the grains securely in position. The other end of the line is made fast in the bow of the boat, and the slack coiled all ready to pay out as rapidly as required. The man who strikes stands in the bow and poises the pole in both hands, and, if necessary, throws it several yards with unerring precision.

By the time that the arrangements for striking were completed, we were within a hundred yards of the fish which had attracted our attention. They were a great school of mullet. They were flashing through the water, and leaping out of it by hundreds, as if terrified by some enemy.

"Starboard," cried Linden, "starboard, starboard, more yet,—hard a-starboard; let's take that channel. Now steer for that tall tree on the little island ahead. By gracious, boys, I see what's the matter with them mullet; it's the biggest kind of a white shark fishing for them, as I'm a sinner."

"Can't you strike him?" I eagerly exclaimed.

"Strike him," said Linden, "why we have got a line that wouldn't hold him easier than a stran' o' silk. He's off anyhow. He's taken that other channel. Jest look at them mullet! By gracious, he's taking in provisions for a month. It seems to me that we'd better be thinking of going back, so as to be within hail. If the wind should spring up, the captain will want to be off in less than no time. Head your boat the other way, Fred; you can see the channel plain enough between the mud flats under water."

I did as I was told, and the boat had barely reversed her course, when I observed a motion in the water about fifty yards ahead. "There's something," I shouted to the Conch, who was just taking his grains off the pole.

"Sure enough, so there is," he replied, readjusting the grains, and resuming his station. "Confound it, it's nothing but a big sawfish!"

I stood up in the stern-sheets, and I could see a huge animal slowly swimming along in the same direction as the one which we were pursuing. It appeared so sluggish in its movements, that I felt sure of our being able to capture it, so I begged Linden to give us some sport. He said that we would lose our grains if we attempted to strike it. But I was too much excited to be reasonable. I had never seen a fish harpooned, and I felt sure, too, that the Conch did not really think that we would lose our grains, but did not wish to strike the fish, because it was unfit to eat.

"Do strike it," I urged. "If you lose the grains, I'll get you another pair when we arrive at Key West."

"Well! here goes," he said, and with that he plunged the grains into the fish, which, by that time, was almost under the bow of our boat. "Port, port!" he shouted, as the line spun out. "Pull men, and let's get more way on the boat."

The line whizzed out like lightning, and the men gave way with a will. Just as the full extent of the line paid out, jerk it went, as if it would break, and the boat rushed rapidly through the water.

"Steady, Fred," shouted the Conch; "keep her head with the line. If you keep her off, it'll part."

"Aye! aye!" said I, feeling quite nautical, and using a seaman's answer to correspond with my dignity as steersman.

The boat rushed along with surprising velocity, the water boiling around her bow. I stood up for a better view. I saw that the line was very tense. Now and then, near the bow, it whipped on the surface of the water and then clove through it, indicating that the fish swam at various depths. Suddenly the Conch shouted in a hurried manner,

"Keep away from the starboard bank. There's a channel on the starboard side, leading right off our course."

Without comprehending why I was ordered to do so, I put the tiller hard a-starboard, so as to keep over towards the bank on our port bow. I had hardly had time to shift the helm, when the boat careened, and "fetched up" on the mud flat, which was only about two feet under water. Over it she went for ten or fifteen yards, stirring up the mud, and spurting the water all over us. Suddenly, snap went the line, and the boat stopped plumb.

I had scarcely breath to ejaculate, "Is the line broken?"

"Parted, sure enough!" said Linden. "We've lost our grains. A line of that size can't hold all creation. It was stronger though than I thought for. If it hadn't been the sawfish took that channel, and hauled us on the bank, the line wouldn't have parted after all."

When the boat stopped, the men sprang to their feet, and laughed and shouted at the mishap, while around about the startled sea-birds wheeled with shriller cry, and winged

49

their flight farther from the boisterous merriment. After many relapses into fits of laughter, the men at last regained their sobriety.

"Better luck next time," said Linden, and with that he commenced with his oar to shove the boat off into the channel, adding, "but you need a harpoon, and a heavier line for that sort of work. When we get up the Reef, I'll show you some sport."

The cause of our losing the fish was that it suddenly entered another channel, which ran off nearly at a right angle with the course which we were steering. The consequence was, that as the boat had some scope of line out, the fish was well up the new channel while we were still in the old one. So, instead of being able to enter the mouth of the former, we were forcibly dragged by a short cut on top of the bank which divided the channels. Here the line, which had scarcely been able to bear the strain when the boat was in deep water, broke, and she rested on top of the bank, in shallow water in which she was not quite afloat.

Afloat once more in the main channel which we had left, the men resumed their oars, and, with now and then a laugh and a sally of fun, headed the boat again towards the inlet. When we reached the inlet, we saw that outside there was a dead calm, and not a soul stirring on the deck of the schooner.

"I move we wait here," suggested Bill Ruggles. "We're not wanted aboard, and what's the use of going off until we're obliged to?"

Nobody gainsaying this proposition, we determined to wait until the wind came up, or the captain made a signal to us. The painter was once more passed over the stake on the beach, and we amused ourselves by rambling off into the mangroves. We certainly had not been absent more than ten minutes, when, on emerging from the woods to return towards the boat, we saw that she was adrift. On reaching the stake, we found that it must have become loosened by using it for mooring the boat. The eddy caused by the tide's flowing into the inlet had carried the boat out from shore, from which, by tugging, she must have withdrawn the stake, and drifted off still farther. She was now fifty yards from shore.

"By gracious, but the captain will be mad," said Bill Ruggles. "Have any of you got a line about you? If you have, I'll put a rock on it, and throw it aboard the boat and haul her in."

No one had a string over a yard long, and there we stood looking at the boat floating quietly out of reach.

"Standing here doing nothing won't fetch her ashore, observed the Norwegian. "I'll strip and swim for her."

"No, you won't," answered Linden. "Are you fool enough to go in swimming off one of these inlets, where sharks are coming and going, 'specially when the tide's rising? Didn't I say that was a white shark I saw in the bay?"

"Well, suppose it was," replied the Norwegian, "I'm a good swimmer, and I haven't got above fifty yards to swim, and—you can't keep me now, here goes, clothes and all."

With that, before anyone could frustrate his intention, he sprang into the water, and struck out for the boat. He was, as he had said, a good swimmer, and he had not proceeded more than half the distance to the boat, when we cheered him. As we did so, a dull splash sounded in the inlet beside us. Looking in that direction, we saw the dorsal fin and part of the back of a great white shark. Startled at our voices, it had given a sudden flirt in the water, and now held on its course straight out of the inlet.

Paralyzed for a moment, no one spoke. Then every one, shouted, "Shark! shark ! shark! Swim for your life!"

The Norwegian gave one glance over his shoulder, and struck out frantically for the boat. We held our breath in suspense. At that instant, the huge fish seemed animated with a sudden perception. Instantaneously, its dorsal fin disappeared below the surface of the water.

We glanced at the swimmer and the boat. The Norwegian's efforts were nerved with desperation. He was within six yards of the boat. In a moment more, his hands were grasping her gunwale. But suddenly throwing up his arms, he fell backward and submerged in the sea. A thrill of horror ran through us. The boat rocked with the tumultuous agitation of the waters on which she floated. Our blanched faces turned on each other as, with one accord, we exclaimed, "My God!"

"PORT, PORT!"

CHAPTER IX

THE DISCOURSE OF BILL RUGGLES—THE ANNOUNCEMENT OF THE NORWEGIAN'S FATE TO THE CAPTAIN AND CREW—THEIR HORROR— THE CAPTAIN'S SERMON—THE BURIAL SERVICE—THE SCHOONER SAILS.

AY I be henceforth spared the horror of a sight like that! Yet we saw nothing but a disappearance, save, as the boat presently swung within the influence of the current flowing into the inlet, and swept near us, we noted, with a shudder, that the water on which she floated was tinged with crimson.

We scarcely spoke for some minutes. Mechanically, Bill Ruggles grappled the boat with a stick, as she passed close to the beach on our side of the inlet, and then sat down on the ground, and Linden and I sat down beside him.

At last Ruggles spoke:

"Well, shipmates," said he, "I've been following the sea this many-a-day, but I don't know as I ever felt quite so cut up as I do this here minute. I've seen men drownded, and some smashed by falling from aloft, and mummoxed up all sorts of ways, but dash me if this don't go ahead." Here he wiped away a tear with the cuff of his coat. "I say," he resumed, "anything but that. You can't pound a man's life out any way that he's afeard of, if he's a lad of spirit, but, dash me, this is enough to scare anyone. I'm not much at prayers, but I feel as if we ought to do something that way. Here's a poor fellow gone to his last account, and not a soul to say something comfortable over him, with an Amen to the end of it."

If Ruggles had not used the most chaste language in his discourse, he had at least spoken to the hearts of both of his hearers.

53

"I feel jest so," replied Linden. "Why, Bill, I've lived, boy and man, on the Reef, these twenty year, and I never see that sight afore, and I pray God I never may again. It don't often happen, for all sharks is so thick in some places. Then I've knowed *him* ever so long, and who'd have thought that was to be the way he was to go."

We were all so absorbed in our thoughts, that we had not observed the wind, which had come up and begun to blow quite freshly. As Ruggles was about to rejoin something in answer to Linden, he happened to glance towards the schooner, from which he observed that signals were being made for the boat to return.

"There!" said Ruggles, "they're hailing us, and there's a breeze stirring that must have been up this half hour! I forgot about the wind, and everything else. Come! Aboard with you! The captain doesn't know what's happened yet. I'm thinking he'll take it as hard as any of us."

In a few minutes we were alongside of the schooner, and jumped aboard of her, just as the captain, who had been walking impatiently up and down the quarterdeck, strode forward and commenced with, "Where have you men,"— Suddenly observing the expression of our faces, and the absence of one of the party, he said quickly,— "What's happened? Is the other man hurt?"

"No, captain," said Ruggles, "he's out of pain. He's took."

"Took! Taken! How taken?—not by a shark? Heavens! You don't mean that!"

"Yes, I do, captain," replied Ruggles, dejectedly. "He was took by a shark afore our eyes, and we couldn't do nothing to save him, not one of us."

The crew drew around the group on deck, and echoed the words of Ruggles,— "Took by a shark!" The captain grasped me by the arm, and led me away to the cabin. "My boy," said he, when he had made me sit down, "this is too horrible for belief. You can tell me how this happened, better than one of the men. Let me hear."

I narrated to the captain, as clearly as I could, how the catastrophe took place, and how powerless we were to prevent it, as the man had suddenly jumped into the water, before anyone divined his intention. I concluded by mentioning how we were all overwhelmed, and what Ruggles had said to us of the horror of such a death, when compared with any other.

"Yes," said the captain, when I came to this part, "Ruggles is a rough, but a good-hearted fellow. What he said suggests something to me. It would be well to take advantage of this opportunity to say a word to the men. Go, Fred, and call them aft. I will meet them on the quarterdeck."

The men quickly assembled, and the captain, approaching the group, addressed them as follows:

"Men: I cannot let this occasion pass without saying a word or two to you. We sailors—you, I, and all of us—are apt to trust too much in ourselves. Here's a lesson of how little strength, skill, and courage, may avail. You now feel how utterly dependent we are on a higher power. Think seriously over this dreadful fate, and your thoughts will be better than anything I can say—better than the best sermon. And now, although we cannot bury your shipmate with the funeral rites which usually attend the dead, we can at least read a portion of the religious service."

With these words, the captain drew a small prayer book from his coat pocket, and opening it at a place which he had marked, he solemnly read the burial service, omitting only those portions which were not applicable to surrounding circumstances.

By the time that the beautiful epistle of St. Paul was finished, the auditors were much affected, and when the captain, reading beyond, reached the words of the service: "In the midst of life we are in death: of whom may we seek for succor, but of thee, O Lord!" two of the sailors fairly gave way, and sobbed aloud. Since then, I have often heard the service read at the grave, but I never heard it read with so great effect as then, when the sudden removal of a companion, by a fate so horrible, disposed all hearts to bow in submission before the Almighty.

"Now, men," added the captain, in a quiet voice, after he had given the concluding supplication, to which all fervently responded, "Heave up the anchor. Let's get underway and leave this place."

CHAPTER X

CAPTAIN BOWERS—KEY WEST—THE CONCHS.

HE scene which was enacted after the occurrence of the terrible event detailed in the last two chapters gave me some insight into the character of Captain Bowers. Chary of speech with regard to his feelings, he was nevertheless imbued with deep religious sentiment.

Although a strict disciplinarian on his vessel, he was always kind to the men, and ever ready to afford them any pleasure that was reasonable. In all my subsequent intercourse with him, I found him to be most considerate to everyone with whom he came in contact.

To me, immediately after the event at the Marquesas, he was particularly kind; and I ascribed his conduct to his belief that a young boy must have been terribly shocked by such an occurrence. In the course of two or three days, he gradually resumed his old manner; and this confirmed me in my previous belief that he did not consider it good for the discipline of the vessel to be seen in familiar intercourse with a person, who, of necessity, was obliged, in most things, to be one of the crew.

We reached Key West without any incident worth recording, and as soon as we had made fast to our wharf, the captain gave me leave to go ashore, and provide myself with the clothes of which I stood in so great need. These I readily found. They were goods made in New York. I soon disposed of my slender stock of cash, but that did not disturb me, for I had obtained all the clothes which I required, and of money for other purposes I had no need, having no other wants.

The town of Key West is situated on the northern part of the western end of an island which bears the same name. The island is situated a little north of latitude 24° 30', and a little west of longitude 80° 40' west from Greenwich. It is between four and five miles in length, and, at the broadest part, is not quite a mile in width. It has an elevation of only a few feet above the sea. Once, when a terrible hurricane prevailed there, the water of the ocean was so heaped up on the coast, by the violence of the wind, that a large portion of Key West was submerged and the inhabitants were compelled to seek refuge on the highest ground, which is about the middle of the island.

The town of Key West was well laid out, and contained some very desirable dwellings. The houses were generally provided with verandahs, similar to those which are usually found in tropical countries. The chief business of the town consisted in fitting out and supplying the wreckers, and all the people were devoted to nothing else, except a few travelers, who came for health, and sometimes left their bones. Everything revolved about that business; and everyone was an owner of a wrecker, or a captain of one, or a mate of one, or a sailor on one, or some female relation of these.

Very little food was grown upon the island. Back of the town, there were a few patches of land under cultivation, but they could not supply more than a very limited amount of food. Groceries came from New York; fruit from Havana; beef from the mainland of Florida. Fish and turtle abound on the Reef, whence Key West receives a surfeit. The most remarkable edifices in Key West were the latteen towers—tall, airy-looking structures of wood, from whose dizzy heights the Reef could be seen for miles. Cocoanut trees grew luxuriantly in the gardens, and limes were found in plenty.

Back of the town, and separated from it only by a narrow intervening space of open ground, the mangrove woods commenced, and covered nearly all the Key, although, in places, the growth was either diminutive or sparse. And now you have a picture of Key West.

The Conchs, of whom incidental mention has already been made, inhabit one portion of the island. Their quarter is called Conchtown. They were originally Bahamans, who settled in Key West, and pursued wrecking for a livelihood. Whether a man is a native Bahaman, resident in Key West, or whether he is born in Key West, seems to make no difference: he is known as a Conch.

The name of Conch is taken from that of the large shellfish which are found in great numbers in the waters of the Gulf. It is said to be applied to the Bahamans of Key West because the popular belief, or pretense, is that they subsist principally upon the food of these shellfish. A Conch, it is asserted, can dive to the bottom of the ocean, where the water is not more than twelve fathoms in depth, and there crack and eat one of his namesakes for breakfast.

However true that may be, and I leave you to judge of the probability for yourselves, I am unable to certify or deny it from my own personal experience. In the case of any other people, we might decide at once that they could not live long enough under water to make the shortest repast; but it so happens that the Conchs are most expert divers, and rules which apply to most men do not apply to them.

To people generally, the following will appear within bounds. It was at least vouched for by many residents of Key West. A gentleman on a fishing party to the Reef became seasick, and lost his false teeth overboard. One of the party noted some bearings of the land, and when they returned to Key West, a Conch was engaged to find the teeth and restore them to their owner, in which extraordinary undertaking he succeeded.

It must not be inferred from the circumstance that the Conchs exclusively inhabit a particular quarter in the town of Key West, or from their having acquired the reputation of being skilful divers and wreckers, that they never occupy stations above the grade of common sailors. Many captains, mates, and owners of wreckers come from these people. However, the majority, as elsewhere, are comprised in the class of ordinary seamen; and these, doubtless owing much to the fish diet upon which they chiefly subsist, are easily recognizable by their appearance and carriage.

They are a long, lanky, and sallow race, tough and wiry, and capable of much endurance in the region where they are acclimated.

CHAPTER XI

CAPTAIN TUFT AND HIS FRIENDS—THE EXCURSION TO SAND KEY—
CAPTAIN TUFT'S COOK, SOL—REFLECTIONS ON THE WONDERS OF THE
REEF—THE RETURN TO KEY WEST.

HILE Captain Bowers was waiting for the schooner's cargo of sugar to be unladen, and was receiving the stores which were to last during her cruise on the wrecking station for which she was bound, he had no need of my attendance, as he lived with his family in Key West.

The leisure which thus fell to my lot enabled me to make a very pleasant excursion to Sand Key, which is about eight miles to the south of Key West, and the southernmost possession of the United States. It contains an area of a couple of hundred square yards. Its surface is barely above the level of the ocean, and it does not possess a single blade of any sort of vegetation. At the time of which I speak, it presented much the same appearance that it exhibits now, except that since then the United States government has built there a huge lighthouse of iron, supported on piles of the same material. Some years before the erection of this lighthouse, another structure, for the same purpose, had been swept away by the hurricane already mentioned, which well-nigh destroyed the whole island.

The opportunity of making this trip to Sand Key was afforded me by a Captain Tuft, the captain of a wrecker which was fitting out at the wharf where our schooner lay. Captain Bowers had happened to mention my story to him, and this seemed to interest him in me; for one morning when paying a visit to Captain Bowers, he mentioned his intention of going to Sand Key on the following day, and asked permission to take me with the party.

The next day, about an hour after daylight, we started in a good stout sailboat, twenty-two feet in length, decked over the bow, and provided with washboards.

She was a staunch little craft, and, for her size, carried an immense spread of canvas. Her sail, however, did not prove too much for her, although she heeled over, and everything strained and cracked, and her mast bent as if it would go by the board. In an hour and ten minutes from the time of our departure from Key West, we landed on Sand Key. Captain Tuft, before starting, had not communicated to me the purpose of his visiting that place; but while we were sailing there, I learned from the conversation of the party, consisting of six persons in all, that the excursion was made for the purpose of having a feast on a certain fish, called sandfish, which frequent the coast of Florida, and are found in large numbers in the waters around Sand Key. The captain had brought the cook of his vessel with him, and had provided himself with all the appliances necessary for preparing the fish, not forgetting those accessories in the way of bread, butter, pickles, and condiments of all sorts, with which such parties are generally provided. I found that I had fallen in with a party of *bons vivants,* who had come down to regale themselves in epicurean style.

We had scarcely beached the boat, before the black cook, Sol, was out with his cast net, and making a straight line for the seaward side of the Key, where he thought that he perceived signs of fish. As this was the part of the day's diversion which pleased me most, I picked up the fish-basket, and quickly followed him. The main body of the Key was quite smooth and sandy, but, on the outside, the shore was broken up, by the action of the sea, into boulders of coral rock, scattered so profusely that, by the exercise of a little agility, Sol and I leaped from fragment to fragment, and thus avoided going into the water. In the pools formed by the absence of fragments in some places, whole schools of sandfish flashed around, and darted in and out through the numerous openings to the sea.

"Whist!" suddenly ejaculated Sol, and with that, he crouched low, and throwing his net over his arm, crept cautiously towards one of the pools. In an instant more, the net had left his hand and fallen fairly in the midst of a school of fish.

Just as I said that the net fell fairly in the midst of the fish, it suggested itself to me that you may not know how a casting net is made, and that it were well if I here describe it, as you cannot otherwise conceive how, by throwing a net on top of fish, they can be entrapped. The seine, the scoop net, and the casting net, are all constructed upon different principles. The scoop net captures fish by being raised from below; the casting net by falling from above; and the seine acts by the intermediate process, and merely encircles the fish, whereupon they can be hauled ashore.

The casting net is circular in form, and about three yards in diameter. For the purpose of keeping its edge close to the bottom of the water, little pellets of lead are placed around it at equal distances. A strong cord is attached to the centre of the net, and in throwing the net, the end of the cord is passed around the left wrist. The mass of the net is then supported in a heap on the left arm, while it is spread across between the left and right arm, the latter of which supports and encircles it around its curve. This partial spread of the net is what enables the caster to throw it so that it will open fully. If he held it otherwise, it would fall in a lump; but he extends one portion in its destined position, and suddenly launching that out into the air, the mass of net held on the left arm follows it, and the whole assumes a horizontal position, and falls flat on the surface of the water.

When Sol cast his net, there ensued such a thrashing and splashing and darting and leaping of fish, that it seemed to me that he must have missed his aim, and I intimated as much when I saw him deliberately hauling the net towards the rock on which he was stationed.

"No, sah," chuckled Sol, "dis niggah hab cotch too

many fish. Dey nose him by dis time, and dey nebber tries to get away."

"How about those that left in so great a hurry, Sol?" said I.

"Yah, yah; you see dey was disapp'inted bekase dey couldn't get in, and dey lef sudden. De fish on dis reef knows dat it's not ebery cook can do 'em up so brown as old Sol, so dere's gin'rally a rush to have the honor of me cookin' 'em."

There had certainly been a rush on this occasion, for as Sol slowly and carefully hauled his net to the rock on which he stood, I could see that it was alive with pan-fish from five to six inches in length. We carefully carried it to the sandy ground back of the coral boulders, and there disengaged its glistening burden.

While I was putting the fish into the basket, Sol made off in a new direction, and by the time I had finished, I saw the net swing out again, and fall into one of the neighboring pools. Carefully hauling in the cord, Sol gathered up the net, and approaching me, deposited on the sand a still bigger catch than his first one.

"I reckon we'se got enough to commence on," said Sol, as I heaped the basket nearly to the top.

"To commence on! Why Sol, there's enough for a ship's company!"

"Dey's ekal to *two* ships' companies any day,—the captain and his friends. I've fished for dem genelmen afore, sah,—yes, sah, dey's powerful feeders on small fry. It'll do to commence on. I'll tote de net, it'll wet you,—you tote de basket, will you, sah?"

We returned to the other end of the Key where, by this time, the captain and his five friends had built a fire in a portable stove, and had put up a shelter of canvas supported by four poles thrust into the ground. Under the shade of this awning, the captain and his friends appeared to be making themselves very comfortable with a bottle of light wine and some biscuit. Some such arrangement as the awning was very desirable, for although, in this region, the temperature in the shade never rises above 96° Fahrenheit, the heat in the sun is excessive, and the glare from the white coral sand intense. Under shelter, the sea breeze, which rarely ceases to blow, renders the ordinary temperature delightful.

"Hurry up, Sol!" exclaimed Captain Tuft. "The sail from Key West has given us all ravenous appetites. I didn't touch a morsel for breakfast, just to save myself up for this treat. I drank a cup of coffee, that's all."

Sol was at that very moment hurrying up, being engaged, with the Gulf for a basin, in cleaning and preparing the fish for the table, or rather, the ground spread with a few napkins. Securing my services, we soon had a couple of dozen fish seething and sputtering in the frying pan. This certainly could not have been more than a quarter of an hour from the time when they were caught.

Sol was right about the quality of the captain and his friends as trencher-men. It is true that none of them had had breakfast; all, like the captain, having avoided eating anything before leaving Key West, for the sake of the breakfast which awaited them at Sand Key. The fish were small, too; but then (indisputable fact) the basket had been nearly full, and no fish were left for me and Sol. Sol soon got over that difficulty, and in five minutes had caught another mess of fish, from which we selected the finest, and let the rest go, at which I wickedly informed Sol that they must be very much disappointed.

I found the sand-fish delicious. The bones are so delicate, that although one might wish them smaller, they are not large enough for one to think of picking them out. The most agreeable method of eating these fish is by removing the head, taking the tail between the fingers, and conveying the fish to the mouth without the aid of knife or fork.

By the time I had finished my breakfast, to which Sol added his society, by standing and munching near the place where I sat in the bow of the boat, the captain and his friends were well underway in sea stories and cigars. Sol had commenced to wash up the crockery, and I, having nothing to engage my attention, wandered back to the coral boulders from which Sol had cast his net.

Some of them lay so closely together that I could sit on one and place my heels on two others. As I sat in this position, I gradually came to notice all sorts of little creeping things and fishes and marine plants which, from their diminutive size, had not at first attracted my attention. I got down on my hands and knees, and then lay prone on my face, and examined the water between the boulders. It was swarming with life of every variety. One little fish particularly engaged my attention. It was very small, not more than two inches long, and its minuteness was probably the cause of its not being alarmed at my proximity. In comparison with it, I was probably so gigantic, that it did not even realize my presence. Its color was the most beautiful mazarine blue, when it paddled into the shadows, and when it emerged into the light, it took a cerulean tint. On the Reef, these fish are called bluefish, and they grow much larger, being, when full grown, several inches in length. They never attain a large size.

I lay for a long time watching this fish, and the other living things that, in great numbers, occupied every little shallow; and then I sat up, and looked along the stretch of Keys and Reefs, and thought how strange was this multiform and myriad life, how wonderful this coral which built solid walls of rock from the waters of the sea, and ceaselessly and harmoniously followed out the Divine Thought, in obedience to the Divine Will.

"Fred! Fred!" I suddenly heard the voice of the captain shout, "All aboard, now; we're off for Key West!"

The wind was abeam, and in a little more than the time taken by our first trip, we reached Key West. After thanking the captain for his kindness, I went aboard of the *Flying Cloud,* which was deserted by the men, some of whom were looking on, while the others were engaged in helping to land wild cattle from a neighboring schooner, just arrived from the mainland of Florida.

CHAPTER XII

THE CHARACTER OF THE SAILOR—LANDING WILD CATTLE—THE MAD BULL—THE CAPTAIN'S INTENTION TO SAIL.

*I*F it is true, as Shakespeare says, that we, meaning men and women generally, are but children of a larger growth, the sailor is always the veriest child.

Doubtless it is the freshness of mind and impulsiveness, which he retains in original purity, that so captivate the popular heart. The strange compound which he presents of diffidence and self-conceit, of superstitious awe and quick intelligence, of sportiveness and pugnacity,—of all, in short, that is ill-regulated and contradictory,—is discovered only in the conduct of the child and of the sailor.

I found our men dancing in glee around the spot where the cattle were being landed. The more the bulls raged and strained to break away, the more the crew shouted with delight.

On the wharf was an open space, on which were congregated some cattle which had been landed. When fairly herded on shore, after being released from the dark and noisome hold of the vessel, and from the fastenings by which they were hoisted to the land, they seemed to find so great solace in companionship, that they stood gazing around them with stupid wonderment, as if striving with their dull perceptions, to take in their situation, and mutely inquiring, "What torture next?" The moment of landing was the fearful period for each beast; and each, in turn, resisted as strenuously as horns and hoofs and bellowing could avail.

The operation of landing the cattle was effected in the following manner: First of all, a block and tackle were rigged aloft on the schooner. The end of the tackle was then fastened around the horns of a bull. Another rope was fastened to the horns, and its end passed through an iron ring in the wharf. When the men hauled away on the tackle, the animal was, of course, gradually elevated through the hatchway, and suspended in mid-air. Hanging thus, it looked as if dislocated in every joint, and stretched entirely out of shape. When its hind hoofs were sufficiently high to clear the rail of the schooner, the men on shore hauled away on the rope which passed through the iron ring, and as soon as the hind hoofs cleared the rail, the tackle was eased away until they touched the ground. But the men who were in charge of the rope on shore then had to be on the alert; for the very moment that the animal felt ground, a complete transformation took place. The meek, piteous beast of the lengthened carcass, became the well-knit, ponderous brute of flaming eye, distended nostril, foaming mouth, and pawing hoof.

With any scope of line, the infuriated animal would have broken away, and taken vengeance upon its tormentors. To avoid the danger of this occurrence, when its hind hoofs touched ground, the tackle was quickly eased away, and the rope passing through the ring was hauled so suddenly that the animal's head was brought into forcible contact with the ring on the ground. In this position, it fell and rose, foamed and bellowed, until, exhausted with rage, its quietness confessed defeat. It was then released, whereupon it abjectly trotted off to join the troop of animals which had gone through the same process, and now, as spectators, stood with fearful curiosity, gazing at the performance in which they had just ceased to be actors.

Our men enjoyed all this vastly, and three of them, as volunteers, were manning the rope which passed through the ring. At last came the turn of a particularly savage black bull. There was great trouble to make the tackle fast to his horns; but it was at last accomplished, and he slowly rose above the hatchway. He was, in form, a splendid fellow, and as sleek as if he had been groomed. The usual operation was coming to an end; the hind hoofs touched; the tackle was eased away; and the men at the ring brought the animal's head down with so great violence, that his fore-feet gave way under him, and he fell on his chest. But with a bellow of concentrated rage, he sprang to his feet, and gathering his body into a heap, in which every muscle was brought into play, he made one superlative effort, and broke his bonds. In an instant, all was confusion on the wharf. The bull staggered from the excess of force which he had put into his effort. Then, shaking his head, and glaring around, purpose seemed to settle upon him. His head lowered, and he rushed at the nearest man.

But the man was a sailor, or else he would never have been saved. Dropping instantly, he rolled over and over like a bundle, and just as he fell over the edge of the wharf, he grasped it with both hands, and held on. All this occupied but a few seconds. The bull was disconcerted at the extraordinary manoeuvre of an enemy who had put his body out of sight, but left a head looking at him over the level of the wharf. Drawing a deep breath, expressive of mingled amazement and animosity, he paused, then glanced around to discover his other enemies. They had had time to take refuge in all directions, and, with a snort of defiance, the bull made straight for the town of Key West.

The men came out of their places of security, rushed on the wharf, and shouted, "Mad bull! mad bull!" As our eyes followed him dashing up the street which ranged with the wharf, we could see the people scampering in all directions, and taking refuge in the porches and doorways of houses, or in any shelter that presented itself. We could see the beast occasionally swerve from his course, as he caught sight of someone, and when disappointed, resume his career. He had not more than a mile to go before he reached the woods, and only a portion of that distance lay through the town. Fortunately, no one was injured, and as we hurried towards the woods with guns, we heard the sharp crack of a couple of rifles which forestalled our intention, for we found the poor bull weltering in his blood, and dead.

When we returned to the *Flying Cloud,* I met Captain Bowers, who had heard of the disturbance, and had come down to the vessel.

He made a few inquiries of me, and then said:

"We are to sail tomorrow, Fred. Are you all ready?"

"Quite, sir," I replied, "I had nothing to do, but what I did on the day when we arrived. Please, sir, don't forget to leave my name with the owners, so that if a letter comes for me, it will be sent up the Reef with your mail."

"Certainly not, Fred; I will attend to that. Have you anything else to ask? Make sure, now, for we'll sail tomorrow, for certain."

"No, sir," I answered,— "nothing but that."

"Good-evening, then," said the captain, as he left me.

"Good-evening, captain," I replied, as I walked away and fell into a thoughtful mood,—revolving in my mind my father's letter, my home, and the mysterious Reef to which, by a strange conjunction of circumstances, I was proceeding as the cabin boy of a wrecker.

CHAPTER XIII

THE EFFECT OF A GALE UPON THE COLOR OF THE WATER ABOUT THE
REEF—THE FLYING CLOUD SAILS FROM KEY WEST—HER CRUISE
BETWEEN THE FLORIDA REEF AND KEYS.

HEN on the following morning, I came on deck, a norther, which had commenced to blow on the preceding night, was still unabated. It blew steadily: neither "lighter nor heavier," a sailor would say. So it continued for three full days. Almost the first thing that struck me was the change that had taken place in the water. It had become a dirty cream-color. On inquiry, I ascertained that the storms on the Reef always produce this effect.

Of course, the sea is always swashing over every part of the Reef, detaching fragments from the massive corals, shattering the more fragile growths, and grinding both together and against the bottom, until they crumble to pieces, and even become reduced to powder. This product of the material of the Reef, and the ceaseless labor of the sea, is called disintegrated coral, and forms the only sand known to the region of the Florida Keys. When a violent wind, like a norther, prevails, this sand along the beaches, and in the shallows, and even in the depths is stirred up; more is added to it by the constant wearing of the sea, and, after a few hours, the whole of the waters about the Reef become turbid and tinged with the cream-like color described, and remain so until some hours after the storm has subsided.

We lay at Key West for three days, when the norther ceased. After shipping a man to supply the place of the Norwegian, we cast loose from our wharf, and set sail up the Reef. On our larboard hand lay a stretch of innumerable

71

Keys, often so close together that we could not distinguish any break in the land, until we came abreast of it, and "opened" the inlets through which other Keys were visible, appearing scattered in the waters, back of the well-defined line that we were coasting. All were low, some of them not being more than two or three feet above the level of the sea, and others were partially overflowed. They all exhibited, in greater or less denseness of foliage, the uniform, universal mangrove trees.

The wind was so fair that we could lay our course along the Reef, and it was now beautiful weather, as is usually the case after a norther, so that I enjoyed the sail exceedingly. I had become so used to my duties, which in themselves were quite light, that I felt them to be only nominal, having plenty of time at my disposal, and luxuriating in the novel scenes by which I was surrounded. At first, there had been two drawbacks to my happiness. In leaving Key West, I realized more than ever that I was indeed cast upon the world, and dependent upon my own resources, and I was ignorant of what were my father's sentiments towards me. I also yearned for companionship. Strictly speaking, I belonged neither forward nor aft, and felt and acted accordingly. These sources of uneasiness marred, but could not altogether destroy, my pleasure. I once more buoyed myself up with the arguments which I had previously used to conquer my dejection, and, at last, came to my former sage conclusion, that if misfortune were destined to come, I ought not to meet it half way, and then if it were not, (and with a father so good and kind, why should I suppose it probable?) I should find that I had been giving myself gratuitous pain. As for want of companionship, I reasoned with myself that it was a small matter, and soon threw off the longing, and gradually resumed my late resigned and contented mood.

O youth, thy griefs are fleeting, but thy hopes and joys perennial!

CHAPTER XIV

FRED RANSOM DESCRIBES THE REEF AND KEYS, IN ORDER THAT THE READER MAY MORE FULLY ENJOY THE ADVENTURES WHICH ARE TO FOLLOW, AND ALSO ACQUIRE SOME KNOWLEDGE WELL WORTH OBTAINING.

AS I draw near those scenes in which I was destined to spend several months, it would be well, for the sake of the better understanding of what is to follow, and for that of general information, if the reader will fancy himself aboard of the *Flying Cloud,* as she sails along the Keys, and, meanwhile, learn something about the present formation of the Reef,—how it was made, and how the work still goes on under the charge of little builders, to whom the task was committed thousands and thousands of years ago by the Great Architect of the Universe.

In general terms, the Florida Reef includes all the coral ledges and neighboring Keys; but to speak more precisely, the Florida Reef is one great ridge of coral, stretching continuously from a short distance north of Cape Florida, to several miles beyond Key West. This is the Reef proper, the Reef which must be distinguished as such for it is the only thing thereabouts really entitled to the name, for the reason that it is the only great coral bank lying under water. Except some patches of coral sand, not comprising more than a few square yards, it is entirely submerged, whereas, the Florida Keys form a long line of islands, covered with verdure, and many of them capable of cultivation.

Commencing at Virginia Key, the northern-most island of the Florida Keys, and just above Cape Florida (for the Cape is the southern end of Key Biscayne, the next Key to

Virginia Key), the Reef, except the few patches mentioned, is a great submerged bank, which runs in a gradual curve to a point west of the Marquesas, where it stops abruptly and forms, with the banks around the Marquesas, the main entrance to the Reef Channel and to the Harbor of Key West. Commencing at the north again, the general trend of the Reef and Keys, for about sixty miles, is south-southwest; then, for about one hundred and forty miles, west-south-west; and then, between thirty and forty miles, including the Tortugas, the rest of the line takes a direction about west-northwest. The line of the Reef and Keys curves so regularly, that it forms the segment of a circle with a diameter of about two hundred and forty miles.

Parallel to the great submerged coral bank, which I have said constitutes the Reef, and varying in distance from two to five miles from it, lie the Florida Keys, the appearance of which has been already described. The southernmost one is Sand Key, to which Captain Tuft took me on the fishing excursion from Key West. The westernmost ones are a group named the Tortugas, so called from the abundance of turtles found in the neighboring waters.*

The Reef is really the left bank of the straits of Florida, through which the Gulf Stream flows into the Atlantic. It also forms a natural breakwater for the Florida Keys, throughout their whole extent; for the top of the Reef, being only a few feet under water, protects the Keys from the violence of the waves, and although there often is surf on their beaches, it is of a very different character from that driven in from an open sea. Ordinarily, the water of the channel between the Keys and Reef is not more agitated than usual in the lower parts of bays.

All that we see here, and all that lies beyond, for miles and miles further than any distance which you can actually conceive, although you may know it to exist, is the work of

*The name formerly used for turtle was tortoise, and the word Tortugas is derived from the Spanish word for tortoise—tortuga.

little animals, a species of polyp, so minute and delicate, that before one constructs its rock castle, a little pinch between the finger and thumb would deprive it of existence. For thousands upon thousands of years, they have gone on untiringly constructing a great peninsula of a continent.

What the present Reef is, the Keys once were. They were a coral Reef, commencing to the northward, at the same point at which the present Reef begins, but extending further, and ending in the group of Keys called the Tortugas. Now, still counting from the eastward, we come to the densely wooded shore of the mainland of Florida. This consists of a line of hummocks, which are neither more nor less than an ancient line of Keys, situated on an ancient line of Reef. Back of this main-shore of low bluffs, and after penetrating the growth which covers a low strip of land called the Indian Hunting Grounds, we come to the first of seven parallel lines of hummocks that have already been discovered. These are all known to be the successive lines that have in turn formed the Florida Reef. From Reefs they became Keys, and from Keys, mainland. This is strange enough, but more wonders probably remain than those which have been revealed; for there is reason to suppose that the whole peninsula of Florida has been formed in the same manner.*

Between the present Reef and Keys, there is now a deep channel, but in the course of time, the Reef will complete its growth, and the channel between the present Reef and Keys will fill up by the same process which is now connecting the present Keys with the mainland, and which has already been completed between the shore bluffs and the lines of hummocks in the interior.

You may ask what the limit of this Reef extension is to be. The answer is very simple. The Reef-building polyps cannot build in water exceeding fifteen fathoms in depth, and

*For the fact as to the number of lines of ancient Reef discovered on the mainland of Florida, as well as for several other facts included in this chapter, I am indebted to Professor Agassiz's work entitled, "Methods of Study in Natural History."

not far from the present Reef, the Gulf Stream rolls its almost unfathomable waters.

Without doubt, in picturing to yourselves the corals, you have always imagined them to be either like those delicate red or roseate ones used for trinkets, or like those whose exquisite whiteness and antlered gracefulness render them conspicuous in parlor or cabinet. The corals, however, are of many colors, and of various kinds of entirely different structure.

The corals build Reefs only in tropical climates. The Reef is a wall of limestone formed by the animals from the lime which exist in a state of suspension in the salt water. These polyps have the power of assimilating the lime,—that is, the animals convert the lime to the purposes of their existence. Digestion, for instance, is the process of assimilating food, and although lime does not become the food of these polyps, but, on the contrary, their dwellings, yet in thus appropriating this substance to the purposes of their existence, they perform one of the acts called assimilation.

The direction of a line of Reef conforms to the shore off which it is situated. If the shore is straight or curved, so, also, in the same degree, will be the Reef. Sometimes as in the Pacific, it has surrounded an island, which, by the sinking of the ocean bottom, has disappeared below the surface, while, at the same time, the Reef has grown until it reached nearly to the surface, and then, gradually collecting a soil upon which a dense vegetation has sprung up, it has been transformed into a verdant ring of land surrounding a lake in mid-ocean.

Now that you have learned where the corals choose the sites for the construction of their homes, it is time for you to become acquainted with the mode in which they proceed. The foundations of a Reef are laid broadly and strongly by a kind of coral which constructs huge knobs of many feet in diameter. These the sailors on the Reef call "coral heads." The present Reef is about seventy feet in height, and the whole base of it is composed of coral heads. When in the commencement of a Reef, these "heads" have multiplied and grown in height, until the water has become as shallow as six fathoms in depth, the condition of their prosperity, which requires a certain pressure of water, ceases, and with it ceases their further development. They give place to another kind of coral, which, in time, gives place to another, and another, until just below the surface of the sea, the top of a Reef is crowned and variegated with a delicate growth of fragile corals, corallines, sea-fans, &c.

The Reef is now finished, and forms a solid wall of limestone, abrupt on the seaward side, and sloping gently landward. Now another process completes the sea-wall. The action of the waves on the Reef has detached great masses of coral, broken them into fragments, and ground them into sand. This sand, and materials composed of shells, decaying animal matter, timber and mud from the mainland, are gradually collected among the light corals on the summit of the Reef, until, at last, a tolerably secure soil begins to appear above the surface of the sea. On this, the waves soon wash up the same material that commenced to form the land, and it is rendered still more secure. Vegetation is now the only thing needed, and it comes by accident: that is, if aught can be accident that so resembles design.

The greatest resource which these spots have is in the mangrove tree, with which nearly all the Keys are more or less covered. In the condition of little stalks with roots at the end, the mangrove seeds float in great numbers around the Reef and Keys, and are, of course, deposited wherever the waves carry them. No sooner do they obtain a foothold, than they begin to sprout rapidly, for salt water does not impede their growth. As they shoot up, they throw out numerous roots, not only below, but above, so that the stem is surrounded by a gnarled, fantastic enclosure, over which it is difficult to clamber. In this uncouth basket-work, which looks like a nightmare of rustic arbor furniture, all sorts of materials collect, and the permanence of the new-born Key is tolerably well assured.

We now come to the process by which a Reef becomes, first, the shore of the mainland, and, afterwards, hummocks in the interior. While the Reef is being built, the channel between the Keys (or former Reef) and the mainland has been gradually filling up with mud flats, and by the time the Reef is completed, and another one commenced outside (for the latter does not commence until the other is finished), the channel between the Reef and Keys begins to fill up, while that between the Keys and mainland will have closed, thus making the Keys part of the mainland.

You do not, of course, imagine that, while I was sailing along the Reef, I gleaned all the information which I have imparted. All I saw was, on one hand, a long stretch of green islands, and on the other, the great ocean, with the surf dashing, in places, on the intervening Reef. What I have told you was learned where most information is gained—from books. Then, too, my life on the coast, during the following months, made me very familiar with that region.

Now you will more readily comprehend, and therefore more fully enjoy the adventures to be narrated.

CHAPTER XV

HOW THE OCCUPATION OF WRECKING IS PURSUED—OBSERVATIONS ON
THE CHARACTER OF THE WRECKERS.

ETWEEN the Reef and Keys the wreckers lie securely at anchor, stationed near enough to one another to enable them, by sailing a few miles in each direction, to survey the whole extent of the Reef. In case of necessity, as soon as they sight each other, they communicate by signals. Imagine this long stretch of Reef with its wreckers stationed at regular intervals along its course. There they lie, ever ready, at a moment's notice, to sail at a signal of distress. Not more speedily do the buzzards, from their aerial heights, descry the distant prey and grow from nothing to specks, and then to distinct birds winging their flight from every quarter, than the fast wreckers spread their canvas wings, and flock towards the vessel of the stranded mariner. But the purpose that actuates them is very different. One comes to quench, if need be, a lingering spark of life, but the other comes to save and restore.

It is a very common, and, at the same time, erroneous belief, that the wrecker is one who, on occasions, does not scruple to show false lights to lure the unwary navigator to destruction, and who, under pretense of saving property and life, is ever ready to resort to pillage and personal violence to secure possession of merchandise. This idea comes entirely from the knowledge which everyone possesses, that, in wrecking, what is the loss of one man is the gain of another. But so it is, in greater or less degree, in all the transactions of life. It is evident, that if this notion about the wreckers is correct, the same influence must corrupt nearly all mankind, and especially it would not be safe to live with lawyers and physicians, for fear of being drugged, or constantly set by the ears. In all my intercourse with wreckers, I found them to be men much like others of their species; and if there was anything objectionable in their mode of life, it was in a particular injurious to themselves, and about which you will learn when I come to the history of our daily life.

Wrecking. according to a system like that established in Florida, by law, should not be confounded with the coast piracy, which, in old times, often existed in what were called civilized countries, and which still exists along barbarous coasts. There was a time, when, even in civilized countries, the wreck was considered the lawful property of the king of the country where it was cast away. Then there was little mercy for the property or lives of the shipwrecked, except that which the *salvors* chose to extend. But in Florida, now, whatever wrecking there may once have been, when the island of Key West was a favorite resort of smugglers and pirates, the business is as regularly conducted as any occupation in which seamen are engaged. The wrecking vessels are there to give aid, but if a captain chooses to refuse it, even if he needs it, he can use his own pleasure. When, however, he puts his vessel and cargo in charge of any one of the vessels that come to his rescue, the captain of the latter becomes responsible for all further proceedings, and takes full command, and employs others to aid him, or not, as he judges fit. When the stranded vessel, or the merchandise, or both, are saved, the amount due to the salvor is awarded by the Judge of an Admiralty Court. The sum adjudged to be due to the wreckers, in proportion to the loss which they have averted, is termed the salvage. If, now-a-days, there is anything nefarious about wrecking, it is generally on the side of the wrecked. Many a vessel, for the sake of obtaining the money for which it was insured, has been intentionally driven on the Reef, during a night of quiet weather, when there was no danger of her going to pieces.

The wrecking vessels being strung at intervals along the Reef, between it and the Keys, every now and then we paused close to one and received a hail and inquiry whether we had brought any mail for her from Key West. But we had none, except for a vessel which we expected to find near to the station for which we were bound; so after shaking the schooner up in the wind, for a minute or two, so as to give the captains a chance to have a short talk, we kept away on our course.

We sailed along most prosperously until about dark, when we came to anchor just off Indian Key, on which there were a number of houses. The captain went ashore to visit someone, but as he did not order me to accompany him, I had no opportunity of seeing more than the general appearance of the Key, on which I could plainly distinguish the houses of the settlement.

CHAPTER XVI

THE FLYING CLOUD WEIGHS ANCHOR—THE KINGFISH—WE COME TO
ANCHOR AT OUR WRECKING STATION—THE WRECKER'S LIFE.

HE next morning I was aroused by the voices of the crew, as they cheerily sang while heaving up the anchor. In a few moments I was on deck and engaged at my duties. The first one always consisted in providing the captain with a cup of coffee. The cook had already given one apiece to the men. This coffee drinking I found to be a regular custom on the Reef. With a good cup of the exhilarating beverage, the men can better perform their duty before breakfast.

Before I could get on deck, the crew had the sails set, and the anchor apeak; and just as I put my head above the companionway, I saw the jib run up, and the schooner's head fall off, as the quick clicking of the windlass told me that the anchor was clear of the bottom, and the schooner underway.

The morning gave promise of as clear a day as the preceding one had been. We had a spanking breeze, but it was dead ahead. However, as we had only about ten miles to go before reaching our station, the direction of the wind did not trouble us.

We had hardly sailed five miles, when, in a vessel bearing down for us, the captain recognized the schooner which occupied the station to the northward of ours. She was now on her morning sail along the Reef, to sight the next wrecker to the southward. Lately she had had double duty to perform, on account of our absence. As she had a fair wind, she soon neared us and luffed up, whereupon we threw her mail aboard of her, and she kept away, and resumed her course down the Reef.

Our black cook, Hannibal, suggested to me that it would be a good plan to troll for some fish, so I got out my tackle, with which I had provided myself at Key West, procured a chunk of pork at the galley, baited one of my biggest hooks, and let it float out well astern of the schooner. It had not been in the water more than five minutes, when I saw a large fish dart at the bait, and, at the same time, the line slackened, and then jerked violently. I gave a shout, and hauled away with all my might and main, but I could not go hand over hand more than twice. I was just able to hold the fish.

"You're got 'um," said Hannibal, running quickly aft, and chuckling at my success. "He too much for you alone, massa, let me lend you a hand."

"He will be too much for both of you," said the captain, emerging from the cabin, "for he'll part the line if you try to haul it in while the vessel has so much way on her." The captain turned to the man at the helm. "Here, luff the schooner up in the wind's eye."

The schooner ran up into the wind, until her sails were all shaking.

"Now," said the captain, as the vessel began to lose her headway, "haul in as fast as you can, Fred. Hannibal, you help him."

Hannibal and I hauled away as directed, and soon got the fish on dock. It was a splendid kingfish, a species of pike quite numerous in the waters of the Reef.

"There, Hannibal," said the captain, "take him forward and make him into a chowder. There'll be enough for the cabin, and all hands forward."

I followed my prize forward, perfectly delighted at my success, as, before that occasion, I had never caught anything larger than a river perch. I suppose that if I had then been called upon to estimate the weight of the fish, I would have set it down at several hundred pounds.

In about an hour, we came to our appointed station off the Reef. The sails were soon furled, and the captain took breakfast. The men had had theirs while we were underway.

Here we were, at last, on our destined station, to remain how long, I had not the slightest idea, for the intentions of owners and captains are not communicated to cabin boys and crews. Shrewd guesses, however, are often made as to matters which are not mentioned. Nice calculations of the probabilities of a vessel's stay are often gathered by the men from mere trifles.

The crew were set to work at scraping and slushing down the masts, and at resetting and tarring down the standing rigging. The day passed in this and other work needed to put the schooner in perfect condition. Aboard of a ship at sea, the work is ceaseless. On a schooner, like ours, of less than a hundred tons burden, the work, of course, bears no comparison with that aboard of a ship. Besides, it is less in proportion; for as a wrecker lies much at anchor, she is not subjected to the wear and tear incidental to a vessel constantly underway. Still, there is always something to be done on the smallest vessel.

The experience of the following few days instructed me in the whole business of wrecking, but it was not until I reached a more mature age that I was enabled to realize the feature to which I once alluded as objectionable in the life of the wrecker. Not being employed at regular wages, he is paid his proportion of salvage. His profession is that of taking a share in a lottery. He may draw a prize, but he is more likely to receive a blank. The case of the whaler, who also goes on shares, is different, for he is sure of something. But the wrecker may serve a long time, and earn absolutely nothing. Meanwhile, where is he? On board of a small vessel with a large crew, and without sufficient work to employ his body or mind. He has high hopes for the future, sustained by some crumbs of comfort from the past.

CHAPTER XVII

FRED RANSOM'S FIRST DAY'S EXPERIENCE AT WRECKING—HE, BILL RUGGLES, JOHN LINDEN, THOMAS DEAL, AND DENNIS BRADY, THE IRISHMAN, GO ASHORE—THEY TAKE JACK, WHO ALWAYS WANTS TO BE ONE OF A PARTY WHERE THERE IS LIKELY TO BE ANY SPORT.

UST at the peep of day, on the following morning, the *Flying Cloud* got underway, and sailed eight or ten miles to the northward, until she sighted the wrecker that had passed us the day before, and afterwards repassed us in order to resume her station on the Reef. The wrecker was underway for the purpose of sighting our vessel. No wreck appearing on the Reef, between the two schooners, they reversed their course, the *Flying Cloud* running past her anchorage, and examining the Reef, until she sighted a wrecking sloop that was underway from the next station to the southward. She then reversed her course for the second time, and ran towards her anchorage.

"Where will we sail now?" I inquired of Ruggles, with whom I was standing on the forward deck.

"Nowheres, today," he answered, "unless it should blow this afternoon, and then the captain might chance to get underway again."

"And is this all that we shall have to do every day?" I asked.

"Well, yes," said Ruggles, "about all, 'cept keeping the schooner in good order, and sometimes getting underway in the afternoon, if it's blown heavy along through the day, 'mounting to a storm. We always take a good squint at the Reef, the first thing every morning; for night's the likeliest time, you see, for vessels to pile on it."

"It seems to me, Bill," rejoined I, "that wreckers must

85

have mighty easy times."

Well," said he, "for sea-faring men, they do have about the easiest times a-going. 'Cept when they gets a wrack, and then a crew has about enough to do in a week to last them for a year. What with getting a wrack off, or a-saving of her cargo, and a-taking on it to Key West, and everything about it, why the crew has a-plenty to do, I tell you."

"How do you kill all your spare time?" I asked.

"We gin'rally get plenty of liberty on shore, and the Reef is fairly alive with fish and turtle, and such like. We can't hardly miss catching something, even when we're off, just for a spell, to cut wood for the schooner. Then a man can stand a precious lot of sleep, if he practices at it. But you ain't a-goin' to complain about not having enough work to do, be you? If you be, I guess you'll find some of the crew as'll accommodate you with some of their'n."

"You had better believe I don't intend to complain about that," said I, laughing, "but I thought wreckers were every day pitching around offshore in a heavy sea, or floating about on rafts and saving people's property and lives, and doing all sorts of desperate things, and when I began to suspect how different it was, I felt like asking some questions— that's all."

"You may see more of jest that sort of thing, of pitching around, etcetery, than you care for, before your time's out," said Ruggles. "But it don't happen every day, because it don't storm every day, and ships isn't lost along the Reef every day it does storm. Wrackers is like an army preparing for battle; easy times in camp, and then blue blazes, and then easy times, and blue blazes again."

"That reminds me, Bill," said I, "to ask you why the schooner has arms aboard. The Indians about here are peaceable, are they not?"

"Oh, yes," replied Ruggles, "the Indians around here is peaceable enough. They're the Spanish Indians; but you know the Seminole Indians, to the northward of them, are at war now with Uncle Sam, and Indians is a curious set. You don't know where to have 'em; they're peaceable with you one day, and your throat's cut afore morning. I expect the owners think it's about as well to be on the safe side, and keep arms aboard the schooner."

"But, Bill," said I, "what is the use of people's having arms, if they are not always ready to use them. We didn't keep any watch on deck last night, did we? What is it to prevent Indians from capturing the vessel at night?"

"Nothing, as I knows on," Ruggles replied, "'cept what I told you just now, that Indians is curious critters. They've a mortal fear of tackling a vessel. There's nothing they be afeard to try ashore, if there's plenty of trees and bushes around, but they don't like the looks of a vessel. Perhaps it's because it seems such a mighty big thing to their canoes, and besides, as I told you, it's against the nature of Indians to do any fighting, unless there's plenty of woods, or other cover around, and if they attack a vessel, they've got to paddle off to her jest as if it was open ground, only worse, because on open ground they could scatter if they wanted to, but in canoes they'd be huddled together."

"Do the men go armed, whenever they go ashore?" I inquired.

"Mostly," said Ruggles, "when they go to the mainland; leastways, it's been so ever since I've been here; but on the Keys, we're not always so partic'lar."

"Why, when you land on a Key," said I, "how can you tell that there may not be Indians from the mainland there, prowling around in the mangroves? Their canoes could be hid, just by hauling them their length from the edge of the shore."

"Well, we don't know, that's a fact," said Ruggles, "but it's jest a risk we run, sometimes. I reckon it isn't much of a risk though, for as I was a-telling you, these Spanish Indians are peaceable-like. Still what's the use of having arms if you don't carry them, I say, and I don't trust an Indian nohow. It's a'most as easy to take the arms in the boat, as to leave them behind, but the wrackers' crews has got used to knowing there's Indians around that seem to be peaceable inclined, and I reckon that's the reason they often forget to carry their arms. But I often says, boys, wouldn't it be safer if we'd bring some muskets along, for, says I, if we meet Indians, says I, and they get to know we're in the habit of going without arms, it mightn't be safe for us. My belief, I says, is, that the Indians gin'rally thinks the crews has arms along with 'em in the boat. I've met parties of Indians several times, when I've been with a boat's crew over to the mainland, but they never troubled us. They're always asking for tobacco, but they're very civil."

"Ready, about!" sang out the man at the helm.

Bill Ruggles left me, and ran to tend the jib-sheets.

"Helm's a-lee," again sang out the man who steered. Then came the rattling of blocks, and shaking of sails, as the schooner ran up into the wind, and went about.

"Draw away!" shouted the helmsman.

Bill Ruggles and the man with him tending the jib-sheets eased them away. Bill returned to me, saying, "We'll fetch our anchorage on this tack."

"Is there anything to prevent our going ashore, when we come to anchor?" I inquired. "The captain has had his dinner, that clears me. Is there anything for the crew to do? Wouldn't you like to go? How do you think that the rest would like to go?"

"I'll go quick enough," said Ruggles. "I'll jest see who else'll like to go, and one can ask for all. It won't be more than ten minutes afore we'll be at anchor, and as soon as the sails is furled, I reckon the captain'll give us liberty, if too many don't ask. I reckon there'll be enough of the crew that won't want to go, for any work that the captain may have to do this afternoon."

Ruggles inquired, and found that John Linden and one of the other Conchs, named Thomas Deal, wished to go, and also the Irishman, whose name was Dennis Brady. They and Ruggles and I would make a party of five,—a very good number,—four to row, and one to steer the boat. I was deputed to go and ask permission of the captain, who readily gave it, on condition that the sails should be furled before we started.

"All right," said I, addressing Ruggles, as I rejoined him. "We can go after all hands furl the sails."

"Come, boys," cried he, putting his head down the hatchway, "tumble up here, and stand by to furl sail the moment we let go our anchor. The captain says we can go."

In the course of a quarter of an hour, the vessel was lying at anchor, with everything snug, and the men lowered away one of the quarter-boats, and began to put various things into her.

"Let's take everything," said Linden, "harpoon, grains, and a couple of muskets, and then we'll be ready for any game that comes along."

Jack seeing all these preparations, was seized with so intense a wagging of his tail, that he almost wagged his hind feet off the deck.

"Old Jack wants to go," said I. "I guess we can take him without asking permission, can't we?"

"Oh yes!" said Ruggles; "here, you men, lend a hand and help him into the boat. That's it, take hold, two of you, e-a-s-y now with him."

"My! but it's the nate way he has to get aboord," exclaimed Brady, as Jack scrambled down the side of the schooner. "But he's the wise one, though, and if he wasn't so cloomsy, bedad! he'd be the image of the dorg I had in the ould counthry."

"Gammon, Dennis!" said Ruggles, very unceremoniously, as he shoved off from the vessel, and took his seat at the tiller. "You never had a Newfoundland."

"It's the thruth that I'm t'lling ye," said Brady, giving way lustily with his oar. "The finest dorgs in the worruld comes from Ireland. Me ooncle has a pack of Newfoundlands."

"A pack of Newfoundlands?" said Ruggles, shouting with laughter.

"Aye!" rejoined Brady, "it's a pack of Newfoundlands; an'

sure, and what is there so quare about that? On an eshtate like me ooncle's, about half the size of Floridy, a great many dorgs is naded."

"Well, suppose there is," said Ruggles, "Newfoundlands ain't hunting dogs, be they? What are you talking about packs for?"

"There's where you're out," replied Brady, "for it's jest for huntin' me ooncle keeps 'em, for the stags in Ireland is so big, that nothin' short of a Newfoundland is equal to pullin' 'em doon."

"Nonsense!" said Ruggles. "If a Newfoundland can pull them down, he can't ketch 'em."

"And that's jest where you're out agin," retorted Brady, not at all disconcerted, "for that's what I was jest a-going to tell ye when I was afther spaking about the dorg Jack being so cloomsy. He's cloomsier nor me dorg in Ireland. Me dorg was one from me ooncle's raising, and, bedad! he'd beat any greyhound ye ever see run."

"That'll do for one," said Ruggles; "I'll swow, if that don't beat cockfighting. Now, jest you tell that to the marines."

"An' sure, and it's the maranes is the sinsible min, compared with the likes of ye," retorted Brady.

Luckily, at this point in the conversation, the landing on the beach commenced, or there is no saying where the dispute would have ended, for Ruggles being an Englishman, and Brady an Irishman, they were always sparring with each other.

CHAPTER XVIII

THE BOATING PARTY LAND—A MISHAP BEFALLS DENNIS BRADY—HE
SPEEDILY RECOVERS—RUGGLES AMONG THE CORMORANTS AND PELI-
CANS—THE PARTY CAPTURE A JEWFISH—TURTLING POSTPONED.

IT had been blowing a pretty stiff breeze since early
in the morning, and as there was some surf beating the beach of the Key on which we landed, the
men jumped out of the boat, and ran her high and
dry ashore.

Brady had hardly leaped into the water, from his side of
the boat, when he gave a cry of pain, let go of the boat, and
hopped and hobbled to the nearest place out of reach of the
surf, where he seated himself, and writhed about, uttering
moans of distress.

We quitted the boat, and ran to his assistance.

"Howly Moses! Howly Moses!" roared Brady, "I'm kilt
entirely." Hereupon, he rolled over and over in a series of
contortions accompanied with cries of "Howly Moses."

"He's trod on one of them sea urchins," said Ruggles.
"I've told him afore that he'd ketch it some of these times, if
he jumped out of the boat barefooted. Here, Brady, my boy,
hold still a bit, and I'll take the spines out with my jack-
knife."

But Brady continued his cries and contortions, and
went on as if he was mad.

"Brady," remonstrated Ruggles, "you'd better let me
pick the spines out: jest be quiet a minute. The longer they
stay in, the worse it'll be for you, and your foot'll swell up the
size of two."

At this, Brady seemed to return sufficiently to his senses to be able to keep still, and hold out the sole of his foot,

91

which was bleeding and quivering with pain. Ruggles knelt down beside him, and commenced to pick at the flesh with his jack-knife. In a few seconds he removed a blackish splinter, as sharp as a needle, and then another, and another.

"Here, one of you," said he, "wet a handkerchief, a piece of shirt, or anything you've got about you, so I can wash the sand and blood away."

One of the men brought a dripping handkerchief, and the sole of Brady's foot, on being washed, exhibited about a dozen black marks where the spines had penetrated. Ruggles now proceeded adroitly, and soon extracted the rest of the spines, although he was often interrupted by the wincing of Brady, who continued to ejaculate, "Howly Moses!"

"Now they're all out," said Ruggles, gently washing the foot again, and depositing the heel on a flat piece of coral ledge, so that the sand could not get into the incisions in the sole, "and I hope you've larnt a lesson about jumping out of the boat barefooted. Them urchins is thick around here."

"An' faix, an' is it urchins ye call 'em," said Brady, recovering his tongue; "but it's the quare name they has. In Ireland, it's the little byes as is urchins. The things in me fut is the divil's own byes, bedad!"

"Why, don't you have sea urchins in Ireland?" said Ruggles, maliciously, seeing that Brady was getting over his pain. "I thought you had everything in Ireland."

"And there's where ye're right," replied Brady, not disposed to acknowledge that Ireland was deficient in anything. "Barring snakes and toads, that Sint Pathrick druv away, there's nothing we haven't in the ould counthry. But, for a moment, I jest disremembered the sea urchins. In Ireland they grow to a wontherful size. On me ooncle's eshtate that raches to the say-shore, he once had a line of thim set, jest to keep smugglers from landin' at night."

"Now, Brady," said Ruggles, "quit that. I believe what you got jest now was a punishment for the whopper you told in the boat, and here you're at it again."

"A whopper, was it, indade," said Brady, "bedad, if you

92

stuck to the thruth yourself, you wouldn't be afther thinking other people didn't tell it."

"Well, it's more'n I can do to believe some of your yarns," said Ruggles. "I say, if Ireland's such a fine country as you make it out, why do so many of you leave it?"

"Why do we lave it: and it's aisy to answer that. We've got a duty to perforrum, to spread ceevilization in the worruld, and carry instruction to haythens like you."

"You've got it, Bill," shouted the men. "He's too much for you!"

"But it's obleeged to ye I be for docthering me fut, and no offince," said Brady, rising, and hobbling to the boat to get his shoes and stockings.

"Now, boys," said Linden, "what did we come here for? There's no game about here. Let's go back of the Keys, on the flats, and see if we can't find something to strike."

"Hold a bit," said Ruggles, "I know what I want to do. I've been wanting for some time to get a pelican's pouch to hold my smoking tobacco, and I'm going through the mangroves to a place where I know I can get a shot at a pelican.

"I'm off now," continued Ruggles. "The place is jest 'round the north end of the Key. I'll walk along the outside beach until I get near the place, and then I'll work through the mangroves until I come in sight of the birds. You'd better launch the boat, and keep along the beach; but don't keep out too far from shore, or the birds'll see you, and I won't be able to get a crack at them. As soon as you hear me fire, you can pull away, and if my bird's dropped in the water, you'll be able to get it for me. I only want one: but I reckon I'll take both muskets along, so if I miss the first shot, I'll have another one."

Ruggles and I walked along the beach for about half a mile, and, as we neared the end of the Key, we turned into the mangroves, and, with much difficulty, made our way among their roots. After going about a hundred yards, and slipping and stumbling around through the dense growth standing in water,—for the back part of the Key was below the level of the sea,—we began to distinguish the edge of the mangroves. Ruggles crept cautiously forward, and I followed him until we got very near to the edge, and then moving a little towards one side, we came opposite to a slight opening, which proved to be a long and shallow inlet leading out to the waters back of the Key.

"Hist!" said he. "Don't make any noise."

I advanced cautiously to the place where he was standing, and thence I could see, through the opening, a little Key which was not more than forty yards off. In the branches of its mangroves, there were multitudes of pelicans and cormorants. They did not seem to be aware of our presence, and rested on the limbs of the trees, as if with a sense of perfect security. The pelicans had a peculiarly grave and ancient appearance, and they and the cormorants seemed to be on excellent terms. The leaves of the mangroves, and the trunks of the trees were whitened with the droppings of the birds, for this was one of their favorite resorts.

"Shall I pop over that old grand-daddy of a pelican," whispered Ruggles, designating, with the muzzle of his musket, a very patriarchal-looking individual. He had hardly spoken before the stroke of oars was heard. The wings of the birds all lifted simultaneously, and they arose in a cloud.

"No time for picking out a bird now," said Ruggles, aiming at the nearest pelican.

Bang, went the gun, and the pelican fell dead in the water, and the other pelicans flew rapidly away. Not so with the cormorants, however, for they continued to stupidly flap about in the air, hovering over the dead pelican, and sometimes descending to take a look at it, and then flying away a short distance, only to return. The temptation was too much for Ruggles, who seized my musket just as a cormorant was returning for another look, and shot it within three yards of the spot where the pelican lay on the surface of the water.

"There!" said Ruggles, "I hope you're satisfied now! You was so curious about it, I thought I'd let you see how it felt. That's not what I did it for, though, Fred: I was only joking.

What I shot him was for to see if the things can be made fit to eat. I've tried 'em, and couldn't eat 'em, but Hannibal says they wasn't fixed right, because the rank part's the skin, and it ought to be took off; so I promised I'd fetch him one some time, and let him show what kind of a fist he'd make at cooking of it."

The sound of the approaching boat grew more distinct, but we kept along shore so as to get to the beach, because it would have been impossible for the men to force the boat through the mangroves to the place where we were standing, and if we had gone to the edge of the mangroves, we would have been up to our waists in water. After going a short distance, Bill Ruggles sang out, "Boat ahoy!"

The sound of the oars ceased, and Ruggles shouted again, "You'll find two birds in the water, abreast of the roost. You'll have to come back to the nearest point on the beach for us. There's no getting out to the edge of the mangroves here."

"Aye! aye!" was answered from the boat, which we could not see on account of the dense growth, and the stroke of the oars recommenced as we resumed our way towards the beach. As soon as we reached that place, we took our shoes off and wrung out our stockings, for the water among the mangroves had sometimes been over ankle-deep. The men in the boat soon landed near us, having found the birds without difficulty. The pelican turned out to be a large one, with a very fine pouch, which contained a fish. Bill Ruggles took the fish out, and then separated the pelican's pouch from its lower bill. Brady commenced to pluck the cormorant, saying that it was the only thing he'd have to do with it, "The rest might ate it and wilcome."

"What kept you so long?" said Deal, "we thought something must have happened to you."

"Something did happen to us," said Ruggles: "we missed our way. But you oughtn't to have come around the point until you heard me fire. You came very near making me lose the birds. If you'd come a few seconds earlier, they'd have

95

been off."

"We gave you plenty of time, Bill," replied Deal. "A pelican pouch may be worth a heap to you, but there's no use of spending all the afternoon getting it, 'specially when I know where we'd be pretty sure to find something worth having. There's apt to be turtle back of this Key. I know the place well. I was once on this station in the wrecker *Susan Day*. Jest back of here, about a quarter of a mile, there's some holes in the mud flats, where I scarcely ever missed finding turtle."

"Well, boys," said Ruggles, "I'm very sorry if I've been a-keeping of you from going there, but you've only got to say the word, and we'll go there now. There's plenty of time. I don't believe it's more'n three o'clock. What would you say it was by the sun? Hold! Fred has a watch. What time is it by your watch, Fred?"

"Lots of time," said Ruggles in reply to my announcement of the time, "we sha'n't have to go off to the schooner until near dark. Come, let's start: be lively, Tom, you were in a big hurry jest now."

The men put out their oars, and were rowing slowly along the southern edge of the inlet, and almost touching the mangroves with the tips of the port oars, when Linden stopped rowing, and held up one hand.

"Did you hear that, Tom?" said he, addressing the other Conch, while we all listened to hear the noise to which he alluded.

"No," said Deal, "I didn't. What was it?"

"I'm certain I heard a jewfish," resumed Linden. "Get out the grains, Tom, you've got the bow oar. Jest slip your oar in gently, and put the grains on the pole. They're ready in the bow, with the line made fast. There it is again, don't you hear that?"

At long intervals, a noise under water, like the sound of a muffled drum, reached our ears. Boom—boom—boom, it went. The men kept perfectly still, and not an oar was dipped into the water, while Deal skillfully unshipped his oar, and stepped lightly into the bow of the boat, as he drew the pole after him, and at the same time adjusted the grains.

"I should judge it must be as much as fifty yards off," said Deal. "Don't make any noise."

Boom—boom—boom—boom, again went the jewfish.

"Give the boat the least bit of headway," said Deal, turning slightly around, and speaking to Linden and Brady: "and you, Bill, steer as you see my grains point."

I left my seat by the side of Ruggles, and crawled cautiously forward, until I could crouch down in the boat, behind the place where Deal was standing high up in the bow, and balancing his grains with the most perfect address. The bow had a stout grating set into it, about six inches below the gunwale of the boat, so that Deal was enabled to stand in a very commanding position. I peered into the water, which was so limpid that I could distinguish old roots and shells lying on the bottom. Once in a while, we heard the jewfish repeat the monotonous boom—boom.

The men gave the boat only enough motion for steerage-way, barely touching the blades of the oars in the water. Suddenly, I saw the grains pointed in a certain direction, as a gesture from Deal, and a half turn of his head towards Ruggles showed that he had discovered the jewfish. I strove to penetrate the obscurity of the water in that direction, but my face was just above the gunwale of the boat, and I looked through the water at an acute angle, whereas Deal had the great advantage of looking from an elevation which increased the angle made by the line of vision with the surface of the water. But more than all, Deal had the advantage of a practiced eye; and we had rowed three or four yards before I could distinguish the fish as it lay in the water under the overhanging boughs of mangroves.

It was perfectly still, except the movement of its fins and tail, and lay just within the shadow of a tree, with its snout almost touching the line in the water between sunlight and shade. The water was at least five feet deep, and at the shortest distance to which we dared approach, it would have been

97

impossible to strike the fish by throwing the pole like a dart. So Deal made a motion to the men to rest on their oars, and quietly dipping the grains below the surface of the water, he gradually extended the pole until the points of the grains were within six feet of the fish, and then, with a rapid shove, he transfixed it.

Instantly, a tremendous splashing ensued, and the fish was darting away, when Deal took a turn of the line around a cleat in the bow of the boat. This proceeding nearly caused the loss of the fish, for it was very large, and the grains were not so secure that its powerful efforts to escape would not have eventually disengaged the tormenting irons. At last, it seemed on the very eve of breaking away, when Deal,—doing what would have occurred to no one but a Conch, or, certainly, what no one but a Conch could have done well,— jumped into the water, which was up to his armpits, and ducking below the surface, bestraddled the fish and, at the same time, thrust each of his hands through its gills. In this position, he appeared above the surface, managing the fish as if it had been a restive horse. At one moment, he had it under control, and at the next, it would make a desperate effort, and carry his head below the surface of the water. If they had been left to fight it out in single combat, the jew-fish's chance of escape would have been quite as good as the Conch's chance of preventing it. But Linden jumped into the water and grappled with the fish and, by the united exertions of the two men, they managed to hoist it into the boat, where it thrashed around as if it would stave everything to pieces.

The capture of the fish was thought to be a sufficiently good piece of luck to serve for the afternoon's sport, so it was decided to defer the turtling until another occasion, in order to have plenty of time to visit all the holes where Deal had stated that he was certain to find turtle. The men thought that if they started on the expedition now, it was so late that they might be chasing a turtle when the time came to go aboard of the *Flying Cloud*, in which case, they would be obliged to desist from the pursuit. All hands agreeing to put off the excursion until another occasion, the boat was turned towards the outer mouth of the inlet, and the men pulled towards the schooner.

When we came alongside, the jewfish, as the most distinguished passenger, was passed aboard of the schooner, and received by Hannibal and one of the crew, with many expressions of admiration.

"You hab had luck," said the ever-grinning African. "Jest right size, too, 'zactly, precise. I reckon he's not over seventy-five, is he? When dey's over a hundred, dey's pretty coarse fish, but smaller size is very nice indeed, very nice indeed."

"And the way he was cotched, was a caution, cook," said Brady, as he came lamely up the side of the schooner. "It's the first time in me life, this blessed afternoon, that I seen a fush rid, barring the little marble byes, widout any clothes on, that sits a-top o' dolphins unthrer fountains. But it's me belafe thim Conchs could live in the wather with aise."

CHAPTER XIX

THE FLYING CLOUD INSPECTS THE REEF—CAPTAIN BOWERS SENDS
THE MEN ASHORE FOR WOOD—BRADY HAS BAD LUCK AGAIN.

THE next morning, at daylight, the schooner's sails were set, her anchor weighed, and she sailed up the Reef, until we sighted the wrecker approaching from the next station. Then she sailed down the Reef, passing her anchorage, and continuing her course until we sighted the wrecking sloop, which was underway from the station in that direction. Then the course was reversed for the second time, and she returned to her anchorage, after having been underway for five or six hours.

This was the daily mode of procedure, but it was not invariable. The object of the wreckers is to survey the Reef, daily, throughout its whole extent; and the only test which can be afforded that it is effectually accomplished, is by sighting each other in both directions, and thus they see that there is no wreck in the intervening space.

On the morning of which I spoke, when we came to anchor, furled the sails, coiled away ropes, and got everything in good order, it was between twelve and one o'clock, and we took dinner. Soon after it was over, the captain ordered the men to lower away one of the quarter-boats, and go ashore to cut wood for the schooner. Probably seeing my wistful look towards the preparations, he said,

"If you want to go, you can go, Fred,—that is, if you have got through with your duties."

"I have nothing to do, sir," I answered; "unless you have something particular that you wish done."

"No," said he, "nothing. If you've finished your regular duties, be off with you."

The men, having provided themselves with axes and a keg of drinking water, placed them in the quarter-boat used for the purpose of wooding, and then lowered her from the davits. Jack was immediately seized with an anxious wagging of his tail, accompanied with alternate prostrations and gambols, in the midst of which he was gratified by being deposited in the boat.

The crew of the boat consisted of Ruggles, Brady, Linden, Deal, and another Conch, and, as she pulled five oars, each man took an oar and I occupied the stern-sheets, and steered for a point to which I was directed to head. The men gave way with a will, and in the course of fifteen minutes we landed on a Key a little over a mile distant from the schooner.

One of the party was left in charge of the boat and the rest proceeded into the thicket, which soon rang with the quickly descending strokes of the axe. Ruggles, Linden, Deal, and Brady composed the party of woodmen. While the first three men were engaged in cutting down trees, Brady was employed in lopping off the branches and twigs of those which had been felled. The party worked steadily for about half an hour, and began to feel so much heated with their exertions, as to wish for the water that had been left in the boat. Accordingly, I was dispatched to help the boat-tender to carry the little keg to the place where the men were at work.

We soon returned with the keg, and the men drank the water greedily. The afternoon was sultry, and, in the midst of the mangroves where not a breath of air stirred, the heat was intense.

"It's so moighty warrum in here," observed Brady, "I think I'll take off me shirrut before I do any more chapping."

"You'll be stung by mosquitoes, if you do," said Linden, as he observed Brady stripping off his woollen shirt, and tightening the leathern strap around his waist.

"The muskatees isn't so bad as the hate," replied Brady, placing his shirt on the fallen trunk of a tree, and seating himself on it, as he hauled a branch towards him, and commenced to trim off the twigs. "And I've a notion, byes, to try the plan a naygur once told me was good for muskatees."

"What was that, Brady?" said Linden, picking up his axe, and taking an occasional chop at a neighboring tree.

"Jest what you see," said Brady, "nothin' shorter, to sit in me buff. I wunst landed on one of thim Kays to the southward, and I see a naygur wid his pants strapped 'round his waist, and widout a rag of a shirrut. I says, 'Ain't ye afeard to go that way for the muskatees.' 'No, indade,' he says, 'for this way they can't get a good holdt o' me.'"

"You wait till sundown dressed that fashion," said Ruggles, "and they'll leave so little of you, they'll have nothing to take hold on, sure enough."

"Be me troth," replied Brady, "I've had enough exparience already, for I fale the varmints stingin' me awful. I'll put on me shirrut widout any more loss o' time."

The woods once again resounded with the vigorous blows of the axemen, as Brady slowly arose, picked up his shirt, and pulled it over his head. As he slipped his arms into the sleeves, he uttered an exclamation, hurriedly tore the shirt off, and dashed it away from him into the bushes.

"What's up now?" said Linden, dropping his axe, and walking up to Brady, as he stood rooted to the ground, and clasping one of his arms.

"The mather is I'm bit wid a scorpion; look at thut," said Brady, exposing the place where the scorpion had struck him, and which was already beginning to swell from the animal's venomous sting. "Murther, but it's the bad luck I have!"

"Be still, Brady," said Linden, "it hurts bad, but it isn't dangerous. I never knowed anyone to die of it, 'cept an old woman in Key West, and the doctors didn't say positive. Put on your shirt, and we'll go right aboard and get some hartshorn from the captain's chest: that's the best thing for it."

The men had all desisted from their work, and grouped around Brady. His shirt was picked up and carefully inspected, and he had again pulled it over his head, and proceeded to about the same point in his dressing as in the former attempt, when he suddenly stopped, and tore it off as rapidly as before.

"It's bewutched! it's bewutched!" he shouted, as he threw it from him. "I'm bitten all over me chist and me arrums."

He was, indeed, stung very severely. The scorpion, or whatever it was, had managed to wound him in half a dozen places, during the short time that he was engaged in extricating himself from his shirt. A couple of the men started towards the boat with him, while the rest picked up the shirt and reexamined it. The second inspection proved more successful than the first, for the scorpion was found in one of the folds of the shirt. One of the men speared it with the point of his knife, and I had an excellent opportunity of examining it as we walked towards the boat. This specimen of the animal was about six inches in length, including the tail, which was composed of several joints terminating in a sharp hook. The body is provided with a pair of crablike claws, with which the animal seizes its prey.

As soon as we reached the shore, we got into the boat, and put off towards the schooner, where we delivered Brady into the hands of the kind captain, who assured him that the stings, although numerous and painful, would not prove fatal, and led him away to the cabin, to undergo the usual treatment of hartshorn.

When we had committed Brady to the charge of the captain, we took another man in his place, and returned to the beach, to load the boat with the wood that had been cut. In the course of an hour, during which we each made several trips between the woods and the boat, we managed to stow her so full that she was almost gunwale deep in the water.

The sun had almost set by the time the men had unloaded their freight of wood, sawed or chopped it up, and thrown it into the hold of the schooner.

Every now and then one of them went to see how Brady

was getting along. He had turned into his bunk, and, although suffering pain from the numerous stings of the scorpion, was not by any means in a dangerous condition. But like most of his countrymen of his class, under similar circumstances, he was despondent. It was useless to tell him that no one on the Reef had ever been known to die of the sting of a scorpion; his ready tongue always had some reply which he considered a reason. When I tried to console him by this statement, he said:

"An' sure, an' thim as lives on the Rafe has got used to it, one bite at a time, but be the powers, I've got enough pison in me to kill an illiphant!"

CHAPTER XX

THE MEN ARE SENT ASHORE AGAIN—THEY RESUME THE WOODING OF THE SCHOONER—HANNIBAL PROVIDES THEM WITH A TREAT FOR SUPPER.

HE next day, after making our usual cruise, the captain ordered a boat's crew to go ashore to procure more wood. The men sent were the same as those of the preceding day, excepting Brady, who was convinced that his wounds were mortal, and persisted in declaring that his days were numbered.

I did not join the party until they had brought several loads of wood aboard the schooner, when, as my duties were finished, and I found myself at leisure, I received liberty to go wooding with the rest. More than that, the captain gave me a general permission to accompany the men whenever I desired to do so, only stipulating that I should be certain that my work was finished.

When we returned to the schooner, it was time for supper, and Hannibal hurried the men to eat it, ostensibly that he might get his pots and pans cleaned before dark. There was not much deliberation on the part of the men. The wood was soon unloaded, and the boat hoisted up to its davits. Two or three of the crew seated themselves on the coamings of the hatchway, and a couple on water casks, while one or two stood or walked around. Hannibal brought supper, and the men commenced to eat heartily. The meal was fairly earned by the hard labor of wood-chopping.

"Here's you' comorant, Bill," said Hannibal, bringing his last dish from the caboose. "He's nice, I tell you, sah. I save him for a treat."

Ruggles received the dish, which had a very savory look,

but the smell of it was anything but appetizing, being decidedly fishy. He looked at it rather dubiously, and then asked Hannibal whether he had skinned the bird.

"Yes, sah; ebery bit of skin is off him," replied Hannibal. "He's mighty good bird, sah; plump as pa'tridge."

"Here, Hannibal," said Ruggles, after giving a sniff at the dish; "I reckon I'll let you eat it: there's hardly enough for all."

"After you's manners, sah," said Hannibal. "I fix him up beautiful, sah. You must take jest small bit, 'cause I cook him 'special for you."

"Cook, I don't like the smell," said Ruggles. "If all hands will try a piece at the same time, I won't object. What say, boys? I've heerd tell they're first-rate without the skin."

The men assenting to the trial, each one was provided with a small piece of the cormorant, and held it between finger and thumb; and it was agreed that, upon counting three, each man should put his piece into his mouth. I happened to glance towards Hannibal, and saw him quaking all over in a fit of chuckles.

"One,—two,—thr-ee," counted Ruggles, and each man smilingly placed his morsel of cormorant in his mouth. Each chewed once or twice, then stopped abruptly, and gazed at the rest with rigid gravity. Human nature could not stand it. everyone's gorge had risen at the revolting dish and, without one word, the whole party scrambled to their feet, and spat and sputtered over the side of the schooner.

"Yah! yah! yah! yah!" screamed Hannibal, dancing a frantic jubah, in the excess of his delight. "I 'spect I put too much pepper in him. Yah! yah! yah!"

The men rinsed out their mouths, then swallowed some water, and gradually joined in the mirth of Hannibal.

"That's my last trial of cormorant" said Ruggles. "I think it's rather worse *without* the skin: it tastes like rancid fish oil. I say, Hannibal, how's Brady this evening?"

"He's ruther better," replied Hannibal. "I reckon he's guv' up the notion he was gwine to die."

"I say," resumed Ruggles, winking around the group, "let's offer Brady some. Brady, my boy," he continued, leaning back, and holloing down the hatchway, "here's a treat we've got. Hannibal understands fixing cormorant so it tastes as sweet as sucking-pig."

"As you've only one burrid," said a voice from below, "I couldn't think o' deprivin' ye of it."

"We've plenty to spare," said Ruggles, winking around again at the group of men, who were nearly suffocated with laughter. "I've heerd tell it's good for the blood, when a man's been stung by a scorpion."

"Arrah, go 'lang wid ye!" replied the voice. "I'll not tech a bit of it! I prefare, like the gintry, to take me mate and me fush on two siparate plates."

"He's getting well," observed Ruggles. "When a doctor prescribes for an Irishman, he needn't never examine anything but his tongue."

CHAPTER XXI

THE MEN GO TURTLING—THEY MEET AN ACQUAINTANCE TO WHOM THEY PAY MARKED ATTENTION—SOMETHING ABOUT TURTLES—WHAT SWITCHEL IS—A GARDEN ON THE BOTTOM OF THE SEA.

IT blew a norther for three days after the day of which mention has been made in the last chapter. An unusually bright lookout was kept on the Reef, but nothing appeared to reward the vigilance of the wreckers.

On the fourth day, the weather was as clear as ever. In Florida, when the weather is fair, nothing can exceed its serenity. The temperature in the shade is delightful, the atmosphere the purest ether.

On the day to which I allude, after returning from our usual survey of the Reef, there happened to be nothing for the men to do, so they asked and received permission to go upon the turtling expedition which had been projected on the afternoon of the capture of the jewfish, and deferred until an occasion when the party could have ample time to prosecute their search. As I had finished my work for the afternoon, by the captain's terms according me leave at all times that my duties were finished, it was permissible for me to go with the turtlers, and I gladly joined their party. The men provided themselves with the usual gear, with one addition,—an instrument called a peg, used for striking the hawksbill turtle. The hawksbill turtle is found in considerable numbers in the waters of Florida. This is the turtle from which the shell called tortoise shell is procured. The material is too valuable to be rudely perforated by the grains, if avoidable, and the use of the peg insures the capture of the animal with the least possible injury to its shell.

The peg is a very simple instrument, consisting merely of a sharp point of iron with a shoulder and socket. The manner of using it is precisely like that adopted with the grains. Instead of the grains, the socket of the peg is secured with a line, and placed on the end of a long pole. When the shell of a turtle is punctured by a blow from the peg, the hole closes tightly after the passage of the shoulder of the instrument, which is thus fastened in the place. In fact, the operation of the peg in securing a turtle is more certain than that of the grains, for the great barbs of the latter often fracture a turtle's shell so materially as to cause the grains to "draw."

When the little turtles are hatching, under the influence of the sun, as fast as they extricate themselves from the sand in which, as eggs, they have reposed, their instinct at once carries them down to the water. I have sometimes seen dozens of them, little black objects, not much more than an inch in length, making their way towards the sea, while, collected all around, perched birds of prey, eagerly watching them, and restrained from devouring them only by my presence.

As we were rowing towards shore, I held my face close over the gunwale of the boat, examining the many objects, beauteous in form and color, that made a garden of the bottom of the sea; and it was not until we had passed the inlet, and our boat's keel commenced to touch the mud flats that I was obliged to relinquish my inspection of the bright borders of that dark, vast, mysterious realm.

Our boat entered the inlet to the southward of the one in which Deal struck the jewfish, and after passing the narrow line of Keys, I, for the first time, found myself in the waters which form the broad and shallow bay between the Keys and the mainland.

The men were all agog to find a turtle. The line was coiled, the grains were adjusted on the pole, and the pole itself was carefully laid amidships, with the barbs pointed over the bow of the boat. Owing to the direction of the wind that had been prevailing for some time, the water was lower than usual, and the boat's keel dragged so heavily that the men unshipped their oars, and used them to pole the boat over the flats. We had progressed in this manner for twenty or thirty yards, when Linden sang out, "Shark!" and we perceived the dorsal fin of the animal appearing above the water on the flat, about a couple of hundred yards in advance of the boat.

In an instant, all thought of the turtling vanished. The boy-nature of the sailors, as well as their unrelenting hostility to the shark, instantly made them oblivious of everything except the presence of the dark object ahead that floundered over the mud flat in its efforts to work its way into deep water. The rudder was of no avail, now that the boat was almost as much on land as in the water, so it was unshipped, and the men stood on the thwarts, and poled vigorously with their oars, while I put out a short scull, and added my mite of strength to aid in catching the monster.

The tremendous noise made by our shouting and splashing soon apprised the shark that enemies were near, and it alternately lashed the water with its tail, and violently wriggled as it used the most desperate efforts to elude the pursuit. Over some places, the water was deeper, and then the shark made better progress, then the water shoaled, and the shark found itself almost fast aground. But through or over whatever the shark went, whether favorable or unfavorable, it was the same for us; for following as we did in its wake, we made good speed where it had met deep water, and were retarded, almost in the same degree, where it had floundered over shallow spots. I say retarded almost in the same degree, because we steadily gained upon the shark, and our only fear now was that it would reach a channel that was discernible ahead, in the direction in which it was swimming.

The men shouted and laughed and encouraged each other to increased exertion. I never saw a more exciting chase. The water began to deepen gradually, where the shark was, and it was observed to make better speed towards the deep channel, which, however, was still a considerable distance ahead. We almost lost hope, the laughter died away, and the poling was, if possible, continued with increased vigor. After going a few yards further, the boat gradually felt more buoyant, and seemed nearly afloat. So was the shark, which had been in the same deep water for two or three minutes.

"Give it to her, boys!" shouted Ruggles. "Lay down to it! Once more, my hearties! There she slides! Never say die!"

The gurgling of the water, as it commenced to ripple against the bow of the boat, and the rapidly shifting oar-blades used in poling, showed our increased progress through the water, even if we had not perceived that we were gaining upon the shark. But the channel was then only about seventy-five yards ahead of the boat, and the shark had the advantage of us by at least thirty yards, so that to catch it before reaching the edge of the channel, we would have had to make nearly twice its speed.

"Take your places, boys, and pull," sang out Ruggles.

Every man dropped into his place, except Linden, who stood in the bow and poised the harpoon, and Ruggles, who seized my little scull, and shoved and guided the boat with it.

We came up with the shark when it was not more than fifteen yards distant from the edge of the channel, and Linden drove the harpoon into its body.

Then ensued a scene that baffles description. The shark was still too much aground to run out the line, and it struggled on, lashing out desperately with its tail. The men, armed with axes, hatchets, and oars, leaped from the boat and attacked it, and, for a minute, there was so close a fight, accompanied with shouting and splashing, that it looked as if, in the excitement, the men could not avoid maiming each other. Presently, the shark ceased to be visible, and the turbid water failed to disclose its position.

Some one halloed, "Take care of your legs!" and then followed another scene of confusion, laughable to behold, as the men themselves perceived after they had tumbled head over heels into the boat; for they roared with laughter, until they were obliged to hold their sides from exhaustion.

Not a soul, however, ventured outside of the boat. The men waited patiently until the turbid water gradually became clear. As the gray clouds in the water slowly floated off, like fog dispersing before the influence of sunshine, a tinge of blood could be distinguished in it, and just below rested the carcass of the shark.

One of the men grappled it with the boat hook, and pulled it towards him, when, as it lay alongside, it underwent critical examination. It was not of the most dangerous species, called the white shark, but it was a dreadful looking creature, about fifteen feet in length, and furnished with formidable jaws and teeth.

It is erroneously supposed that the shark always uses several rows of teeth. It has several rows of teeth, but the inner ones lie flat, and seem to be designed by nature to provide the animal with the means of capturing its prey, in case of accident to the outer row.

Sailors are not always so merciful to a shark, as to deprive it of existence without subjecting it to prolonged torture. Regarding the animal as their most deadly enemy, they not infrequently catch it and fasten to it a billet of wood, to serve as a float. With this appendage, the shark finds it impossible to sink so as to procure food, and dies a lingering death of starvation. Whatever opinion one may entertain as to the propriety of killing a shark,—and I think there can be no difference of opinion as to the right of man to destroy an animal so rapacious, there ought to be no difference of opinion as to the practice of torturing it. The object of killing it is to prevent future depredations, and man's right and duty end with that act, which should be executed without the refinement of torture.

The chase had been so long and fatiguing, that the men felt like resting before starting on the turtling expedition, from which they had been diverted by discovering the shark. Besides, the party had made enough noise to frighten away any turtles, had they been in the vicinity. The men therefore sat down quietly in the boat, wiped the perspiration from their brows, and passed around a tin cup filled with switchel from the keg.*

In the course of a quarter of an hour, they began to show signs of moving, and, by common consent, the boat was shoved off the flat into the deep channel, into which the shark had so nearly escaped.

Here, after a short consultation, it was determined to remain back of the Keys, and to row along the channel, until we arrived opposite to the next Key towards the southward.

I was allowed to steer, and Deal was stationed in the bow. With these dispositions, the four men at the oars gave way, and we shot rapidly along the deep channel. On this occasion, the boat had a yoke on her rudder, to which were attached long tiller ropes, which enabled me to steer as I stood up in the stern-sheets and thus commanded a view of the whole bay.

We had rowed a mile, when Deal said:

"I see something ahead, but I can't make out what it is."

I strained my eyes in vain. I could not even see anything. I still needed the practiced eye which enabled Deal to see an object long before I could distinguish it and then to recognize it, when to me it was only faintly visible.

What I have just said, was proved on this occasion. Deal sang out, "Turtle asleep on the water," at the very moment I could do no more than detect the object which he had for a long time seen.

"Ease your oars, and pull as even as you can," said Deal, after the men had rowed for some distance. The boat glided noiselessly along, until we came within twenty yards of the turtle, when Deal whispered, "Rest on your oars."

The boat glided on, and Deal's hand, brandishing the pole, gradually raised higher, until we were within five yards of the turtle. Then the turtle gave a nervous flirt as if it had

*Switchel is made of water with a little molasses and vinegar.

suddenly awakened. But it was too late: Deal's well-poised lance left his hand, and pierced the turtle's panoply, back-plate and breastplate, through and through. There was little struggling. The wound was so severe as almost to paralyze the animal, which was dragged aboard and dispatched. It proved to be a small green turtle of about fifteen pounds in weight.

This, the men considered a very small prize, although to me it seemed magnificent, and I could not sufficiently admire the animal. Everyone is so familiar with the appearance of the green turtle, that it needs no description here. I should say, however, that whatever points of beauty the green turtle may have (and who can deny that the glossy, rounding shell, the symmetrically sealed flippers, the cream-colored throat, the white undershell, are points of beauty), it possesses them, when fresh from the water, in a far higher degree than after it has made a long voyage, and lain for hours subjected to the heat, dust, and plaguing encountered in the streets of a city.

The men, as I said, not being quite satisfied with so small a turtle, decided to keep along the channel, which still continued to run towards the southward, about parallel with the line of Keys, and about a mile distant from them. After rowing for a considerable distance, and finding nothing, we commenced to cross the flats, heading for one of the inlets that lead into the Reef Channel. Deal kept a lookout, and was soon rewarded by seeing something dash through the water.

"Green turtle, boys," he sang out, "give way strong. It's a buster."

I now understood steering so well, that I was permitted to retain my place at the tiller. When I did not see the turtle, I was guided by observing the direction that Deal's grains indicated. The flats, over which we were going, were much lower than the ones over which we had pursued the shark, and the boat did not draw enough water to make her touch bottom. The men gave way with a will, and sometimes we almost overtook the turtle, which seemed to swim by spurts.

When we came within a few yards of it, it darted off with a quick cant to the right and then to the left; and so much, under these circumstances, does the swimming of a turtle resemble a bird's flight, that one can almost imagine that he sees a huge hawk, with outstretched wings, darting over the bottom of the sea.

Rapid as the movements of the turtle were, they lacked continuous effort. Perhaps the animal became exhausted. Its flights became shorter and more spasmodic, until chancing to come across a hole, it no doubt deemed itself comparatively safe in the obscurity of the deep water, for it stopped and remained motionless on the bottom. And, in truth, it was very nearly out of our reach, for as the boat passed over the spot, Deal was obliged to lean, in an awkward position, far over the bow, and plunge the pole perpendicularly at the dark object on the bottom.

But the stroke of a Conch is unerring, and the poor turtle was transfixed. It was off this time with all its remaining strength. The line spun out until it grew taut, and the boat commenced to be towed through the water. But as she was towed along, three of the men got into the bow, and slowly, hand over hand, hauled in the line, until the turtle, still towing us, was brought close to the bow. Then a tremendous struggle took place, and the turtle, with the aid of a hampering line and the strength of four men, was hoisted into the boat.

It was a fine animal, and must have weighed quite a hundred and fifty pounds, for I know that, when we reached the schooner, the men found it so heavy to pass up the side, that a tackle was lowered, and it was hoisted on deck amid the congratulations of the captain and cook. To us, often condemned for days to a diet of fish and salt provisions, the capture of a turtle meant more than the mere gratification of appetite. It meant health.

CHAPTER XXII

THE FLYING CLOUD RIDES OUT A GALE—A DISASTER ON THE REEF—
THE FLYING CLOUD ARRIVES THE DAY AFTER THE FAIR.

HE month of November passed away amid scenes similar to those last described, alternated by the morning duty of carefully inspecting the whole Reef for several miles in each direction from our station. Towards the latter part of November, there was one terrific storm, whose fury in the open sea we could realize by the stress that it put on our ground tackle, even as we lay protected, in a measure, behind the huge breakwater formed by the Reef. Experiencing the effects of the wind, without a heavy sea, we managed to hold on by letting go our sheet-anchor in addition to our other bower.

The main violence of the storm expended itself at night, and was disastrous along the whole coast. When day broke, the ocean was a mass of foam driven by the still-raging tempest. We took a double reef in all the sails, got underway to examine the Reef, and at last sighted the sloop towards the southward by overhauling her slightly, for she was under sail, and standing away from us. This fact apprised us that she had sighted something to the southward, and we kept on our course, knowing that we could not reach the scene of disaster as soon as the wrecker on the station below, but hoping that we would get there in time to be employed by those who took the wreck in charge, and needed assistance from extra crews.

We were disappointed again; for when we reached the place, quite a little fleet of wreckers was already assembled, and no assistance was needed, in addition to what could be rendered by the first-comer. The vessel which had struck upon the Reef was a small brig that had been so fortunate as not to strike until the storm had been blowing from the northward and eastward for several hours. In consequence, the water had by that time been driven towards shore in so vast a quantity, that it was quite high on the Reef. In addition, the brig struck at a place where there was ordinarily rather more than the average depth on the Reef,—in fact quite a little channel. The vessel did not draw many feet of water, so that everything had conspired in her favor. She struck beam on, and, for a few seconds, all hands thought that they were lost. In the darkness, nothing could be ascertained, except that she was on shore, and the heavy shocks of the vessel, as she pounded on the Reef, seemed as if they would break her asunder. All the time she was nearing safety. After thumping violently for half a dozen times, she was found to be in deep and comparatively smooth water. The lead was hove, six fathoms were found, and she cast anchor. The brig had pounded across the narrow Reef, and lay in the Reef Channel. Had the water not blown in from the ocean; had the brig not happened to run aground in a place where there is a shallow channel; or even, with both these favoring circumstances, had she been a large ship, instead of a small brig, she would have gone to pieces.

Instead of that, she was saved, although leaking badly; and, when morning dawned, the first wrecker that discovered her was engaged, and relieved her crew, who had been all night at the pumps, and were nearly exhausted. When we arrived, the pumps were still manned, but the water did not gain on them. The captain of the wrecker having the brig in charge had just been trying to stop a leak in her bow, and having been partially successful, he got her underway for Key West, with one crew at the pumps, and the other navigating the vessel.

Thus ended the first wrecking scene that I witnessed. Subsequently, the *Flying Cloud* was more fortunate.

CHAPTER XXIII

FRED RANSOM GIVES SOME EXTRACTS FROM HIS JOURNAL, WHICH RECORDS SOME CURIOUS THINGS THAT HE SAW AND SOMETHING OF WHAT HE DID AND THE NEWS THAT HE RECEIVED.

EVER since I had left Key West, I had kept a journal in which I jotted down the incidents of the day. If there was nothing except the regular routine of duty, I wrote it down in a short, business-like way; but if anything of particular interest occurred, either aboard or ashore, I wrote it out at my leisure, feeling that the day might come when it might prove of interest to me or to others.

On the 4th of December, my journal simply says:
"Wind N.N.W. Temperature moderate, atmosphere clear.

"Got underway at daylight; sighted the wreckers in each direction. Came to anchor in our usual berth. Afternoon very cool for Florida."

The record of days about the same period so vividly recalls my thoughts and actions, that I prefer to quote from it for a while, rather than to attempt to change its frankly written expressions.

DECEMBER 6TH.
"The wind has been all around the compass today. We had hardly reached our usual turning point at the northward, when the wind came out ahead, and that made it fair down the Reef; and we had hardly sighted the wrecker there, when the wind hauled sufficiently for us to lay our course

back to the anchorage.

"At the anchorage, the water was remarkably clear to-day. In five fathoms of water, I could see every little shell on the bottom. I saw the most curious thing there. The men call it a sea cat (there is also a fish of that name), and it did look like a cat. It was about ten or fifteen fathoms astern of the schooner. It looked like a tortoise-shell cat coiled up, for it had yellow stripes. I asked permission to take the dinghy and get it, and the captain said I might, and Ruggles went along and helped me to grapple it with the killick.

"We took it aboard the schooner. The nearer we went up to it, the less it looked like a cat; but, at a certain distance, it was the image. It was nothing, either, but a sort of a sack of a substance about the the color of dirty flannel, and marked with tawny stripes and spots; and it was these marks that shaded the thing off so well that it looked like a cat. There were the eyes and nose and legs and tail. We cut it open, and it moved up and down as if it was breathing (but of course it was not breathing, for there were no lungs to breathe with), and everything that it had inside of it was a thick concern like an entrail, and that was full of coral sand."

DECEMBER 7TH.

"The captain keeps a fish-car, fastened by a line to the stern of the schooner. He generally has lots of groupers (that is the most common fish about here, and they make first-rate chowder), and they attract sharks to the vessel. I made up my mind to try to catch a shark, so I took three codfish hooks, and put their shafts together, and barbs pointing out. A shark took hold right away, and carried the hooks off as if they had been sugar plums. The captain had given me permission to fish from the stern of the schooner, and, as he was in the cabin, he heard me halloo to Hannibal that I had lost my hooks, so he walked two or three steps up the companionway and handed me a big hook, which he called a shark-hook. It was about nine inches long, and had a short chain and swivel fastened to the end of the shaft. The captain says

119

there must be a chain, because a shark will bite off any ordinary line, and there must be a swivel, even if there is a chain, because a shark will turn around so fast in the water that it will break or injure the line by twisting it, and with the swivel on the chain, it may turn as much as it pleases, it cannot twist the line. Hannibal baited the hook with a whole grouper, and I jerked the line as hard as I could. The shark did not pull heavily at first, and I began to think that I was going to haul it on deck all by myself; but I had scarcely got its nose out of the water, before it gave a dash, and whizzed out the line so as to burn my hands. I managed to stop the line with my foot, and give it a turn around a cleat, and then I called for the men, but the captain hallooed to me not to let them haul the fish on the quarterdeck; so I took hold with three men, and we led the line outside of the main shrouds, then hauled the fish alongside of the schooner. One of the men passed a running bowline, or slipknot, over the slim part of the tail, just in front of the flukes, and the shark was soon hauled on deck.

"The men would cut it open (they always want to do that the first thing), to see what was in it. It seemed to me that we found almost everything that had been thrown overboard for the last day or two. Hannibal found two old dishcloths that he had thrown away this morning, and there were Bill Ruggles's rusty old tin coffee cup that had been tossed overboard, and a pair of tarry overalls that had belonged to Linden.

"The stories that I used to read, that the position of a shark's mouth obliged it to turn over on its back to seize its prey, are all nonsense. I recollect one that describes this position as favorable for stabbing the animal. A shark's mouth is a big, ugly slit, some distance from the animal's snout, but the shark, in seizing its prey, does not always stop, and it *never* turns over on its back. If it swims from a depth to seize its prey, it rises perpendicularly, like any other fish. If it and its prey are at the same depth, it darts horizontally, and, in passing, turns like lightning on one side, and uses its jaws. It is not a quick fish. Sailors say that it can-not catch a bowline towing in the water. But that is an exag-geration. It is only a slow fish when compared with the quickest."

DECEMBER 8TH.

"The captain got Ruggles to row him off in the dinghy. He told me to come along, as he was going to fish, and I might keep him supplied with conch cut up for bait. We fished just abreast of the inlet, near the anchorage, and caught eleven groupers, two barracudas, and some grunts.

After we got through fishing, the captain told Ruggles to row slowly along the edge of the mangroves in the inlet, so as to keep in the shade of the trees. Here I found some shells called mickleemocks.* I had often seen them as ornaments in parlors, on sideboards, or on mantelpieces. It is a sort of turtle-shaped shell with an even slit in it on the under side. The queerest part of finding them is, that I found them on trees (some of the boys at home would not believe that). They were stuck fast to the mangrove roots and boughs that were under the water, and the animals in the shells had such a power of suction, that you had to pull them pretty hard to get them off. The captain told me not to take more than two or three, because they would make so much smell on the schooner before I could get the shells perfectly sweet. A couple of days ago, he told the men that if they wanted to clean any more sponges, they must do it on shore, as he would not have such a smell on the schooner. The sponges, when drying, do smell awfully, that is a fact.

"We went off to the schooner about five o'clock, and I gave my shells to Hannibal to put in hot water, so as to kill the animals. Tomorrow I will gouge them out as well as I can, and let the rest dry out, and take the shells home to—I was going to say,—to my father, but I do not know yet whether he will ever accept anything from me. I wish that a letter from him would come. This suspense sometimes makes me very unhappy. 10 p.m. by the cabin clock. It is so late that I must turn in."

DECEMBER 9TH.

"This afternoon a sail was lowered in the water, so as to make a 'belly,' as the men call it, and all hands went in bathing. The captain says that the men shall not go in swimming off the vessel, on account of the sharks about. The other afternoon I was looking overboard, thinking there

*Mickleemock is the sound of the word. It is a local name, is probably of Indian origin, and without fixed orthography.

were no sharks about, and wishing I could strip off and take a plunge, and I saw a thing, like a black shadow, coming from under the vessel, and it was a big shark. I guess I thought the captain was right after that. We often talk of the poor Norwegian."

DECEMBER 10TH.

"Bill Ruggles taught me to box the compass today. It seems hard at first, but it is very easy when you come to look into it. The mariner's compass is divided into thirty-two points. It is divided into quarters by the four cardinal points, north, south, east, and west. The quarters are divided into eighths, the eighths into sixteenths, and the sixteenths into thirty-seconds.

"To recite the points in order, commencing at the first one west of north, is called boxing the compass backwards.

"Seamen speak of half points. For instance: midway between south, and south by east, the place is called south by east, half south."

DECEMBER 11TH.

"This afternoon the captain had a new suit of sails bent on the masts of one of the quarter-boats; and to try them, he took me and a full crew on a sail up the Reef, so as to have plenty of live ballast and crowd sail on, and to row back in case of necessity. The wind died away almost as soon as we left the schooner, but the captain kept on up the Reef Channel, until nearly dark. Before dark, it was almost calm for a couple of hours, and the water was as smooth as glass. It was quite dark before the men had rowed halfway back to the schooner. The water is more luminous tonight than I ever saw it. When the oar blades dipped into it, it looked as if a scum had been broken through, and showed below a lake of molten gold. On each side of the boat, a wing of flame spread out from the bow, and in her wake, she had a long fiery tail like a comet's. The captain calls this water phosphorescent, and says that it is caused by immense numbers of little animals that give out light.

"As we were rowing back, I asked the captain whether he did not think it was time for the arrival of our mail from Key West, and he said that he did. He said that he thought that if any letter was coming for me, it must have reached Key West, and the next mail from there would bring it.

"Until the captain said this, it had never struck me that I might not receive some letter, good or bad. No letter would be the worst thing of all."

DECEMBER 12TH.

"This is a black day in my calendar. The captain told me that he wished me to prepare a spare berth in the cabin, as he expected his son within a few days. He said that he could not tell within a few days, but, that when last in Key West, he had told his son that he might come up the Reef at the first opportunity that offered about the middle of December.

"I do not know what kind of a fellow the captain's son will turn out to be. If I was only an officer of the vessel, or one of the crew! If the captain's son is a nice fellow, and I belonged in the cabin, it would be splendid. It won't be pleasant to be bossed by a boy no older than I am. I wonder whether it would offend the captain to ask him to let me go forward? I am neither fish, flesh, nor fowl here."

DECEMBER 13TH.

"No signs of the captain's son yet. The berth is ready for him. The captain has mentioned to me that his son alternately goes to school, and sails aboard of the *Flying Cloud,* as he is to follow wrecking for a livelihood. He is to be aboard during all this winter."

DECEMBER 16TH.

"The captain's son not arrived yet, and there is no mail yet. The captain's son's name is George,—George Bowers. I don't know whether that sounds as if he was a good fellow or not."

DECEMBER 18TH.

"Shall I never get a letter? The captain says that a mail must be coming along pretty soon. Why doesn't that fellow George come, if he is coming?"

DECEMBER 19TH.

"Captain's son and my letter have both come together. Hurrah! I am the luckiest fellow in the world!"

CHAPTER XXIV

GEORGE BOWERS AND THE LONG-EXPECTED NEWS FROM HOME—THE TIDE IN THE AFFAIRS OF FRED RANSOM IS AT THE FLOOD, WHICH, SHAKESPEARE SAYS, "LEADS ON TO FORTUNE."

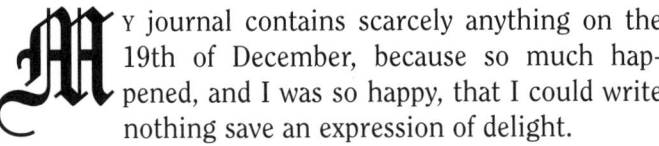

Y journal contains scarcely anything on the 19th of December, because so much happened, and I was so happy, that I could write nothing save an expression of delight.

We were lying at our anchorage when, about four o'clock in the afternoon, a schooner hove in sight. I felt sure that on board were the captain's son and my long-expected letter. My heart failed me at the thought of what trouble the former and what sorrow the latter might bring. In half an hour, the captain discovered that someone was making signals from the deck of the schooner. He closed his telescope, and calling me to him, said:

"I feel sure that George is aboard. I make out the schooner to be the *Kate Ramsey,* which was to leave Key West about this time, and aboard of her I see someone waving a handkerchief."

In half an hour more, the *Kate Ramsey* was flying by us, with the Captain's son standing on the quarterdeck, shouting, and waving his handkerchief. She rounded to, let go her anchor, and lowered a boat. George Bowers descended into it with his seaman's chest. In a minute he was clambering up the side of the *Flying Cloud,* and shaking hands with his father, who led him away to the cabin. I was left on deck in ignorance as to whether there was any mail. I asked one of the seamen who was passing young Bowers' chest out of the boat, whether he knew if there was a mail from Key West. He said that he believed there was. Just at that moment, the captain put his head above the companionway and said,

"Fred, tell the men to fetch that chest aft."

The chest was taken aft, and down the companionway, and my anxiety continued for a brief space longer, when I heard Captain Bowers call, "Here's a letter for you, Fred."

I ran eagerly aft. The captain handed me a letter, and then retired into the cabin. I was alone on the quarterdeck. With an irresolute feeling, I turned the letter over once or twice, fearing to examine its contents. Then I desperately broke the seal, and took out a note directed to Captain Bowers. Thrusting that into my pocket, I commenced to read my letter, the first words of which thrilled me with joy. This is it.

NEW YORK, November 18th.

"MY DEAR FRED:—

"However good a son you may be (and I believe you to be a good son), you cannot comprehend a father's love until you have been a father. Had I to forgive even disobedience, I would cheerfully do so, if you showed contrition. But you have not thus offended me, and I have not that to forgive. I have found you ever truthful, how could you then suppose that I might disbelieve your story? I thank Heaven that I can truly say I do not doubt your word. Grief I have experienced, for when it was ascertained that you were missing and had probably sailed on the *Cygnet,* I thought that, in an unguarded moment, you had been betrayed into committing an act of disobedience; but when I received your letter, my son, it completely reassured me, and brought such joy to my heart as none but a parent can know.

"You have been in fault, in not submitting to my judgment, and have had your punishment in the sorrow which you entailed upon yourself, and which I accept as full amends for your fault.

"If I knew exactly how you were situated, and what were your feelings, I could speak definitely. If I thought that you were radically cured of the desire to pursue an adventurous career, I should say, at once, come home. Or, if I knew that you were suffering hardship, even if I thought you still imbued with the nonsensical spirit that possessed you, I would say, at once, come home. But I do not know how you are situated, or what your sentiments are, and, therefore, I must trust to that honor which I have said that I believed you to possess, and say to you this: If you are not suffering hardship, or if you cannot conscientiously state that you believe yourself to be cured of your disposition towards adventure, do not return at present, but remain, in order that reality may blunt the keen edge of imagination.

"I enclose a letter to Captain Bowers, thanking him for his kindness in taking you on his vessel, and requesting that if he does not desire to retain you longer, he will get you on board of some vessel on the Reef. As lads of your age may not be given anything except their board, I have told Captain Bowers that any owners in Key West may draw upon me, and I will be grateful to him if he will manage so that, wherever you are, you shall receive ten dollars a month. Good-bye, my son, and believe me that you have never forfeited my confidence or love.

Your affectionate father,

DAVID RANSOM."

While reading these lines, they appeared to become more and more blurred, as my eyes became suffused with tears, and when I had finished the last word, I could see nothing but a blank sheet of paper. Then welled up in my heart a thousand thoughts of mingled pleasure and pain. Memory poured its floods upon me, and, disembodied, I crossed my father's threshold, once more listened to his and to my dead mother's voice and counsel; and then, at last, came a soothing sense of relief, and high above all my thoughts, sat enthroned the resolution that the future should prove me not unworthy of their patient love. I had passed through one of those crises which mold the conduct of a lifetime. I wiped away my tears, calmly folded my letter, and, after waiting for a few minutes, that all traces of agitation might disappear, I went down into the cabin, handed the captain the letter that had been enclosed in mine, and, with my usual deportment, withdrew.

While in the cabin, I could not avoid seeing George, who was examining me with boyish freedom. Despite the feeling I had had towards him, because I feared that his presence might materially affect my situation, I could not now help being prepossessed with the appearance of the fellow. He had a strong likeness to his father; the same good-natured face, the same florid complexion. I took him to be about a year younger than I was, and I felt sure that he was, mentally, rather younger than his actual years. He had a towy head of short curly hair that looked like the skin of a yellow poodle. He had blue, roguish-looking eyes, which seemed to indicate that the owner had a good deal of fun in his composition. All this I saw at a glance, and left the cabin, saying to myself, "He isn't such a bad-looking fellow after all." But I thought to myself, an instant afterwards, that it probably made no difference to me; for my father had himself suggested to Captain Bowers the idea of my discharge, and, under present circumstances, and as the captain must feel that he had done his duty towards me, he would very likely avail himself of the opening that my father had afforded.

The captain called me, and I returned to the cabin. He sat at the table holding my father's letter in his hand, and beside him was George, leaning both elbows on the table, and having an expression of great interest in his face.

"Sit down, Fred," said the captain.

At this unusual request, I sat down on the nearest chair. Although I had always had a berth in the cabin, my use of the cabin had never extended beyond occupying it during the evening and night.

"Your father's letter to me," said the captain, addressing me, "apprises me of what is very gratifying to me to learn— that I have not been harboring a scamp. I did what I thought to be my duty in taking you aboard. You yourself must know that your story was very unlikely, but I gave you the benefit of the doubt. I did all that I thought was warranted by circumstances. Now, circumstances have changed. I *know* you to be unfortunate, instead of culpable, for your father tells me that he has implicit faith in your word. Of course, you can't any longer be a cabin boy aboard of this vessel (how sadly that made me feel); you are free to go by the first opportunity, and I will say in your praise, that I think, considering the trying position in which, for a boy of your bringing up, you have been placed, that you have shown remarkably good sense. Your father tells me that he has given you permission to come home, if you can honestly say that you are suffering hardship, or that you are completely cured of your craving for adventure."

"I cannot go then, captain, for I cannot honestly say either," I replied. "When must I leave the vessel, captain?"

"You are not *obliged* to leave it at all," replied the captain. "You do not intend to go home, then?"

"No, sir, I cannot," I answered.

"Then I myself have an offer to make you," said the captain. "George and I were talking over it before you came down, but I did not think it right to make it to you before, for fear of influencing your decision about returning. What would you say to remaining with me?"

"I would not ask anything better," exclaimed I, wondering how I could stay aboard of the *Flying Cloud,* as the captain had said that I could no longer be his cabin boy, and he knew, as well as I did, that I was not fit to be one of the crew.

"This is my offer," continued the captain. "My son George, here, is to be with me all winter on the Reef. When he comes, he is obliged to lose schooling, in acquiring other knowledge. You are farther advanced in your studies than he. How would you like to stay with us and study with George and help him along? Would you consider your services paid by your board?"

I involuntarily started up from my seat, half-extending

my hand, and then withdrawing it, with the feeling that I had taken a liberty.

"Give me your hand, my boy," said the captain, perceiving my embarrassment. "You are no longer the cabin boy, and you never have been, as far as my feelings were concerned."

"Give us your hand," said George, jumping up, and imitating his father's example. "Won't we have jolly times!"

No wonder that I wrote almost nothing in my journal that night.

CHAPTER XXV

THE KATE RAMSEY RELIEVES THE FLYING CLOUD ON THE STATION NORTH OF INDIAN KEY—THE LATTER SAILS FOR CAPE FLORIDA—FRED RANSOM AND GEORGE BOWERS LISTEN TO THE MEN SPINNING YARNS—BRADY EXCELS ALL THE REST.

HAT a change had come over my prospects! One day the cabin boy of a wrecker, and perhaps a disowned child; the next, the associate of my employer, the companion of his son, and a boy happy in the knowledge that he was still loved at home. I felt that I could not be sufficiently grateful to God for his mercies to me,—for having guided me to these kind friends, and blessed me with such confiding love.

The *Flying Cloud* and the *Kate Ramsey* belonged to the same owners. The latter had orders to relieve us on the station, and we were ordered to occupy a station off Cape Florida.

The *Kate Ramsey* brought us a supply of various articles of which we were in need, and also a very acceptable addition of tropical fruit. There were two barrels and a couple of boxes, containing cocoa-nuts, oranges, pineapples, yams, bananas, limes, sapodillas, and mameys. The last two I never fancied. They always tasted to me like a mixture of strawberries and turpentine.

On the morning after the arrival of the *Kate Ramsey*, the men were engaged for two or three hours in transporting the stores from one vessel to the other. Meanwhile, the captain wrote to his owners and family in Key West; and I availed myself of the chance to write a long letter to my father, and add it to the captain's mail, which was left on board of the *Kate Ramsey*. That vessel, occupying our station, would soon be able to send the letters by some vessel sailing from Indian Key. Bidding a long farewell to our old anchorage, we set sail up the Reef.

I found that George was very well acquainted with the men, having frequently seen them when the schooner was in Key West. On inquiry, I ascertained that the reason I had not met him in Key West, was that he had been absent, having been at school at St. Augustine. George was a very communicative fellow, and the men learned of my promotion within an hour of its occurrence, whereupon they congratulated me with mock ceremony, but without the slightest appearance of envy. Since then, I have associated with men of all ranks in life, but under homespun or broadcloth, never knew better hearts than those possessed by that little knot of rude seamen.

The wind was ahead, and we did not make more than thirty miles before night set in; and then the breeze gradually died away, and we were forced to let go our anchor. The nights are exquisitely lovely in Florida. On that particular one the stars shone out brightly; the gentlest zephyr played over waters that broke in phosphorescent waves. Nature seemed hushed in repose, and the low laugh and murmuring voices of the men collected on the forward deck seemed to indicate that they felt the quiet influence of the scene.

"Where do you sleep?" said George to me, as he reclined near me on the quarterdeck, where we had been enjoying a long boy-talk.

"Your father permitted me to occupy a berth in the cabin," I replied, "and I have always slept there."

"Didn't you ever sleep on deck?" inquired George.

"No," said I, "although I must say that on some nights I felt like it. I was afraid that your father might think it out of the way."

"That was all very well then," said George, "but now you needn't be afraid. I never sleep below on a night like this, when the schooner's at anchor. Wait a bit, and I'll show you my rig."

Saying this, he went down into the cabin, and brought up a mosquito bar with long strings fastened to the corners of the top, which was formed of a stout piece of muslin. The strings on one side, he made fast to the main boom; of the other two, he made one fast to the shrouds, and the other to a boat davit. The net then hung evenly, with its lower edges trailing on the surface of the quarterdeck, which was a trunk-cabin. He brought up his bedding and placed it under the bar and tucked the edges in all around, excepting one place to crawl under, and then said,

"Isn't that bunkum?"

"Splendid!" I replied.

"Well, if you like it," said he, "why can't you fix yours on the other side of the boom?"

"Because," said I, laughing, "I haven't got any to fix."

"Oh! that's the idea, is it?" replied George. "Wait a while! There's an old one of mine aboard, full of holes, but you can mend them tomorrow."

We rummaged in a locker, and having found the old net, it was rigged up on the other side of the boom.

"You must look out for the moonlight!" said George, as he assisted me in putting up my bar.

"Look out for the moonlight?" echoed I. "Why should I look out for the moonlight?"

"Why, don't you know," said George, "that if you sleep with the moonlight on your face, it will draw it up so badly, that you wouldn't know yourself in the glass?"

"No!" said I, "you are joking, are you not?"

"Not a bit of it," he replied. "You ask father how one of his men, called Tom Barton, caught it one night, when he came aboard drunk, and lay all night on his back, with the moon shining right in his face. Ask Brady, he knew the man: I hear Brady's voice talking there forward."

"Brady's word," said I, "would not go far with me, for he tells the biggest yarns I ever heard."

"Very well," said George, "then ask my father tomorrow: he has turned in now. The bars are fixed, what do you say to going forward and hearing some of the men's yarns? I don't feel like sleep yet."

"Nor I, either," I replied, "the night seems too beautiful to sleep it all away."

We found the men sitting near the windlass. There was no moon yet, and the picture lay in dark patches, except where the starlight, shining here and there, lighted a face, a bit of cordage, a block, or a spot of glossy rounding spar. The men had evidently been telling a succession of yarns, each one taking his turn in producing the most marvellous story in his budget. As George and I approached, the voice of Bill Ruggles ceased, and then said,

"Here's the boys. Begging pardon, the young captain, and the professor," he added, with mock respect. "I was taking my turn at spinning a yarn. Would you like to hear about an alligator that I once saw killed on the Mississippi?"

"Go ahead," said George, "that is just what we came for."

"The alligator, you see," said Ruggles, resuming his story, "was as much as fifty yards from the edge of the marsh, and we were six men. Hows'ever, I believe if he'd been able to turn quick, which they can't, being kind of hampered by a bone on each side of their necks, he'd have killed one or two of us. Sometimes, he'd stop and make a short fight, and then off for the water again. It didn't seem as if we could stop him, until three of the party fetched a heavy timber of drift-wood, and pinted it up and dropped it on the critter's head. That stunned him like, and you never see such a rolling round and gasping and making awful swipes with his tail. We had to stand clear of the tail. We ran in with a hatchet and an axe, and put in two or three cuts on his neck. Then he was past getting away, and we got in two or three more cuts with the axe, and, at last, chopped his head right square off.

"Now I'm coming to the curious part of the thing. We left the head and body, and went down to our boat, and sot there as much as a half hour, and was going off to the vessel with the water casks, when we thought we'd take one look at the alligator. One of the men was just going to feel of the head with the toe of his boot, and, as luck would have it, I thought how long snapping-turtles' heads lived after they were cut off, and I says, 'Avast there, Tim, jest try the blade of your hatchet.' He hadn't more'n touched the critter's head with the blade of the hatchet, when, my sake! its eyes opened, and sparkled with fire like, and its jaws shut on the hatchet blade, so that some of its teeth were ground to flour. Some one says to Jim, 'You didn't give him a fair shot, jest touching his nose.' So Jim put the hatchet down again and the alligator's jaws shut on it so fast we couldn't get it out, and had to take hold of the hatchet handle and carry the head along to the boat, where we stowed it out of the way of our shins, and rowed off to the vessel. I'd be afeard to say how long the head lived afterwards. And that's a true story, every bit of it, for I see the thing myself, with my own eyes."

"It's your turn now, Brady," said Deal.

"I think ye must have an illigant sufficiency for the night," replied Brady.

"No, we haven't," said Linden. "Honor bright, now, Brady! It was to be turn and turn about."

"Well, byes," said Brady, "I've no objection to spell yees a bit. But whinever I tell ye anything, ye're always screwin' up yer eyes, and distartin' yer fatures at a'most every ither word I say, and botherin' me with yer 'is that so, Brady,' and 'till that to the maranes,' when the thing's not strange at all, at all. What 'ud ye be afther doin' if I till yees a right wontherful story? I guess I won't waste me breath."

"Oh, yes, Brady!" exclaimed the men, with one accord.

"Yes, Brady," continued Ruggles, "it's too dark to see us, so there's no danger of your knowing it, if you come to anything rather tough; and we won't interrupt you."

"Yis," replied Brady, "but whin I get through, it'll be, 'is that so, Brady,' and 'till that to the maranes.'"

"Not a bit of it," replied Ruggles, "we won't say a word. Will we, shipmates? It's agreed, isn't it?"

Everyone agreeing to the terms, Brady commenced, "Spakin' of th' alligator, reminds me of somethin' I once saw in Ireland."

"On your uncle's estate?" said Ruggles, gravely.

"On me ooncle's eshtate it was," replied Brady. "It takes in the best pashture-land in the county, but me ooncle has a patch o' bog, about sax be three mile, jest for diggin' pate for the farm tinants. I was spindin' me time at the place, shootin' and the like o' that; and the first night sich a roarin' come from the bog, as made the ground trimble. I says to me ooncle in the mornin', 'What baste is that ye've got in the bog? Last night the roarin' was awful.'"

"'Did ye never hear one of thim?' says me ooncle, 'it's a kraken, and he's ate 'most two flock of sheep on me.* One of me shipherds was here yisterday, and said he'd fixed a conthraption that would ketch the baste beautiful, and I'm going prisintly to see him drawed out o' the bog. If ye'd like to g' lang, jest say the worrud.'

"Says I, 'I'm wid ye, faith I'd like to see the baste as could murther me rest!'

"'An' me shape', says me ooncle, 'but here's the bye and the nags, let's be aff.'

"Afther ridin' a mather of tin mile, we come to the bog, and on the idge of it was some tinants with ox-tames and carts, and in one of thim a shape newly slaughtered, and a big coil of cable wid a hook on the ind of it. The min threaded the shape on the hook, and sint a bye galloping over the bog to drop it in a big hole quite convanient to where we was standin'.

"In less nor tin minutes, the cable comminced to wark, and the tinants clapped to it, and made it fast to the pole of an ox-cart, and goaded the oxen; but they couldn't stir a peg, and out of the bog came a roarin' to make yer hair stand on ind.

"'Anither yoke of oxen, me byes,' says me ooncle, and the min hitched anither yoke, thirteen foot girth, not an

*The kraken was a fabulous sea-monster, reputed for a long time to frequent the coast of Norway.

inch less; an' the two yoke hauled till their noses teched the ground, and I see the head and fore legs of the kraken coming out of the hole, and its roarin' was frightful to hear, and it twisted its snout and fore legs in the bog, so the oxen stopped short to blow.

"The oxen was *dead bate,* and me ooncle says, 'byes, clap on anither yoke, and we'll fetch the spalpeen.' The tinants hitches them on, and the noses of the three yokes goes down to the ground with the strength of the haulin' they done; and the roarin' made the bog quake all around, and jest as the oxen was a'most spint, the line slacks up, and sinds thim a-sprawlin.'

"'Be the powers,' says me ooncle, 'we've drawed him.'

"'No we haven't, bad cess to him,' says one of the tinants, 'we've drawed the *shape* out of him.' An' sure, an' when we'd hauled the shape up to the place where we was standin', there was nothin' on the hook, barring itself and a pace of an intrail."

Silence ensued, unbroken, except by suppressed laughter and a few prolonged whistlings.

"Well, Brady," said Ruggles, at last, "I thought Saint Patrick drove all the varmints out of Ireland; it seems to me he left a pretty big one."

"Bedad!" said Brady, scratching the side of his head, "there was one varmint the Sint never got out of Ireland, and that's sin, and it's me belafe, byes, that the kraken was Sathan himself."

At this, the suppressed laughter burst forth, and the whistling found free vent.

"Be still wid yer whistlin'!" said Brady, "or ye'll rise a storrum."

"The captain will, if we make so much noise," said Ruggles. "Come along, boys, be quiet! Let's turn in."

The men arose, and began to disperse; but every now and then they went off into fits of laughter, interspersed with whistling so significant, that it was hardly worthwhile for them to have made their agreement with Brady.

138

George and I retired to the trunk-cabin. With a delightful sense of perfect contentment not experienced for many a day, I chatted with him under the boom, until we both fell into a drowsy state that a few seconds converted into deep slumber.

CHAPTER XXVI

THE ANCHORAGE AT CAPE FLORIDA—FRED RANSOM AND GEORGE BOWERS, WHAT THEY DID, AND WHAT THEY SAW, AFTER THEY WERE PUT IN COMMAND OF A DINGHY.

ARLY in the afternoon of the next day, we came to anchor off Cape Florida. The Cape, as the reader will remember from my description of the Reef, is the southern end of Key Biscayne, north of which is Virginia Key, and north of that, the southernmost point of the Atlantic shore of the mainland of Florida.

On the mainland, in a northwesterly direction from Virginia Key and Key Biscayne, is Miami River, a small stream that effects part of the drainage of the Everglades of Florida.

On the western side of the southern point of Key Biscayne, the water is bold up to the very beach, and affords a secure anchorage, from which the Reef and Key Biscayne Bay can both be seen.

It was here that we let go our anchor, in this snug little harbor, from which, looking towards the eastward over the low point of Cape Florida, we could see a portion of our cruising ground, and, looking to the westward, command a long stretch of the mainland. On the point of Cape Florida was a tall lighthouse, of the old-fashioned conical form. Except its keeper, and a few soldiers in a military post at the mouth of the Miami, not a soul inhabited the region, save the Indians lurking in the forest on the distant mainland.

On a calm morning, rowing gently along the margin of the Keys or Reef, gathering shells, sponges, anemones; then spreading sail to drop the killick of our dinghy on some fishing-ground, where the fish never nibbled, but seized the bait; then, spreading sail again to see some distant spot, where the marsh hen, with quickly-throbbing note, sought cover, but found no protection from our eager guns,—these were our sports, these the pleasures of which we never seemed to tire.

One of the prettiest sights to be seen in the inner bay was the fish hawk mounting on high and soaring in wide circles, until some tempting prize made it close its wings and descend like the thunderbolt. Then came the splash, the brief struggle, the fierce bird mounting on sluggish wing, bearing in its deadly clutch the struggling fish, which gleamed and glittered like polished silver.

Of all the birds that we saw, the most graceful in outline was the frigate bird, or man-of-war hawk, as it is called on the Reef. Its tail is remarkably long and forked, and its wings, capable of great extension, taper to the finest points. The bird can be recognized by its shape, almost at the greatest distance at which it can be seen. It soars at a great height, and one may watch in vain to detect the slightest movement of the wings. It ascends and descends in graceful spiral flight, in which it seems as if moved up and down on gentle currents in the air.

One day we had the great good-fortune to find the shell of a paper nautilus. This light, graceful object, with its high curving prow, really looks so much like what one might fancy in a fairy gondola, that it is no wonder it was fabled to rise from the ocean bottom, spread tiny sails, and waft across the bosom of the deep. But, alas! the fable is gone, and we now know that the nautilus *crawls* on the bottom of the sea, *with its shell on its back.* The argonaut is the true name of the paper nautilus. It possesses an exceedingly white and fragile shell. When inhabited by the animal, the shell is elastic.

The pearly nautilus belongs to another order of mollusks, and is the only remaining representative of several extinct species of animals. The pearly nautilus is the one of which Dr. Holmes wrote the beautiful verses, commencing,

"This is the ship of pearl which poets feign
  Sails the unshadowed main—
  The venturous bark that flings
On the sweet summer winds its purpled wings
In gulfs enchanted, where the siren sings
  And coral reefs lie bare,
Where the cold sea-maids rise to sun
                          their streaming hair."

The Portuguese man-of-war sails in little fleets about the waters of the Reef, and we often passed through hundreds of them merrily dancing over the waves. They are filmy little boats, like pods of glossy violet silk; and on one side they at pleasure raise or furl their delicate lug-sails which speed them on their way, while below, hang numerous filaments that stream astern like tiny cables. It is often supposed that the boat is the animal itself, and these cables only so many appendages, to serve as rudders to keep the sail braced against the wind. The streaming cables do serve that purpose, but they form a whole community of beings that use the little boat to tow them through the sea. Thus, you observe, that if anything is subordinate, where everything is mutually dependent, it is the boat, and not the crew who float astern.

Sometimes we rowed our boat through a little inlet, so narrow that the oar tips scarcely cleared the foliage on the banks, and, with a few strokes, darted into the waters of a placid lake studded with green islets. We found many Keys like this. From the outside, they seemed a dense growth of trees extending from shore to shore; but they were really nothing but a rim of land encircling waters which ebbed and flowed through obscure inlets. These places always had great charm for me. Coming from the seaward side of a Key, where the breeze drove on the restless, chafing sea, which frets at every barrier, day and night, and never ceases its hollow murmuring or thunderous crash upon the shore,—we could come with one swift glide into waters unruffled by a ripple; where there was not a sound, save the scream of a wild bird; where the brilliant flamingoes stood in gorgeous troops, and the solitary heron watched moodily beside the bank.

CHAPTER XXVII

THE TWO QUARTER-BOATS ARE SENT TO THE MAINLAND TO PROCURE
WATER AT THE PUNCH BOWL—A STORM—A SHIP IN SIGHT—CAPTAIN
BOWERS SAILS TO GIVE HIS ADVICE AND RENDER ASSISTANCE—THE
SHIP GOES ASHORE ON THE REEF.

ECEMBER ended, January came and passed away, and February was verging to its close. I had again heard from home and written in reply, and George and I continued our studies and sports, and we were the best friends and happiest boys.

On the 20th of February, the schooner being short of water, the captain ordered both quarter-boats to go to the mainland and procure a supply. We took all the water casks, and set off from the vessel, as soon as she came to anchor after her morning cruise. No one but the captain and Hannibal remained on board. George steered one boat, and I took the helm of the other. After rowing about seven miles, we landed on the shore of the mainland, at a place called the Punch Bowl, not far south of Miami River. This was the place from which we were accustomed to procure water for the schooner's casks and water tank. It required four boatloads of casks to fill the tank, and after it was filled, the casks were usually replenished. A full supply of water used to last from three to four weeks, as, excepting for the purpose of drinking, in which the men were not restricted, a very small amount of fresh water was allowed.

The Punch Bowl is worthy of description. On the straight and wooded shore of the mainland is a little bluff which has been described as the remains of an ancient line of Keys which were once an ancient line of Reef. In the face of this bluff, which is separated from the water by a beach

144

not exceeding two yards in width, is an excavation like a little cave, and in this excavation is a deep hole, called the Punch Bowl. It is filled with pure water that filters through the ground from the Everglades, which lie a few miles to the westward. It is an exhaustless spring, so close to the ocean that a high tide washes into its basin.

We ran the bows of the boats close to the Punch Bowl, and, taking the bungs out of the casks, stationed two men with buckets at the spring. Each man dipped his bucket and passed it along a file of men reaching to his boat. In this way, the buckets constantly going to and fro, in the course of an hour the casks were filled.

We started off immediately with our deeply-laden boats, and put up sail to aid our progress, as the casks so obstructed the thwarts that the men could not pull all the oars. The boats had for some time labored along through the water, when the breeze began to freshen and they became almost as unmanageable as logs. I saw Ruggles and Linden glance several times at the sky, and at last Ruggles said:

"It looks kind of squally."

"Worse than squally," replied Linden, "we're going to have heavy weather."

"Think so?" said Ruggles.

"I do," rejoined Linden. "Did you ever see the clouds bank up that way without meaning something? Look out for a storm, I say. I wish we were aboard. If it comes on afore we make the schooner, we'll have to heave the casks overboard, if we don't intend to lose casks, boats, and ourselves too."

The day began to darken, and the wind to come in blasts. There is certainly language in a storm. Even before the wind commences to blow heavily, it has an angry tone, and the gentlest sounds seem to articulate in fierce whispers. Perhaps it is because the seafaring man knows many signs which mutually throw light upon each other, that each has a significance, which, singly, it would not possess.

The boats began to plunge and to roll almost gunwale under, until I began to fear that they would fill; but we were

145

now only about a mile distant from the schooner, so I hoped that we should be able to accomplish the remaining distance in safety. I observed the captain walking rapidly up and down the quarterdeck, by which action, as I knew him so well, I perceived that he was uneasy.

At the distance of a few yards from our boat, the other boat sailed and rowed along in no better plight. Brady, after putting some seizings around a couple of casks, hallooed to us:

"I'm thinkin' ach one of uz will soon be tendin' a buoy widout any pay."

"We'll weather it, Brady, never fear!" shouted Ruggles; "But, boys, we'll have to douse our sail now; the wind's hauling so much that we're not standing within ten points of the schooner."

Both boats took in sail, and, in each, the men managed to get out an additional oar. Although the oars were not equivalent to the sails, the boats were now able to head directly for the schooner and their actual progress was about the same, although their speed through the water was not so great. They wallowed through the sea as if they had no buoyancy, and every moment a wave broke over the gunwales, so that in each boat a man had to bail constantly. What a relief it was when we reached the schooner! There was no need of orders. The men leaped aboard, lowered tackles, and quickly hoisted the casks on board. The falls were then hooked to the boats, and in a few seconds they were triced up to the davits. While the men were engaged in these operations, the captain, George, Hannibal, and I all lent a hand by rolling the casks on the skids placed along the schooner's rail; so that by the time the men had hoisted the boats to the davits, the deck was all clear. The captain, who had been violently exerting himself, at last stood up. He at once glanced seaward. Following the direction of his eyes, I saw a large ship, which, when approaching the schooner, we had observed about a mile outside of the Reef.

"Heave up the anchor!" shouted the captain. "Double

reef the mainsail; unlace the bonnet of the jib! Here you, Ruggles, take the helm!"

Although Ruggles lived forward, he was a sort of sub-officer, and, in any emergency, he was selected for the post of responsibility. In the course of five minutes, the anchor was tripped, the *Flying Cloud's* head paid off, and we were underway, with the falls of the windlass still clicking, as the men hove away to get the anchor to the cathead. For a few seconds, the captain shook the schooner up in the wind, to clear the anchor flukes when they were awash under our bow; and then, as the men put a stopper on the anchor, he kept her off again. Before they could accomplish that, the schooner was heeled over and rushing through the water. I had never been underway in the *Flying Cloud* in a gale, when she was close-hauled. When we sailed for the wreck south of Indian Key, we had had a fair breeze. Now the vessel had a chance of showing her sailing qualities, and well did she maintain her reputation on the Reef. The water swashed over her deck, but the gale was so heavy that her lee scuppers were always beneath the surface; yet while she thrilled in every timber, she tore through the water, gracefully riding the seas, laying her course close in the wind's eye, and holding it in one unswerving line.

There had been so much to attend to on the *Flying Cloud*, that we had all paid comparatively little attention to the ship; but now that everything was snug on our decks, and the vessel fairly underway, all hands stood at their stations, and speculated upon the fate of the ship on that lee shore.

George and I were standing near the captain, who had remained near the wheel, and had not spoken, except to give his orders to the crew, when he said half-musingly, and half as if addressing us, "There's scarcely a chance for her."

"Isn't there?" said George, glad to avail himself of an opportunity to gratify his curiosity. "What are you going to do, father?"

"I'm going to try to get out to her by one of the channels across the Reef," said the captain, "but nothing can save her unless the wind shifts. It'll be close sailing for the schooner to get through the channel, with a headwind, but I'll try it. If we go on the Reef, someone will have to wreck us. Ready, about!" added the captain, in a stentorian voice.

"Ready!" shouted the men at the jib sheet.

"Helm's a-lee!" sang out the captain. Ruggles put the helm hard a-lee, and the schooner turned around like a top, with the blocks rattling, and the sails flapping as if they would split.

"Draw away!" added the captain, almost in the same breath, so rapidly did the schooner go about.

Over we heeled on the other tack, and went whizzing through the water, with the spray flying all over the schooner.

Once more we went about, and steered a little to windward of the entrance to the channel across the Reef, so as to be certain of fetching it, in case the wind should veer a little; but without that, we were almost certain to do it, for the wind blew so hard that Ruggles was constantly obliged to ease the schooner by running her up slightly into the wind, by which process, with the tremendous way that she had, we were always shooting up to windward.

"Keep her off," said the captain, as we neared the channel, and the vessel, being now brought with the wind full on her sails, careened so much that I thought she would either capsize or carry away her mainmast.

"Steady, at that!" said the captain, to Ruggles. "Here, one of you men, lend him a hand. It's pretty hard steering now, boys," said the captain, addressing us.

"Linden and Deal!" sang out the captain again. "Stand by the peak halliards!"

The schooner entered the channel, and we could see, by the roll of the waves, that the water was very shoal.

"Now, men!" shouted the captain, looking astern, to get a range that he knew on shore, "stand by; a moment's time may lose the schooner!"

Every man was at his post, and we flashed through the channel, while, combing up astern of us, came a wave that proved the shallowness of the water through which we were passing.

"Ready, about!" roared the captain, as we almost struck the edge of the channel; and about the schooner went on her heel. In a few seconds more we were in the Gulf. The captain drew a long breath, as if infinitely relieved, and said to us:

"I wouldn't want to try that again for anything you could offer me."

While we had been passing through the narrow channel, our attention had been once more distracted from the ship, but now that it was again plain sailing, every gaze was riveted upon her. She was a large ship and evidently a good sailer, but she was tasked to her utmost. She had not apparently gained much to windward since we first sighted her. She was sailing under close canvas, with double-reefed topsails. The captain kept his glass constantly directed towards her, but we could see her distinctly with the naked eye.

All at once her topsails split, part of them blew out of the bolt-ropes, the ship's head paid off towards the Reef, and her crew let the jib go by the run.

"Lower away the peak!" shouted the captain to Linden, "lower,—lower away! Mind your helm," said he to Ruggles, "and run the schooner up into the wind, if I sing out! We'll catch that squall presently. That ship's as good as lost," said he, addressing us boys, as he saw the sailors climbing aloft and trying to bend a new storm sail, while the ship swept rapidly to leeward. "There's no time to bend a sail, before she'll be on the Reef. They see it now, for the captain's trying to get up the jib and a piece of the spanker; there they go, torn to ribbons! It's all up! Ease the schooner," said he quickly to Ruggles, "here comes a snorter."

The blast struck us, and made everything hum; but Ruggles had put the helm hard a-lee, and that, with our lowered peak, saved us from destruction.

The ship came drifting down towards us. We went about

149

again, and as we came up with her, we backed our jib and laid the schooner to, so that she drifted to leeward side by side with the ship.

"Where am I?" shouted the captain of the ship, through his speaking trumpet.

"Abreast of Cape Florida," Captain Bowers replied through his trumpet.

"What's best to be done?" said the captain of the ship.

"Let go both anchors," replied Captain Bowers, "and give them all the scope of chain you've got. You're almost on the Reef."

We heard the trumpet on the ship speak in a lower tone, and then one anchor after the other was let go, and the cables ran rapidly out of the hawse-holes; but it was some time before the men could manage to give them a turn around the windlass, and then one of them parted, and the ship commenced dragging slowly to leeward.

Meanwhile, we had been lying to and slowly drifting towards the Reef, but, seeing the ship dragging, Captain Bowers ordered the men to ease away the jib and lower the mainsail. The *Flying Cloud* went off before the wind, under her jib and in a few minutes darted through the channel across the Reef. When she came into the Reef Channel, we hoisted a piece of the mainsail by the throat halliards, and ran along the inside edge of the Reef, until we were opposite to the place where the great ship was slowly drifting down upon the outside of it, just where there was one of those spots of sand found at rare intervals on its crest.

In a moment, our sails were let go by the run, and we came to anchor. Without any delay, the men furled the jib and the mainsail, and, as the last gaskets were being made fast, we saw the ship strike.

CHAPTER XXVIII

RESCUE OF THE SHIP'S CREW—ALL ABOARD THE FLYING CLOUD—THE STORM CONTINUES—THE FLYING CLOUD LYING AT HER ANCHORS AND RIDING OUT THE GALE.

HE ship struck on her bilge, fell over on her beam-ends, and the sea dashed over her in a mass of foam. In this position she rolled heavily from side to side, and, with one surge heavier than the rest, two masts went by the board.

"We must save her crew, my men!" claimed Captain Bowers. "Who volunteers to man a boat?"

All the men eagerly rushed forward, and the captain said:

"You, Ruggles,—Linden, Deal, and two others. Lower away the starboard boat!"

More quickly than it is told, the men lowered the boat and unhooked the falls. The captain ordered a coil of rope to be thrown into her, and then leaped aboard with his speaking trumpet in his hand. The oars fell into the rowlocks, and the boat went plunging through the heavy sea.

The captain steered for the little spot of sand, on the outside of which the breakers were dashing in long lines, like gigantic cavalry charging from the sea. Fortunate, indeed, was it for the crew of the ship, that she had drifted on the Reef at a point just to windward of that sand island. Using the telescope, I saw the captain land on the leeward side of it, run to the windward side, then stop and put the trumpet to his lips. At the distance at which we lay in the schooner, I could not distinguish what he said, but a movement instantly took place among the forms that clung about the ship's deck. In a few minutes, I could perceive a couple

151

of men making a line fast to the ship's stern, and then, after a pause, a sailor, holding the line, dropped into the water. There I lost sight of him in the engulfing waves, and intently watched the boat's crew on the beach. Suddenly they rushed forward, and I saw them drag a dark object from the edge of the breakers. They supported it. It stood erect and walked. The sailor was saved!

"Hurrah!" exclaimed I to George, who stood beside me, and to whom I described every movement that I saw. "One saved; hurrah!"

"What are they doing now?" said George to me, "can you make out? They're at the boat."

"No," I replied, looking through the telescope. "I can see them as plainly as I can see you, but I can't make out. They seem to be bending the line from the ship to the middle of the boat. Yes, that's it; now they are rolling the boat over and over, and the line is getting taut. I see what it is now! They are rigging up something on the ship. It's a sling of heavy stuff, with a line made fast to it. Now the captain is saying something through his trumpet. Now I can see a sailor getting into the sling. There he comes, don't you see?—sliding down, working his way hand over hand, while the slack line pays out behind him. There he is, just at the edge of the breakers, and the line swags so much that they'll carry him away. No they won't! Our men have given the boat another turn over on the beach. He has cleared the breakers! Hurrah! One more saved!"

Here George and I engaged in capering about deck, shaking bands with each other and shouting to Hannibal.

"Look again, Fred," said George to me, "or let me have the glass."

"I've got it on them again," said I. "The captain is bending his line to the sling. Now he is speaking the ship again. There goes the sling back to the ship. There's another man getting into it. Our men on shore are pulling him down as fast as they can go. They've got him safe ashore. I see him getting out. There goes the sling back again. Now there's another man getting into it. Here he comes, hurrah! that's quick work. There goes the sling back again. They'll all be saved, George, won't they? Won't they be saved, Hannibal?" hallooed I to the cook, who was standing near and participating in our excitement.

"Lor' bress um, and watch over um, Massa Fred! I believe you'se right," said Hannibal. "But I wish dey was all ashore, for ebery one make dis chile feel as if dat would be de lass."

But down came another and another and another; and we watched them through their perilous journey, and, at every escape, capered and lugged each other around, bestowed some hearty slaps upon Hannibal's broad shoulders, and then quieted down and renewed our observation of what was happening on shore.

At last, there was a pause, and the scattered pigmies on the beach collected in a group; and I could distinguish the men engaged in unbending the line on the boat and righting her again. Then some of them seized her by the gunwale, and ran her down to the leeward side of the beach, and a number crowded in and shoved off, leaving the rest on the island.

In five minutes, the captain was alongside, and a portion of the ship's crew jumped upon our deck.

"Shove her off," said the captain; "there's not a moment to be lost, the water's commencing to rise on the beach."

The boat shot away again, and George and I addressed ourselves to the wants of the shipwrecked men. They had saved nothing: it was hardly worth while to ask the question, for we had seen all. Wet, exhausted, and miserable they were. We sent them below, and Hannibal instantly supplied them with hot coffee, which he had prepared in anticipation of its being needed. The three men on board opened their kits, and made the newcomers welcome to everything in their possession. The Norwegian's clothes, now, for the first time, came into play; for not one of the men had ever been willing to wear the clothes of the poor fellow.

153

By the time that the captain returned with the second and last boatload, including the captain and mates of the ship, who had preferred to remain on the beach, the first set of men were tolerably comfortable. Captain Bowers took the captain and first officer into the cabin, to fit them out with his wardrobe, while the crew of the boat provided the last-comers from their kits.

We had both anchors out, and it was as much as they could do to hold; but we gave them all the scope of cable that we had, and lay plunging up and down, and buffeted about as if we had been in the open sea.

The ship rolled so heavily, that every minute I expected to see her go to pieces. Her third mast soon snapped; and there she lay, a great dark hulk that was every now and then obscured by a dense whirling cloud of foam.

The ship's crew, fourteen men in all, were saved. They consisted of the captain, the first and second mates, and eleven men. George and I gave up our berths to the captain and the first mate, and the other mate stayed forward with the crew, as is quite usual on board of ships. As it was storming so violently, all hands, except a watch, had to stay below. It was quite crowded forward; but, in the cabin, the only difference in comfort was that George and I shared, in common, the extra berth of the cabin, which, by spreading a couple of boat-sails in it, we managed to make quite comfortable.

The captain of the wrecked ship was in very low spirits, as may well be imagined, for he had no hopes of saving her cargo, and Captain Bowers was not able to offer him any consolation on that point. We spent the evening drearily. The schooner lurched violently from side to side, and every now and then, in the intervals of frantic pitching, the captain of the ship would ask some question, to which Captain Bowers would respond, and then, after an attempt to keep up a conversation, silence would settle down upon the occupants of the cabin, and their energies would be confined to steadying themselves in their seats or berths.

If one has never spent a night aboard vessel in a storm, either in a roadstead or in the open sea, he can have little conception of what a dismal scene the interior of the vessel on such occasions presents. In the best time that can be properly termed a storm, on deck there are the creaking spars and shrilly-whistling cordage and masts playing wildly to and fro over the laboring hull that every instant experiences a heavy shock and besprinkling from stem to stern. In the cabin, things are in disorder; clothes thrown hastily aside; broken glass; the faint light of the lamp clinking in its gimbals; disorder, discomfort, everywhere. But in severe storms, the very nature of things is reversed. Then the ship groans as if in agony; the shocks fall like those from a battering ram; the cordage shrieks and howls as if demons filled the air; the tall masts bend like wands. There is darkness, with fitful gleams of light, whence coming or whither gone, impossible to tell. Sailors run quickly over the decks, or clamber aloft; and all that interposes between the ship and destruction, are those dark flitting forms, that binnacle-lamp faintly glowing and shedding its light on the compass and on a calm, observant face.

We experienced not all of this on that dark tempestuous night; but we were on a lee shore, plunging into the seas, with every timber cracking and straining, as the vessel surged at the cables and brought up with a jerk hard enough to disengage our grasp of the supports which we were all forced to seek in every posture. Then everything would rattle, and then would come a horrid shock: then a roll on one side, then a shivering in every timber, the ring of metal, the crash of glass, the sough of the wind, intermingled with the shrieks and howls of the demons in the cordage. And in the cabin sat two forlorn men, whose ship lay beating, scarce five hundred yards away, on the roaring, pitiless Reef.

There was no sleep that night for anyone, either forward or aft. The watch was on the alert, and every few minutes Captain Bowers was on deck, and the poor captain of the ship followed him and strained his eyes in the gloom to try to obtain one glimpse of his ill-starred craft.

Towards morning the gale began to abate, and long before dawn every soul was on deck and anxiously waiting to discover what the first light would reveal as to the condition of the ship.

At last day dawned, and showed us the state of affairs. The storm had so raised the level of the water along the coast, that what with the increased depth and the violence of the waves, the ship had been canted around on her bilge, until she lay athwart the Reef, with her bow pointing seaward. In this position, she presented a comparatively small surface to the action of the waves, which, before, had struck her fairly on her beam. Now, they struck her bow, raised it slightly, and dropped it as they sped onward; and then she swayed heavily from side to side, until the next great billow came rolling in, raised her, and dropped her as it rushed by her sides, and roared away over the Reef.

By twelve o'clock, the storm was decidedly abating, but the same sea still swept in from the ocean, which was a grand sight. As far as we could see, it rolled in maddened turbulence. There was a war of the waters. Groups of white-capped waves rushed frantically at each other, and then all went down together in the struggle; and in a moment their dark forms and white angry crests appeared, arose, and dashed together again desperately, in unyielding and tumultuous strife.

No wreckers hove in sight. It was impossible for them to leave their anchorages. But we did not concern ourselves about them. Even if our thoughts had not been absorbed with pity for the unfortunate situation of the rescued sailors, we would have been easy in mind in regard to the disposition of the wreck, for the captain of the ship had authorized Captain Bowers to take charge of whatever the elements might spare.

Once more night closed upon the scene, with the wind gradually lulling, but the seas still maintaining their ascendancy, and, on account of the diminution of the wind, as distinguishable in the darkness, to the ear, as they had been by day to the sight. All night long the wind gradually lulled, until, by morning, it was almost calm. But all night long, the seas rolled on in a chorus of blending, hoarse, and menacing roar.

CHAPTER XXIX

THE WRECK DRIVEN HIGHER ON THE REEF—WRECKERS HEAVE IN
SIGHT—TWO ARE RETAINED BY CAPTAIN BOWERS—THEY TAKE A LOAD
FROM THE SHIP AND SAIL FOR KEY WEST—BRADY'S QUARREL ON
SHORE WITH THE "BIG INGIN," AND HOW IT ENDED.

ORNING arrived at last, and showed us the ship
in a higher position on the Reef than the one
which she had occupied during the previous
day. The storm had gradually subsided, until
the wind had become a gentle breeze, and nothing remained
but the effects of the gale, in the still agitated sea and the
stranded ship.

Then, towards the north and south, appeared the distant and approaching sails of the wreckers, which, before
long, arrived, came to, and boarded us to know what was to
be done. Our captain had his plans matured, but the sea was
still too boisterous to put them into execution. The services
of two of the wreckers, that were of greater tonnage than the
others, were secured, and the rest made sail again for their
stations.

In the afternoon, the two quarter-boats and the dinghy
went ashore, carrying all hands except a crew left on board
of the schooner. George and I went in one of the boats,
which were provided with axes, and switchel in a keg for the
men, and with water in a monkey, a porous earthenware jug,
for the officers. Parts of the crews of the two other wreckers,
equipped in the same manner, went ashore in their own
boats.

We landed on one of the Keys, not far to the southward
of Key Biscayne, and found, on its southern point, a place on
which there was a good sandy soil, covered with a sparse and

stunted growth of bushes. The men, who numbered about thirty, went to work with their axes and hatchets, and by nightfall they had managed to cut down the growth and heap it around the edge of the clearing. When this was done, the crews pulled off in their boats to their respective vessels.

Throughout the whole day and night of the 22nd, the same gentle breeze prevailed, so that, by the following morning, the sea was quite placid. In two or three hours after daylight, it was almost calm on the Reef, but still remained deeper there than usual, owing to the violence of the gale which had been blowing towards the coast.

Captain Bowers and the captains of the two wreckers had concerted measures in advance so that, the moment the sea became tranquil, the vessels, which had been lying with loosened sails and anchors apeak, got underway and steered for the ship. The *Flying Cloud* arrived first, and the water was so tranquil that Captain Bowers was enabled to make her fast alongside of the ship, merely getting his fenders out to avoid chafing the schooner's bulwarks. During the latter part of the blow, the ship had been forced farther on the Reef, and had settled in a hollow, in which, by working, she had gradually embedded. With the increased depth of water on the Reef, she had then righted so much that she now lay almost on an even keel.

Our crew soon forced a convenient entrance into the hull of the ship, by going to work with their axes in a place on the side where she had been so violently pounded that the planking was broken and beaten into a fibrous pulp. The other wreckers followed our example and, soon, almost every man belonging to the three vessels was engaged in unloading the ship. The cargo was from Boston, and consisted of common furniture for one or two of the ports in the Gulf. Soon the decks, holds, and cabins of the three schooners were crammed with cabinet ware. All three then cast off from the ship, and Captain Bowers ordered the two, which he had employed, to sail immediately for Key West, and return as soon as they could unload their cargoes. The

Flying Cloud sailed in close to the Key where we had made the clearing, and the whole afternoon was consumed in transferring her cargo to the beach, and in spreading sails over it to protect it from the weather. At sundown Ruggles was left ashore with an armed party, consisting of Linden, Deal, Brady, and a couple of the crew from the ship. The captain took this precaution on account of having observed an Indian canoe paddling from the mainland, in the direction of the Key. We left the men a little coffee, salt pork, and hard tack, with which to prepare their breakfast for the next morning.

In the morning, at daylight, all hands aboard of the schooner had their coffee, and without visiting the party on shore, proceeded at once to the wreck, and recommenced to unload her. By twelve o'clock, we had our cargo completed, and sailed for the beach, to which, as on the day before, we transferred everything. From curiosity to know what was going on there, George and I, accompanied by Jack, went ashore with the captain in the first boat that left the schooner. As we neared the shore, we saw three or four Indians standing near our men, and, on landing, distinguished by the tone of Brady's voice that he was angry. As George and I approached the group, I caught sight of Brady shaking his fist under an Indian's nose, and heard him exclaim:

"Ye dud! ye dud! I see the graise around yer chaps now, ye botherin' old parrot-toes. Go 'lang wid ye; do ye think I come to Ameriky to be cook to an Ingin, bedad?" Here Brady flourished his fist within an inch of the Indian's nose.

"What's all this row about?" said the captain, brushing past the outskirts of the group, and elbowing his way up to Brady and his opponent, just as the latter was making a low guttural response, of which I could understand nothing. "What's the matter, I say? Speak, Brady!"

"Spake, is it? an' sure, an' it's little spakin' I fale like doin' this minute, yer honor, the captain. I want ye to see him git fair play wid fist or shillelah; and if he won't fight, wid yer honor's permission, I'll give him a taste of me fut."

"But the matter, the matter?" said the captain, impatiently.

"Ah! it's the mather, the mather, you'd be afther knowin'? Well, there's enough the mather! I'll till ye ivery worrud. This blessed minute, the min had all done their dinner, and was gone to worruk ayont, and I was frying me bit porruk; and, thinks I, the fire's not hot enough, I want some of thim dry brush-wood I see over there, and I goes to get it. And as I was a-coming back, I see this coppery thafe wid his chakes stuck out, and chawing very speedy, an' not a bit of me porruk in the pan. I says to him, 'ye're a thafe;' and I put me fist till his nose, and I says again, 'ye're a thafe;' and the chawin' he kep' up was awful to behold, and all to wunst he give a swaller, and stared at me as if he was a-chokin'. 'Ye're a thafe,' says I again, for the thirrud time; 'won't ye be afther answerin' me?— Ye stole me porruk.' And he says to me:

"'Ingin no stale. Big Ingin, great chief Mickewakes-tamekakekyme.'

"Chafe, indade, ye spalpeen, says I, ye staled me porruk,—and don't I see the graise rinnin' down yer chaps? Go 'lang, wid yer chafe. And, yer honor, the min came rinnin' around uz, and I was jest going to lay the heft of an Irishman's vingince on him, when yer honor came up."

While listening to this recital, and looking at the excited and pugnacious Brady, contrasted with the stolid Indian,—who despite his denial, was glistening around the mouth from the effects of his hasty repast,—the captain was seized with several convulsive twitches of countenance; and as Brady concluded with an attempt at the name of the chief, and his own reply upon its dignified announcement by the owner, the captain burst out laughing, and went into such convulsions of merriment, that he had to cast himself on the ground. The contagion spread to the whole party, who roared in concert with the captain, until the puzzled Brady broke forth into a succession of broad grins, alternated by eclipses of serious expression; and even the greasy mouth of the much-injured Indian, who, despite his tell-tale appearance, had maintained an air of dignified composure, melted into something like a smile.

At last the captain arose, almost exhausted, and after having taken Brady aside, rejoined the group, and addressing the Indian, said:

"Friend, he much sorry. He no see buzzard takee."

"Yah, yah," replied the Indian. "Buzzard much plenty here, much takee pork."

"And, by the way," said the captain, "Indian man want eatee, here plenty."

"Yah, yah," replied the Indian, "chief tankee much."

The Indian was evidently pleased at this intimation of the captain, and he, with the three companions who had accompanied him to the Key, walked quietly away to the place where they had left their canoe.

The captain then turned to Brady, and said:

"Now, Brady, I'm not surprised that you were provoked, but you and all the men—do you all hear?—must keep on the right side of these fellows, or they'll give us trouble. I don't want you to let them steal the furniture, sails, or anything valuable; but don't have any difficulty with them for the matter of a piece of pork. Let them have what they want to eat, and I'll furnish you with a larger allowance. All you have to do is to keep a bright lookout for the property on shore."

Saying this, the captain returned to the boat with us, and pulled off for the vessel. Jack sat in the stern-sheets, and kept up the growling and suppressed bark with which he had been affected ever since he caught sight of the Indians, around whose calves he had walked and snuffed until he almost disconcerted the chief of the greasy chin and unpronounceable name.

CHAPTER XXX

THE WATER SUBSIDES ALONG THE REEF—THE FLYING CLOUD CON-
TINUES THE WRECKING—THE IRREPRESSIBLE BRADY DESCRIBES THE
APPEARANCE OF THE IRISH INDIANS—THE RETURN OF THE TWO
WRECKERS—ALL THE WRECKERS WEIGH ANCHOR—FRED RANSOM
MAKES THE ACQUAINTANCE OF THE FAMILY OF CAPTAIN BOWERS.

By the following morning, the water along the coast had subsided to its usual level, and the depth on the Reef had so decreased that the *Flying Cloud* was no longer able to approach the side of the ship. This was of little consequence, for the principal part of the furniture that had escaped damage sufficiently to render it worth removal had been saved in the four cargoes which had been taken from the ship. The two quarter-boats were now employed in transporting all that remained undamaged, and even the little dinghy did her share in the work. The water was now sufficiently low to enable us to get at the kits of the sailors, and they were immediately removed to the schooner, whose rigging was soon dressed with garments hung out to dry. The clothes of the captain of the ship, and of his chief mate, had been saved upon the first occasion upon which the three schooners had lain alongside of the wreck. The level of the cabin being much higher than that of the forecastle, they were out of reach of the water after the waves ceased to break over the ship.

By night-time, we had collected quite a number of other things that were worth saving, and had stowed them aboard of the schooner. On the following morning, the *Flying Cloud* sailed as near to the Reef as she could approach without danger of grounding, and the boats went to and from the wreck, until almost everything above water, and portable, had been removed.

The next day, the 26th, as the weather after the storm was becoming quite hot again, and the addition of the ship's crew to the small accommodations forward rendered the place so close as to be almost intolerable, some men were sent on shore and rigged up awnings made of spare sails that had belonged to the ship. Under the protection of these, a portion of the ship's crew spent that night, in company with the party on guard. While the men were engaged on shore, with the party of Ruggles, in constructing these makeshifts for tents, Captain Bowers got the *Flying Cloud* underway, and ran through the channel which crossed the Reef. On reaching the Gulf edge of the Reef, he laid up along it, until opposite to the wreck, and let go his anchor in seventeen fathoms of water. He then lowered the remaining quarter-boat (the party on shore had been allowed to retain one), and sent it aboard the ship to get the chain cable.

Meanwhile, we passed out of one of the schooner's hawse-holes the end of the cable of the anchor that was hanging at her bow. In a short time, the men who had been dispatched to the ship had made a line fast to the end of her cable, and lowered it into the stern-sheets of the boat. They then hauled into the boat a little of the slack, and with much difficulty rowed to the schooner; for, although the cable was quite slack, for the reason that the ship had changed position after having struck on the Reef, be it remembered that any chain-cable is a very heavy thing, and that of a ship particularly massive. With some trouble, we managed to pass the end of the cable through the hawse-hole from which we had removed our cable. The men then hove away at the windlass. As our own chain came home through one hawse-hole, a large gang of men hauled in the ship's cable through the other; and just as our anchor broke ground, the ship's cable was passed around the bitts, and the men continuing to heave at the windlass, we at once swung at the ship's anchor. As it was lying outside of the place for which the schooner had headed, in weighing her own anchor, her stern fell off, and she headed towards the Gulf. We took in over a hundred fathoms of chain before we got the ship's anchor apeak. For the ship to have dragged ashore with over a hundred fathoms of scope out shows what must have been the violence of the gale in which she was wrecked.

When we got the anchor to the cathead, we found that it was too heavy to be carried there, for it put the schooner entirely out of trim; so we hoisted it aboard, and placed it about amidships, just forward of the main hatchway.

There was little hope of getting the other anchor. It had been cast in about twenty fathoms of water. When the chain had parted, it was at a point so far from the Reef, that it would have been difficult to find the end of the cable, unless upon such an occasion as one already described, when the water was so limpid that it resembled molten glass. The short piece of cable, which still hung through the hawse-hole in the ship's bow, was secured by our quarter-boat; and we then ran down the edge of the Reef, sailed through the channel across it, and came to anchor in the Reef Channel.

Here, after everything was made snug, we again lowered our quarter-boat, and sent the rest of the ship's crew ashore, with directions to remain there with their shipmates, and to relieve Ruggles and the schooner's men who were stationed there. They were told to keep one of the quarter-boats, but were cautioned to haul it up on the beach, beyond the reach of the sea. In the course of half an hour, Ruggles and the rest of the party, detailed for the first guard on shore, came aboard. Very glad they were to be relieved from their duty. Brady, in great glee, climbed up the side of the schooner. When he got on deck, I asked him how he liked it ashore.

"Musha! musha!" said he, working his shoulders around inside of his shirt, "the muskatees and sand-flies is enough to ate a man up be night."

"And the Indians by day," said I, jokingly.

"It was the porruk he ate," retorted Brady. "Bad luck till him."

"In Ireland," said I, "you are not bothered with Indians.

You've got the advantage of us there."

"We're not," answered Brady, "that's thrue for ye, Misther Fred; but if ye mane to say there's no Ingins there, ye're meestakin'. In Ireland they're dacent drissed and behaved—that's the difference."

"Do they look at all like the Indians here?" said I, choking down premonitory symptoms of a laugh.

"Wid graisy clothes on, and leather poorses on their fate? Indade they don't! I wunst see a tribe of thim, and ivery mither's son of 'em a chafe, and had a complate shoot of black, wid a satin waistcoat to match."

This picture of a tribe of Indians was too much for me. I burst out laughing, much to the affected surprise of Brady, who kept saying,

"An' what's so quare about their drissing that way? It's jew to the riches of the counthry."

"But, Brady," suggested I,—thinking that I could nonplus him once,— "how could each man be chief?"

"Och! how should I know the arringements they has?" replied the immovable Brady. "In Ameriky ain't ivery win of uz a sovereign?"

With this unanswerable argument, Brady joined the gang of men, who, by this time, had hooked the falls to the boat, and were engaged in hoisting her to the davits.

On the morning of the 27th, the boat from the schooner, and that from the shore, again visited the wreck to get the few things which still remained above the level of the water in the hold. About ten o'clock, they had collected a number of small articles, and put them aboard of the *Flying Cloud*. The *Flying Cloud* then got underway, and sailed across to the Key; and there she commenced to take in a cargo. About two o'clock in the afternoon, the two wreckers, which had been dispatched to Key West, hove in sight, and by four o'clock they came to anchor near us. Then, for the rest of the afternoon, the place presented a lively scene, as the men busily loaded the boats, and rowed them to and fro between the schooners and the shore.

Early on the 28th, the loading was resumed, and, by evening, everything had been removed from the beach to the schooners. That is, everything except some small articles which our Indian friend had chosen to pilfer. As they were of very small value, both Captain Bowers and the captain of the ship judged it expedient to wink at the theft, rather than, for the sake of obtaining their restitution, run the risk of a disturbance which might make enemies of the neighboring Indians, and perhaps result in a collision between them and the wreckers.

On the following morning, the three schooners got underway about the same time, and ran down the Reef. The *Flying Cloud* was the last to get underway, but she soon overhauled and passed her consorts.

We did not anchor at night. Having a fair wind, we kept on our course down the Reef Channel, and early the next morning, after a pleasant voyage, came in sight of Key West. Here, the three schooners hauled alongside of the wharves in front of the warehouses belonging to our owners, and the unloading and stowing of the goods commenced.

The captain and George took me up to their house, where I was introduced to the family, which consisted of Mrs. Bowers, a son, and a daughter. George and I continued to sleep aboard of the schooner, but when we were not obliged by duty to remain aboard, we went up to the house; where Mrs. Bowers always greeted me so kindly, and appeared to take so lively an interest in me, that I knew there was no danger of wearing out my welcome.

CHAPTER XXXI

THE SALVAGE SETTLED BY THE ADMIRALTY COURT IN KEY WEST—THE
FLYING CLOUD SAILS FROM KEY WEST—SHE COMES TO ANCHOR OFF
INDIAN KEY—THE CAPTAIN, GEORGE, AND FRED, GO ASHORE AND
SPEND THE EVENING WITH THE FAMILY OF DOCTOR CLUZEL.

IT will not interest you to know the particulars of
our stay in Key West, so I shall not dwell upon
them. At first, our time was taken up in unloading
the schooner, and in storing the goods in the
warehouses in which the first cargoes had been placed. Then
came the decision of the Court in regard to the amount of
salvage due, and until that matter was decided, the attendance of Captain Bowers was necessary. The underwriters
were in Court to attend to the interests of the insurance
companies, for the ship had been partially insured. The captain, officers, and crew of the ship, were also detained for
some time to give their testimony. Finally, the cargo was
sold, the amount of salvage was awarded, and the whole
business closed. Each of the men was paid his share of the
money received for salvage, and upon Captain Bowers' repre-
sentation to our owners that I had performed duty in steering the boats, and in doing whatever else had lain in my
power towards saving the cargo, they were so generous as to
make me a present of a hundred dollars. This sum I asked
that they would allow to remain on deposit with them, so
that I might draw upon it in amounts that my necessities
might demand. The request was granted, and I found myself
the happy possessor of a bank account made up of a sum won
by my own exertions. This money, added to what remained
undrawn of the monthly stipend allowed by my father,
amounted to nearly one hundred and fifty dollars.

As soon as everything was settled, and just before our departure from Key West, I wrote a long letter to my father, in which I described the events that have been narrated in the last few chapters. I mentioned the money which I had earned, and told him that he need no longer furnish me with an allowance. Captain Bowers, observing me about to seal my letter, said that he would like to add a postscript. I handed my letter to him, and he scribbled a line or two.

In the next letter that I received from my father, he said: "I am rejoiced to learn from the postscript which the captain added to your last letter, that he thinks well of you." It was not until many years afterwards, that, among my father's papers, I chanced to see the postscript. The captain had written, "Have no fears for your boy. You will be satisfied with him."

While I was in Key West, feeling that I was now quite rich, I purchased an irresistible basket, made of milk-white shells. The framework was constructed of delicate silver wire. The shells were threaded on the body of the basket, so as to form imitations of roses and other flowers; while, on the handle, the most minute of minute shells were used to represent delicate clustering tendrils. Some of these baskets, which are made in the Bahamas, are formed of shells of a uniform color. Others are made of shells of colors so intermingled as to present a most variegated appearance. The most handsome baskets that I ever saw were those which were either roseate or white; and, of these, the white are the handsomer, owing to the extreme delicacy and pearly lustre of the shells.

After making a few repairs, and taking in a supply of provisions and water, we set sail from Key West early on the morning of the 26th of March. Late in the afternoon, we let go our anchor off Indian Key; the same Key near which we had anchored on my first voyage up the Reef, and just north of which we for some time afterwards occupied a wrecking station.

On the former occasion, when we anchored off Indian

Key, the captain, it will be recollected, went ashore, but I did not accompany him, and had no opportunity of seeing the place, except what I could distinguish from the deck of the *Flying Cloud.* This time, as soon as everything was made snug, the captain ordered the men to lower one of the boats, and took George and me ashore with him. We learned with pleasure that we were going to spend the evening with a family named Cluzel, with whom the captain and George were acquainted. The family was composed of Dr. Cluzel, his wife, and three children, two of whom were young girls, and the other was a boy younger than George.

The doctor was an extremely well-educated man, being, in addition to his general attainments, a naturalist of no small learning and repute. His residence on the Florida Keys afforded him an opportunity of pursuing his favorite study, and he indulged in it with all the ardor which actuates those who have once contracted a love for that science. He had a fine collection of works on natural history and kindred topics, as well as a very fair library of general reading. In fact, his house on Indian Key was an intellectual oasis. To a man fond of any other branch of study, the isolation of such a residence would have been intolerable; but with his family, his books, his papers, and the world of knowledge that the Reef laid at his feet, the doctor craved no addition to his society, excepting the transient visit of a friend. As for his wife and children, they did not feel the loneliness of their situation; for the latter had never known anything else, and the world of the former, as may be truly said in praise of most women, was in the affections.

We rowed, I might almost say, up to the doctor's very door. His house was built on the shore of the Key; so near that one end was supported by piles, which formed a secure foundation for the structure, and enclosed a sort of flooded cellar, into which the tide washed through the interstices. This wharf-like cellar was used by the family as a bathroom. Below the contiguous wharf was a large turtle crawl, from which the family could always draw a supply of turtle, fresh from this little fenced-in bit of ocean.

On landing, the captain and George walked with me a short distance beyond the beach, for the purpose of allowing me to get some idea of the character of the settlement; but fearful lest the doctor's family might happen to perceive us from the windows of the house, and suppose, from our straying past, that we were not eager to see them, we returned to the house and knocked at the door. I had, however, seen enough of the settlement to ascertain that it was very small, that the houses were of an humble character, and chiefly tenanted by fishermen and their families.

On being admitted, we were very kindly received by the doctor and his wife, who devoted themselves to the entertainment of the captain, while George and I were committed to the care of the two young ladies and their brother. It was soon dusk, and tea was served. After tea, Captain Bowers and the doctor and Mrs. Cluzel continued to converse, and we younger folks played checkers and backgammon. Wearying of these, and being at the same time attracted by some of the words which reached us from the other group, we left our games, and collected around the elder people. The doctor was discoursing about some of the many strange things which he had observed during his residence on the Reef; and, in the course of the evening, he disclosed a store of knowledge so varied and abundant, that he had no more attentive and charmed listeners than the younger members of the party. It was eleven o'clock before we bade the family good night, and, accompanied by the doctor, walked down to the beach, and hailed the schooner to send the boat ashore.

CHAPTER XXXII

THE FLYING CLOUD SAILS FROM INDIAN KEY—SHE ARRIVES AT HER OLD ANCHORAGE—THE CAPTAIN VISITS THE WRECK—THE CREW SET TO WORK TO SAVE THE IRON ABOUT IT.

A T daylight we were again underway. Whenever we anchored at night, we always weighed anchor at the first streaks of light in the eastern horizon. The wind was ahead, and the schooner was obliged to beat all day. Towards night, the wind freshened and shifted, enabling us to lay nearer to our course. Before morning, it hauled again, so that we were obliged to recommence tacking. The captain therefore cast anchor for three or four hours, and, just before day, got underway again. Late in the afternoon of the second day of our departure from Indian Key, we came to at our old anchorage and station off Key Biscayne.

There, on the Reef, a few miles away, lay the hull of the wreck. I could hardly refrain from apostrophizing the thing as something from which life had departed. More to the ship, than to anything made by man, does it seem as if he had imparted a ray of his intelligence. The ship is so beautiful in its symmetry; its career is so adventurous and checkered; it so promptly and unerringly obeys the slightest impulse from the will of its master,—that it seems more life-like than a mere mass of timber, iron, and cordage. And when fate decrees that it shall be stranded on the shore, it seems like some huge departed leviathan that cumbers the spot with its colossal skeleton.

On the following day, we made our usual cruise up and down the Reef; and after we came to anchor, the captain took one of the boats and went on a visit of inspection to the ship.

George and I accompanied him, and were very glad to revisit the scene of our first wrecking exploit. Since we had been at the place, the sea had made sad havoc with the timbers of the great structure, which, for many a year, had sailed from continent to continent, and defied the elements. The merciless waves had vengefully battered in the sides, and rent and scarred the bottom, by grinding it against the sharp-pointed coral. Masses of bulwarks that had once been timber and plank, so securely jointed and battened, that nature itself could scarcely have wedded them more closely, hung at the ship's sides, and swayed helplessly to and fro. The rudder was gone; the figure-head, the crew's *beau ideal* of female loveliness, was washed away. Nothing was left of all the beauty with which, on that fatal afternoon, the graceful object had careered to its tomb upon the Reef.

And we, insatiate mortals, were not to be satisfied until we had secured the last vestige. Money was again to produce something else; perhaps help to produce something identical; to go, perhaps, through the same ordeal, and to encounter, perhaps, the same fate. What of that? Should we object to imitate a law of the universe— the economy of Nature? Nothing is absolutely lost. "Imperious Caesar dead, and turned to clay, might stop a hole to keep the wind away."

The captain said to us, as we rowed slowly around the wreck:

"Well, boys, there's a good deal of stuff about her yet, that's worth saving. We'll commence tomorrow. I reckon, too, we'll be able to get the other cable, by grappling for it."

The result of the captain's inspection of the wreck was that instead of coming to anchor after our next morning's cruise, we ran out through the channel across the Reef. The captain sent one boat's crew aboard the ship, for the purpose of detaching all the planking that was loose, while, with another boat's crew, he commenced grappling for the cable which we had not saved. We had so good an idea of the direction from which the ship drifted on the Reef, from our knowledge of the direction of the wind at the time, that although the water was not clear, and we were obliged to rely entirely upon the grappling irons, we managed, in the course of several hours' persistent dragging, to get hold of the cable. As upon the previous occasion, the end of one of our cables was removed from its hawse-hole, and we hove the ship's anchor to the cathead, hoisted it aboard, and stowed it just abaft the foremast.

Meanwhile, the boat's crew at the ship had, by using axes, managed to detach great pieces of the bulwarks, which they lowered into favorable positions for drifting ashore. These would not have been cut away and set afloat, had not the wind been blowing towards shore. On the following morning, the boats visited the beaches along the Keys, made lines fast to these rafts of timber and plank, and took them in tow to the Key where the clearing had been made. Then, with the aid of purchases rigged to trees, they were hauled ashore and fired. When they were reduced to ashes, the iron with which they had been fastened was carefully collected and deposited in rough lockers on board of the schooner. We found the ship's masts, and a good many stray bits of cordage which would serve as old junk. All those things were carefully preserved, for everything of the sort is valuable.

By sending axemen to complete the work which the sea from time to time partially executed for us, we made so thorough work with the wreck, that, in the course of a few weeks, nothing of it was left but the great mouldering ribs, in which the worms were making extensive ravages.

CHAPTER XXXIII

GEORGE BOWERS AND FRED RANSOM MAKE A VOYAGE—THE OAK
FORESTS ON THE ST. JOHN'S RIVER—THE CAPTAIN'S INVITATION TO
THE BOYS ON THEIR RETURN—FISHING AT NIGHT, WITHOUT HOOKS
OR BAIT—THE SPORT, AND HOW IT WAS ENJOYED.

OWARDS the middle of April, a sloop stopped at our station. Her captain was acquainted with Captain Bowers, and came aboard of the *Flying Cloud* to say, that as his vessel was short-handed, and he had to go up the coast to St. John's River, he would be obliged if the *Flying Cloud* could let him have a man for a few days. This request Captain Bowers could not grant, but he offered the captain to let George and me go, if we were willing, as we, he was pleased to say, were supernumeraries. The captain of the sloop accepted the offer, and we boys, always ready to welcome any novelty, went aboard of his vessel. We were gone just nineteen days.

The course of the St. John's is peculiar. A few miles from its mouth, it takes a sudden turn to the southward, and runs parallel with the coast. The shores are densely wooded, and, in the broad parts of the river, the scenery is very agreeable.

We saw great forests of oak covered with Spanish moss. In their dense shades, the moss hung in flowing masses that looked like long gray giant-beards. When the rays of the sun struck aslant through them, they were penetrated and suffused with light so rich, yet so soft, that they seemed dripping from a bath of silvery-gold. Nothing can be imagined more funereal, more weird, than one of these dense forests, at sunset when the darkness of night has settled on the ground, and stolen around the huge trunks of the oaks; while above, in gentle gradations of light, the long, waving,

175

gauzy drapery grows brighter and brighter, until, on the top-most branches and twigs, it shines resplendently.

After procuring the lumber for which the sloop had entered the river, we set sail for the mouth, put to sea, and, in three days from that time, George and I were once more on board of the *Flying Cloud*. We were rejoiced to get back to the schooner. Life on the Reef had more charm in a day than our voyage of over half a month had afforded. As we had shipped to supply the place of one man on the voyage to St. John's River, we were paid what one man would have received for wages, and divided the sum between us.

Although the month of April was nearly spent, there was not a marked change in the climate on the Reef. As for the appearance of the country, the verdure is the same throughout the whole year, and summer is perennial. Under our mosquito bars on the quarterdeck, George and I luxuriated in the coolness of the nights. In all my experience, I recollect no couch so delightful as that quarterdeck. In clear weather, the water was so tranquil that we could just feel the undulation of the schooner, as she dipped her bow into the glassy waves. Looking upward, we beheld the pure firmament bespangled with brilliant stars; and the gentle breeze fanned us, and sang a lullaby that mingled pleasantly with the dull roar of the breakers on the far-off Reef. What more could two boys of our age desire, than all that we possessed? We had studies to give zest to recreation, and recreation and repose surrounded by romance.

A few nights after our return, the captain, who did not often indulge in sporting, said to us boys that he would show us a kind of fishing that we had never seen. We jumped at the offer, not only because there was novelty attending it, but because the captain was to be of the party. George eagerly exclaimed: "What day is to be, father?"

"It is not to be any day," replied the captain, "it is to be at night, tonight, if you like. What do you say to tonight? What do you say, Fred?"

"We are ready," we both answered.

"What bait shall we prepare?" inquired I.

"No bait at all," replied the captain.

"No bait!" exclaimed George. "Fishing by night, and with no bait!— well, that is strange fishing!"

"Perhaps it is because it is at night," said I, laughing, "that we don't need any bait, because the fish couldn't see it if it was on the hook."

"How is it, father?" asked George, jocosely. "Do the fish get caught by running afoul of the hooks in the dark?"

"We sha'n't need hooks!" replied the captain, making his eyes as big as saucers, staring from one of us to the other, and enjoying our puzzled expression.

"We give it up, father," said George, "now don't tease us any longer."

"You will see," said the captain, mysteriously. "Tell the men to lower one of the boats."

Captain Bowers ordered some very mysterious looking apparatus to be stowed in the bow of the boat, and in five minutes we were pulling for the shore. The Captain steered along the Keys, towards the southward. We rowed close to the line of mangroves, just within the verge of their shadows, cast by the faint starlight. After having passed three or four Keys, the boat headed for the entrance to one of the inlets. Keeping towards the Key on the port hand, the Captain suddenly shot the boat into an obscure inlet which led into a lake comprising nearly the whole of the Key, and which George and I imagined to be our possession by the right of original discovery.

"Do you know this place?" said George to his father. "I thought no one but Fred and I knew it."

"Boys are very apt to think similarly about many things," replied the captain, drily.

The oars were unshipped, and the men, grasping the overhanging boughs and twigs, dragged the boat through the inlet, until she shot out upon the placid bosom of the lake, whose shores the starlight faintly revealed in dreamy outline.

"That'll do, my men," said the captain. "Now fire up."

On each side of the boat, the men hooked a couple of iron things, like little grates, into which receptacles they put pine knots and tarry pieces of rope. They then struck a light, and ignited the stuff. The flames sprang up, and in a minute we had a couple of bright bonfires, crackling and smoking and dropping their embers with a seething noise into the water. In and immediately around the boat, the scene was brilliant in the extreme; but, beyond, a circular wall of impenetrable darkness shut in the view.

"Here are your hooks," said the captain, handing George and me a pair of short spears with several barbs on them. "What are you looking up in the air for? Look at the bottom."

Hereupon, George and I, who had been gazing around, charmed at the brilliant spectacle, cast our eyes towards the water. Imagine our surprise, when we found that we could see the bottom as clearly as at noonday; and that, over it, darting about in all directions, were fish of every description. We were so delighted at this sight, that we began to shout and strike wildly into the water. The captain commanded silence, and stationing a man astern, with a long pole, the boat was urged gently through the water, and we were cautioned to make allowance for the refraction, when we were about to strike at a fish. The grates were constantly replenished with pine knots, tarry rope, and oakum; and we went blazing along, harpooning, and struggling with our prizes, some of which were so huge that they were as much as we could master. Just as we had made the circuit of the lake, a great barracuda, terrified at the fiery dragon of a boat, which was sweeping resistlessly along, leaped into its maw. As we had secured plenty of fish, and it was neither the captain's wish, nor ours, to indulge in wanton destruction, we desisted from our sport, and laid aside our spears. A few handfuls of water, thrown into the grates, soon quenched the fire. The grates were then unhooked, emptied, and stowed away in the boat, and the men rowed until we arrived at the inner mouth of the little inlet, through which, as before, we hauled the boat. We came out upon the ruffled waters of the Reef Channel, and within hearing of the sound of the distant surge. There was no merrier laughter along the coast than that with which George and I, on our return, counted our spoils, and talked over our exploits in spearing.

CHAPTER XXXIV

HOW TO FIND A TURTLE'S NEST—HABITS OF THE TURTLE—TURNING TURTLES.

IT was on the night of the 7th of May that we speared fish by firelight. George and I were so fascinated with it, that, only two or three nights afterwards, we begged the captain to indulge us with a renewal of the sport. It was by far the best in which we had engaged. We fancied it, not solely on account of the novelty of using short trident-like spears instead of fish hooks, but because the accompaniments were so charming. The ruddy glare of the fire; the glowing stretch of water; the dark shadows of the woods; the sight of the fish as they dart over the bottom,—all these circumstances combine to render the scene in the highest degree picturesque.

Our first excursion was our last, for the captain could not be prevailed upon to go again, and he would not let us take the boat at night. We had ample amends, however, in some new enterprises which I must describe.

One morning, about the middle of the month, George and I did not go with the schooner on her morning cruise, but rowed off, ashore, to have a day's fishing and gunning. The tide was rising, and had almost reached high-water mark. We were rowing along one of the beaches, when George said to me:

"Fred, do you see that mark on the sand, between the edge of the beach grass, and where the water is now? Do you know what that is?"

"No," said I, "what is it?"

"Guess," he answered.

"A piece of brushwood, or perhaps drift timber, that has

scraped down the beach at the last ebb."

"No it isn't," said he; "it's the track of a turtle. There's a turtle's nest near there."

"A turtle's nest," shouted I, pulling on one oar, so as to bring the boat's head on the beach. "I'm bound to have it."

We jumped on shore, and George whittled a straight stick, so as to make it more slender, and adding a sharp point to it, he went opposite to the place where the mark appeared on the beach, and walked about, carefully examining the sand above high-water mark. At last, he said:

"Here it is. Now come here before I disturb the sand, and I'll show you how to find a turtle's nest. The Conchs taught me; and what they don't know about fishing, turtling, and egging, isn't worth knowing. You must know that turtles choose a moonlight night and high-water to come upon the beach to lay their eggs. How they can tell it's a moonlight night, I can understand, but how they know it's high-water is a peg beyond me. It takes them only a few minutes to lay their eggs, and then, down they souse into the water. But as they come up at the top of high-water, the tide falls a little before they can get away, so they leave their tracks on the beach below high-water mark. The next tide washes them all away, but we came across this place before the tide had risen again. The tracks are one sign. The other is this. Do you see a kind of crescent, cut into the loose sand among this beach-grass, above high-water mark? That's the place the turtle touches with the hind end of its shell, as it turns to go back to the water, after it has covered its eggs, and smoothed the sand over them. If we had been ten minutes later, the tide would have washed away the tracks on the beach; and if there had been any wind, this loose sand would have shifted so that there wouldn't have been any sign at all here."

"I think that you had better set about finding the nest," said I. "It would be a joke, if, after all your directions for finding turtles' eggs, you couldn't find any."

"You never mind," replied George, good-humoredly, "I

181

have to take your instruction every day, and it's my turn now. You don't know everything. I'm just as sure that there's a turtle's nest where that crescent in the sand is—well, now look!"

Hereupon, he commenced to punch the sand with the sharp stick, and every now and then examined the point of it. After jobbing it down several times to the depth of about a foot, he held the point towards me, and said, triumphantly,

"What do you call that?"

"It looks exceedingly like egg," said I.

"That's just what it is," he replied, going down on his hands and knees, and commencing to dig a hole in the sand.

I followed his example; and when we had dug to the depth of a little over a foot, we came to the eggs.

"Ten, twenty, thirty, forty, fifty," cried I, in amazement. "Here is another layer underneath; sixty, seventy, eighty, ninety. Why, there are over a hundred!"

We found a hundred and seventy; and then George ran hastily along the beach to see if he could find any more turtle tracks before the tide rose to high-water mark. He found a place about two hundred yards off, and after the usual jobbing with the stick, we discovered the nest, and took a hundred and forty-one eggs. Three hundred and eleven eggs in two nests! We found a secure place in which we buried them slightly under the sand, to secure them against birds, and then went off on our projected expedition. In the evening, we stopped at the place, and carried the eggs aboard of the schooner.

On the following morning, when the schooner was underway, George and I were on deck talking over our good luck of the preceding day. The captain, hearing part of our conversation, joined us, and inquired how we would like to turn a turtle on the beach. "For then," continued he, "you will have the eggs, and the *hen* too."

It was agreed that we would go ashore that night, and turn turtle. The season being that when the turtles commence to lay, the captain was certain that we would capture at least one. He told me many interesting things about turtles. It seems that, numerous as the eggs were in the nests which we found, they form only a portion of those laid by a turtle in the course of a season. The green turtle lays three sets of eggs, two in May, and one in June. The sum-total of eggs is about two hundred and fifty. The hawksbill turtle lays two sets of eggs, one in July, and one in August. The whole number of eggs laid is about three hundred. The loggerhead turtle lays in May and June, three sets of eggs, which amount to about five hundred. The trunk turtle lays three sets of eggs, which amount to about three hundred and fifty.

The habits of the turtles, in laying, are very different. The loggerhead and trunk turtles, being the largest and fiercest species, are not nearly so shy as the green and hawksbill turtles. The last two resort to the most unfrequented places, although the green turtle penetrates the indentations on the coast. The hawksbill turtle lays only on the wildest Keys, far distant from the mainland.

About nine o'clock that night, one of the quarter-boats was lowered, and the captain, George, and I, pulled by five oarsmen, rowed towards shore. The moon was full, and shone with that silvery lustre which sheds a beautifying influence upon the most commonplace objects, and invests the really beautiful with a charm so mysterious and solemn, that the observer feels as if in a scene of enchantment.

Our keel soon grated on a beach which stretched away for two miles, with its white coral sand reflecting the soft light which bathed it throughout the whole of its graceful sweep. We leaped ashore, and hauled the boat above high-water mark, until it was almost hidden among the beach grass and low brushwood.

"Now," said Captain Bowers to the men, "scatter along the beach, about the same distance apart, just above high-water mark; lie low, and don't make any noise. You Conchs understand the business better than I do, but you, Brady, if you've got any yarns to tell, keep them till you get aboard."

The five men walked off along the beach, and, occasionally, we could see one of them leave the party and disappear in the shadows of the brushwood above high-water mark. At last, in the far distance, was discernible a single figure wending its way along the bright beach; then it vanished, and the scene lay silent and deserted in the silvery sheen of the moonlight.

The tide crept slowly up the beach, and commenced, with a gently plashing sound, to lave the jagged points of coral which cropped out of the sand just below high-water mark.

"You must be very quiet, boys," whispered the captain, as we all crouched behind the high tufts of beach grass. "If a turtle comes near us, it will be off at the slightest noise."

"Aye, aye, sir," we whispered in reply, as we kept a strict watch on the beach.

"There is one," said the captain.

"Where? where?" we eagerly whispered.

"On the beach, about a quarter of a mile off," replied the captain; "near that dark-looking thing like a drift log. Don't you see it move? There it shows."

We saw it, then, as the moonlight shone on its wet shell. In a few seconds it was out of sight.

"Now let me caution you again, boys," reiterated the captain. "Not a word above your breath."

The captain adjusted his night-glass, and commenced to examine the surface of the water.

"Pshaw!" said he at last, closing the slides of the telescope, and shutting it up. "We're not in luck tonight."

He had hardly uttered the words, before a prolonged, loud, and startling hiss came from the water; and, as we crouched still lower, and looked between the tufts of beach grass, we saw the head of a turtle appearing above the surface of the sea.

"Hist!' said the captain; "Lie as close as you can."

We obeyed his instruction and, at the same time, kept our eyes directed towards the turtle, fearing that it might not land near us. But it swam rapidly towards shore, and dragged its unwieldy body out of the water. Its wet shell gleamed in the radiance of the moonbeams, like a silver shield. The monster stretched its neck out of its shell, to the full extent, and crawled sluggishly up on the beach grass, just on the other side of the boat. The captain kept his fore-finger to his lips, by way of enjoining silence, and we scarce-ly breathed. At last, the turtle made so much noise, that the captain cautiously arose and peered over the edge of the boat. Having apparently satisfied himself that we would be secure from observation, he touched us, and motioned to us to look over the boat.

Raising our eyes just above the level of the boat's gun-wale, we saw the turtle hard at work, scooping a hole with its hind flippers. As soon as it had collected a heap of sand, a violent flirt of the flippers scattered it in every direction. When the hole was about a foot and a half deep, the animal commenced to deposit its eggs. The operation of digging being finished, and that of laying commenced, the captain ducked his head behind the boat, and saying, "Now's our chance," ran quickly around it. We followed at his heels, seized the turtle, and, by our united exertions, turned it on its back.

"I don't think that the men can beat this," said the cap-tain. "It is one of the biggest that I ever saw. If we hadn't caught it when it was laying, I'm not sure that we would have been able to turn it. When turtles are laying, which does not take more than ten minutes, they do not seem to be able to stop; but they are powerful things, and when they're making for the water, it's some thing of a job to turn them."

"Hollo! Hollo-o! Hollo-o-o-o-o!" shouted the captain, walking out on the beach, of which the rising tide had left but a narrow strip.

One after another, five dark objects emerged from the shadows, and commenced to move slowly towards us. By the time that the last man arrived, the first-comers, with our assistance, had hampered the turtle's flippers with a piece of marline. We lifted the turtle into the boat, and rowed to the place where one had been turned by a couple of the men. Its captor had accommodated it with a pillow of coral rock, a plan which is sometimes adopted to prevent the animal from reversing its position. On a favorable slope, it sometimes uses its powerful neck to so great advantage as a lever, that it has been known to regain its liberty.

We hampered the second turtle in the same manner in which we had secured the first one, and lifted it into the boat. It was not more than two thirds of the size of the other. The aggregate weight of the two was probably about three hundred and fifty pounds.

"Well, Brady," said the captain to that individual, who was pulling the stroke-oar as we rowed off towards the schooner, "don't mind me, you must be nearly dead from having had to hold your tongue for two hours. What about the turtles in Ireland?"

Well," said Brady, "there's this about toortle toorning in Ireland; it's pleasanter sport there nor here, for the muska-tees."

"You own up, then," said the captain, "that you can't beat America in turtles, and you haven't got any mosqui-toes?"

"Troth, no!" replied Brady; "the bigness of the toortles there would astonish ye, captain, and"—added he, with a sly glance at the captain—"the muskatees too; but they're amazin' kind-hearted be the side of Floridy galli-nippers."

The turtles were so heavy, that a tackle was used to hoist them aboard of the schooner. The next day, one was dispatched, and, with the eggs, served as our principal food for three or four days. The other turtle was put in a shady place, and brine was occasionally poured over its head and body. By pursuing this treatment, a turtle can be kept alive for a long time, without food, and yet preserve its healthful condition.

CHAPTER XXXV

THE MIAMI—THE EVERGLADES—THE DEER-HUNT—THE SIESTA—
THE FIGHT WITH THE PANTHERS—INDIANS PROWLING IN THE FOREST.

URING the remainder of May, and in June and July, the captain occasionally indulged us in a turtling expedition by moonlight, and we captured specimens of all the various kinds of turtle. As he always accompanied us, and seemed to share in the excitement of the sport, our pleasure was very much enhanced.

Daily we got the *Flying Cloud* underway, and sighted the Reef for miles on each side of our station, but nothing rewarded our vigilance. This daily duty at last became exceedingly monotonous, and had we not had recourse to expeditions for the purpose of procuring turtles, fish, eggs, and birds, we would have experienced ennui, despite the admirable collection of books which I have mentioned that the captain possessed. Independently of the spirit of adventure which prompted us to make these expeditions, they were absolutely necessary, in order to obtain food of a kind that would ward off scurvy, which infallibly attacks those who are for a long time exclusively confined to a diet of salt provisions, with a disproportionate amount of vegetable food.

All things, however, must end, and George and I, eager turtlers though we were, tired of the moonlight excursions to the beaches, and craved some novelty. The stay of George was drawing to a close, and the intercourse of the occupants of the cabin commenced to be tinged with a shade of gloominess, brought about by the anticipation of his approaching departure.

How little we all know even of the future which is almost the present! George's going was not nearer than mine. Our departure took place soon and simultaneously, by a train of startling events, transpiring with so great suddenness, that they left us in a maze in which it was difficult to collect our thoughts.

At daylight, on the 5th of August,—owing to the approaching departure of George, and in fulfillment of a promise which had long before been made to him, to the effect that before he went, he should have a deer-hunt,— Captain Bowers committed the vessel to the charge of Ruggles. Giving him instructions in regard to the day's cruise, and taking George and me and Brady in the dinghy, the captain set sail for the mainland. We were provided with two good fowling-pieces, two fine rifles, and an ample supply of ammunition. We did not neglect to take fishing tackle, including the grains, although none of us were capable of using them skillfully.

About eight o'clock in the morning, we landed at the mouth of Miami River. On the left bank, near the mouth, was the little military post first established in 1837, garrisoned by a few men. Here the vegetation was not dense, and a beautiful grove of lime trees surrounded the quarters of the soldiers. Proceeding up the Miami, for a few miles, we at length arrived at the place where it leaves the Everglades. This was a spot which I had long desired to see, and one which, at that time, had seldom been trodden by the foot of the white man.

George and I climbed the roof of a solitary mill which was built at the head of the stream, on the verge of the Everglades; and when we had mounted to its ridge, we commanded a view for many miles.

We had penetrated the Miami to its source, about three miles from its mouth. This, therefore, at that point, is the width of the encircling rim of land which bounds the Everglades, or, as it were, the wooded shore of a vast sea of swamp, covered with long, waving, yellowish grass, and dotted with a perfect archipelago of wooded hummocks. Some of the hummocks were quite diminutive. Others seemed at least half a mile in length. I now realized how difficult it was to prosecute the Florida War, then being waged in portions of these Everglades, where the Indians could lurk in almost impenetrable fastnesses, and when approached by a superior force, seek safety in flight. In fact, the Florida War, from the difficult nature of the country, had been a bloody game of Hide and Seek.

The Spanish Indians, who had been long peaceful, had, for some months, been engaged in committing depredations on the settlements of the whites, and on shipwrecked sailors: so that the practice of providing the wrecking vessels with arms had ceased to be a mere form. No apprehension, however, of immediate danger in our vicinity, appeared to exist in the mind of anyone with whom we had intercourse.

After George and I had remained perched up on the mill for half an hour, the captain hailed us to say that the morning was swiftly passing away, and that, if we intended to hunt before noon, we must immediately descend.

During the heat of the day, deer generally lie down in the place where they have been grazing. In the open spaces of forests like those of Florida, the undergrowth affords concealment, and the animals remain quiet until the coolness of the afternoon invites them to renew their browsing upon the herbage. The kind of hunt upon which we were proceeding, is called a still-hunt. This consists in advancing quietly through the forest, in search of the feeding deer, and whenever they graze, the huntsman is enabled to advance unperceived; but when they raise their heads, he stands stock-still, when, although they no doubt often perceive him, they do not recognize him as a living object.

Being without hounds, we could not hunt in any other manner, for, notwithstanding the presence of Jack, and Brady's authority on the subject of Newfoundlands as hunting-dogs, the captain, if he had ever heard of that sage opinion, preferred to attempt a still-hunt. This requires nothing but a cautious approach and a steady hand, and is practiced by the solitary, keen-eyed rifleman as successfully as if he were a king with a court at his heels.

We entered the boat and rowed across the Miami, and when we reached the other shore, the captain took a rifle, and gave us boys the two double-barreled fowling-pieces, each of which he loaded with sixteen buckshot. Filling our pockets with luncheon, and a supply of bullets, buckshot, and percussion caps, and slinging our powder-flasks over our shoulders, we left Brady in charge of the boat, and plunged into the recesses of the forest.

The morning had slipped away in a most strange manner. Our various delays, principally caused by rowing up the Miami, viewing the Everglades, and increased by all sorts of little distractions,—among others by examining curious objects to which the captain called our attention,—had consumed the time from eight o'clock, when we landed at the mouth of the river, until past noon; and before we had penetrated two miles into the forest, the captain, on consulting his watch, found that it was verging on one o'clock. Not a sign of a deer had we seen. The heat was very oppressive, and our eagerness began to languish. At last, the captain, perceiving that George commenced to lag, suddenly threw himself on the ground, exclaiming:

"Come, boys, we may as well take lunch. We'll not find any deer now, unless we stumble over them."

We sat down, and spread our stores on the ground. They consisted of a few ship-biscuit, some sliced tongue and ham, and a canteen of switchel, quite warm, but as it was, it sufficed to slake our intense thirst.

Not a leaf stirred. The air seemed clogged with heat. Not a sound was heard, save—to use a paradox—that mysterious voice of silence, seeming infinitely distant, yet all-pervading, an inarticulate murmur that fills all space, like blended voices speaking in some distant sphere, and faintly borne within the confines of the earth. Who has not heard it? And if any have not, go where there is silence, and listen, and you will hear its voice. The hot air, the motionless leaves, the deep shade, the repast, the fatigues of the day, affected us all with a languor to which we offered no opposition, but disposing our heads on our coats, rolled up so as to serve as pillows, we were all soon in the enjoyment of a profound siesta.

The captain was the first to awake, and on looking at his watch, found that it was past four o'clock.

"Come, boys," said he, "up with you. Now is the time to find deer, if there are any in the neighborhood."

At this summons, George and I, with some slight effort, threw off a disposition towards sluggishness, and shouldered our guns; while Jack, who had been indulging in a nap, and like us at first, seemed little disposed to make exertion, joined us, and, by his actions, manifested his understanding that the hunt was about to be resumed. Before we had gone a hundred paces, the effects of our sleep wore off. Revived by the cool breeze, we stepped along gaily, peering in every direction to descry the game.

We had walked about half a mile, when we arrived at the opening to a beautiful glade. The tall trees shut in the spot so effectually, that only here and there the sunlight struck through the leafy covering, and sent a long narrow beam athwart the ground, or flecked the low bushes with a few spots of golden light. As the captain preceded us through the opening which served as as ante-chamber to this saloon of the forest, he suddenly halted, and motioned to us to be cautious. Proceeding with a stealthy pace, in obedience to the motion of his hand, we came in view of three or four deer grazing at the extremity of the glade. At that moment, two of them had raised their heads, and were evidently in the act of chewing the mouthfuls of grass which they had last cropped. We all stood like statues until the animals again lowered their heads, when we separated slightly, and cautiously advanced, taking great care to avoid treading upon branches that might crackle under foot. Slowly we drew nearer, each step well calculated, each gun well poised, so that if the deer took alarm, we could fire as they fled.

At last, we came within about a hundred yards of them,

and then our precautions redoubled. The captain's rifle would have been effective at that distance; but George and I, inexperienced sportsmen, who could not rely upon a single bullet, had therefore been provided with fowling-pieces, which are not sure at a range exceeding fifty yards. The captain was to reserve his fire, and make use of it in case ours proved ineffectual.

More slowly, and more slowly still, we advanced, until I judged that we were within the prescribed distance.

I heard the sharp click of George's lock, as he cocked his piece. With a sidelong glance at him, as he was in the act of levelling his gun, I slowly aimed mine at the foreshoulder of a stag which had just raised his head from the spot on which he was feeding, under the overhanging boughs of an enormous tree. But the moment that the sights of my gun showed clearly defined against his red hide, and I was about to pull the trigger, I restrained my hand, for I saw a great animal pounce upon him from the tree. At this astounding sight, George also withheld his fire, and we both dropped the muzzles of our guns.

"A panther!" shouted the captain. "Be steady, now, boys."

The deer stood, for a moment, in startled attitudes, and then plunged madly towards the thicket. They vanished like a flash. Meanwhile, a tremendous commotion was visible among the grass and low bushes in the place where the panther and stag had fallen to the ground together.

"Cock both barrels, boys," said the captain. "Here, George, give me your gun, and take my rifle. This is going to be close quarters, and may need a cool hand. Advance steadily, with your guns ready to fire at an instant's notice. Keep cool!"

We advanced steadily, but with rapidity, towards the place, and came in full view of the scene, which was rather different from our anticipation. Instead of the single panther and stag which we expected to find, and found, just as we reached the place, another panther was in the act of emerging from the thicket.

As our heads appeared above the surrounding bushes, the male panther, or cougar, which had sprung upon the stag, and was then greedily engaged with his muzzle buried in the animal's flank, heard a signal of alarm from his advancing mate, desisted from his work, glanced up, and, with a quick bound, diminished his distance from us by several yards.*

"Steady, boys," muttered the captain, and, levelling his gun, he fired. The panther reared and pawed the air, and George and I, taking advantage of the opportunity, fired at his chest and foreshoulders. He rolled over and over and tore up the ground and bushes in his death agony.

The captain, seeing that there was no danger to be apprehended from one antagonist, glanced towards the other animal, which had been advancing with ferocious aspect to the aid of her mate. Her agile form and snarling jaws had changed at the sight of her companion's fate; and far from seeking to avenge it, she had turned tail, and was slinking away with a rapid lope, when the captain again fired, and her raised hind paw and limping gait showed that she had been lamed by the shot. Jack sprang after her, and I fired simultaneously. She instantly rolled over on her back, then arose; and as if my shot had given her increased vitality, instead of depriving her of it, she bounded for the thicket. Just as she neared the edge of it, she fell, rolled over once or twice; and then, as if endowed with renewed strength, rushed at the trunk of a large tree and climbed it rapidly. As one fore paw grasped the lowest limb of the tree, her hold suddenly relaxed, and she fell heavily to the ground.

---

*It is common for the male and female panthers, when paired, and raising cubs in their lair, to hunt in couples.

The animal known in the United States as the panther, vulgarly *painter,* has been incorrectly named, for the reason that it is a different animal, and does not at all resemble the real Panther, from which it derives its designation. It is the Felis Concolor or Cougar, the same animal as the Puma of South America.

Thinking that she might rend Jack, in her expiring rage, we shouted to restrain him from approaching her. We were too late. The brave fellow rushed at her, and fastened his fangs in her neck. Then as suddenly loosing his hold, he uttered a joyful bark, and looked towards us as we came running up. The panther was dead.

We remained masters of the field, and stood leaning on our guns, and striving to regain our breath, exhausted by the excitement and the chase.

As we returned towards the place where the male panther lay, we boys kept up an animated discourse, recounting to each other what we had all seen. We found that the neck of the stag had been broken by the force of the panther's spring. Even without that, the animal would have had no chance to escape the clutches of its powerful enemy, for the wounds on the delicate hide exhibited fearful laceration effected by the panther's claws.

The panther was riddled with balls. The captain had fired between his eyes, and the load of buck-shot had completely blinded the beast, and caused the rearing which enabled George and me to discharge our pieces at his chest.

The captain drew his hunting-knife, and commenced to dismember the stag. He took one haunch of venison and laid it aside, and placed another in security, by tying it to the bough of a tree. After that, he went to work, with our assistance, and skinned the male panther. This was quite a long operation, and by the time that we finished, cleaned the skin, rolled it up in a bundle, with the hair outward, and provided a branch on which to carry the haunch of venison, the sun was getting quite low.

"Come, boys," at last, said the captain, wiping his gory hands in the long grass; "we must be packing. We've got a mile and a half to walk, and a long sail or row before us. tomorrow we'll get the skin of the other panther."

George and I slung the haunch of venison on the middle of the branch which had been provided, and he shouldered one end of it, and I took the other. The captain carried the panther's skin, and we trudged off through the woods, in the direction of the boat. We felt pretty well fagged with our day's exertion. Now and then, the captain took a turn at one end of the pole, and, in that way, we divided the labor among us; except that the captain continued to carry the skin, which, in its undressed state, was quite a heavy bundle.

When we arrived at the boat, we found Brady, shouldering his rifle, and pacing the bank in a martial manner, while his countenance betrayed the greatest alarm.

"Be yees all safe," said he, anxiously scanning the party. "Be the powers, but I thought yees was all murthered and scalped."

"Pooh! Brady," replied the captain; "what is the matter with you? I hope you didn't get anything to drink from the post?"

"Indade no!" answered Brady;—"bad luck to the military regulations, that has no regard for the wakenesses of human nature. It's sober I am; but I've been a'most out of me mind with thinking yees was kilt and massacred intirely by the Ingins. Yees hadn't more'n went, the mornin', when I heerd a nize in the bushes, and rins on tap o' the bank, and sees two Ingins, one of thim, the chafe, he calls himself, that stole me porruk, yer honor remimbers."

"Aye, aye!" said the captain, "what then?"

"I looks at thim, and they looks at me, and the porruk thafe comes up to me, and says:

"'What you do here?— more men in wood?' and I says to him, 'Mind yer business, or I'll wallop the pair of yees;' and wid that I gets me rifle and says to him, 'be aff wid yees, or I'll shoot yees widout benefit of clargy. I don't like the looks of yees,' says I, 'nor yer manners ayther,' I says. And whin I said that, the spalpeen muttered some gibberage to the other one, and they goes off into the brambles."

"I'm afraid you've been hasty, Brady," said the captain. "Once before I cautioned you to be civil to this very fellow."

"Well, yer honor, the captain, I tried to obey yer orthers, but the sight of thim varmints snaking around when yer honor and the byes was away in the wuds, a'most took away me power of spache."

"I'm thinking," rejoined the captain, "that your power of speech will be an endless trouble to you, Brady. It can't be helped now. Get aboard the boat; the sun has almost set."

"And whin I heerd the shots that was fired so quick," resumed Brady, at the same time obeying the captain's orders, "I made sure that yees were all murthered, and yer scalps shaved off as clane as a whustle."

"I pardon your indiscretion, Brady," replied the captain, "in gratitude for the interest that you have shown for our safety. Pull away, my man, and as soon as we get out of the river we'll loosen the sail, for I see that the breeze is fair." So saying, the captain took the other pair of sculls, and rowed lustily. When we reached the mouth of the river, we set our sail, and, with a free wind, sped away over the bay, in the direction of the Keys. It was ten o'clock before we reached the *Flying Cloud,* and George and I had fallen asleep, several times, in the boat. When she came alongside of the schooner, we awoke in so drowsy a state, that we had scarcely energy to clamber up the side, stumble into the cabin, and throw ourselves into our berths, so entirely were we overcome with the fatigue and exciting adventures of the day.

CHAPTER XXXVI

THE RETURN TO THE FOREST—THE SURPRISE BY INDIANS—THE CAP-
TURE OF GEORGE—THE PURSUIT—THE RESCUE.

HE captain's complaisance, in making and performing the promise to indulge George in a deer hunt, entailed, as is often the case, a further sacrifice of inclination. The captain had passed the age at which such expeditions have the power to charm, and if he had any pleasure in them, it was principally in contributing to that of his son. It must be granted, however, that the exciting character of the sport in which we had actually engaged, had so far exceeded his anticipation, that he did seem to share our enthusiasm. The measure of our satisfaction was complete, except that the coming night had prevented our securing one trophy of the chase, the skin of the female panther.

The captain, it will be recollected, had reconciled us to leaving the forest, as the light was waning, by saying that, on the following day, we could procure the other skin,—a promise from which he was not likely to be released by our indifference. Thus it happened, as I hinted just now, that the captain, having been once gracious, was "in for a penny, in for a pound."

In the morning, George and I were among the first who were astir on the schooner, and the captain had hardly opened his eyes, before we brought him to a realizing sense of his indiscreet promise of the preceding day. With a hearty yawn, and a slight hesitation, he jumped out of his berth, saying,

"Well, boys, a promise is a promise. Besides, to please you, I would have seen the sport out. It will be something to

197

talk over, and I know that you'd never cease to regret that skin. There will be one for each of you to show as the spoils of the chase."

The captain's orders to Ruggles were communicated in a few words. Then, telling Brady, who seemed to think that he was to make one of the party, that his services were not required, as the wind would probably remain in the same quarter; and it would be fair both ways, the captain ordered the dinghy to be lowered. Hannibal stowed some provisions in the stern-locker of the dinghy, and when George and I, accompanied by Jack, got into her, after handing our arms and ammunition to the captain, who had taken his place, Hannibal passed aboard a biggin full of steaming coffee. The boat's painter was cast off, and with sheet unbrailed, we skimmed away towards the mainland, while the schooner, which had been lying with sails set and anchor apeak, got underway and stood towards the southward.

Day had not quite dawned. The breeze was of that faint and fitful character, which frequently heralds the coming sun; and, with it, freshens, until the ruffled water sparkles in the renewing light of day. Thorough wreckers as we were, as soon as our little sail was well set, and the articles in the boat stowed away in the most convenient places, we addressed ourselves to the hot coffee. Without the usual intermission to which we were subjected aboard of the schooner, we then partook of breakfast, consisting of the cold viands which Hannibal had deposited in the locker.

We soon passed the slender line of Keys, and the breeze freshening as the sun showed his red disk above the horizon, we began to glide rapidly through the water.

"I did not bring Brady with me," observed the captain, after we had got clear of the vessel, "because, after previous experience, especially yesterday's, I don't judge it safe to have him with us when there is any possibility of meeting Indians. I don't positively think there is danger from them, or else I would consider myself absolved from the promise I made to you boys; but the Spanish Indians are becoming restive, and any provocation might result in some act of revenge. My feeling of security, among those inhabiting these parts, comes from an acquaintance of years with some of their leading men. I have always been cautious in my dealings with them. But a quick-tempered fellow, like Brady, might mar everything. I'm very sorry that I took him yesterday. To be on the safe side, I brought no one today."

During the sail to the mouth of the Miami, the captain entertained us with some anecdotes relating to the war with the Seminoles, in which some of his friends had at various times participated. His accounts of the atrocities committed by the Indians, unlike those of some novelists, did not afford an agreeable picture of the character of the "noble children of the forest." The captain was in the midst of one of these narratives, when we entered the mouth of the Miami. On the left bank, the stars and stripes floated over the quarters at the little military post. At the sight, I experienced the emotion that thrills the breast, whenever, in a foreign land, or in one's own, in some sequestered spot, the banner of one's country displays its folds, shedding a mystic influence on the soul.

The captain's story continued as we progressed up the river. We soon took in sail, and resorted to rowing; for the river was so completely shut in by trees, as to render the breeze uncertain. Besides, in some of the reaches, we could not lay our course. We had proceeded about a mile up the river, when the captain abruptly ceased his recital, and commenced scrutinizing the bushes on the right bank, near to which we were rowing.

"Ease your port oars, boys," said he;—"more yet. Pull the boat's head into shore."

Obeying his directions, we pulled the bow of the boat in towards the bushes, backed water and then held water, so as to keep her in the same position.

"I thought so," said the captain, looking into the bushes; —"it is an Indian canoe."

George and I stood up to look at it, and then, by the cap-

199

tain's order, backed water, pulled the boat around, and continued on our course.

We asked the captain to continue his story; but he declined, saying that he would finish it at another opportunity. He seemed plunged in a musing mood. When we had gone about a mile and a half up the stream, he told us to pull the boat in towards shore, and land, as he judged that we must be about opposite to the place where we had shot the panthers. We were much further down the stream than the place from which we had started on the hunt; but our course, after striking into the forest, had been nearly parallel with the stream. We had returned by the same way, and the place at which we had had the adventure was also a great distance from the river.

The captain sprang out of the boat, with one of the fowling-pieces, and told George to accompany him. I expected to go, and was therefore surprised when the captain added, "You, Fred, stay with the boat." Then, after a pause, he resumed: "I'll be frank with you. I don't know why, it's ridiculous, perhaps;—but I feel what is called a presentiment. Pshaw! Mind the boat, Fred. Keep a sharp lookout."

And then quickly turning on his heel, as if ashamed of his extreme caution, he walked rapidly away, accompanied by George, who relieved him of his fowling-piece. Jack followed them, frisking around through the undergrowth, crushing it with his burly strength, and uttering short barks, indicative of delight.

They had scarcely gone, when the sense of loneliness, and the captain's last words induced me to pick up the rifle, and examine it, to try whether it was loaded and capped. I found that it was ready for use; and after raising the hammer once or twice, and letting it down on the cap, so as to press the cap firmly on the nipple, I amused myself by sighting the piece at various objects on the opposite shore of the stream, and in the woods on the bank to which the boat was fastened.

Ten minutes elapsed, when I heard the quick barking of a dog, followed by the report of a distant rifle. Then silence for a short interval ensued, and from the distance came borne to my ear, a long and dismal howl. I was standing in the stern-sheets of the boat, still grasping the rifle with which I had been firing imaginary shots. As I heard these sounds, my hands clutched the rifle with a nervous grip; my blood curdled; my hair seemed to stand on end; and my ears strained to catch another sound. At that moment I heard a crackling and crushing noise in the bushes, then a rush, and before me, on top of the bank, stood a stalwart Indian, brandishing his tomahawk. With a whoop, he dashed down the bank. A moment lost, and his tomahawk would have been buried in my brain. With a coolness born of desperation, I raised my rifle, and sent its bullet straight into his breast. With one low moan, and without a struggle, he fell dead at the bottom of the bank.

I dropped the butt of my rifle, and leaned on it for support. The moment of action over, the terror of the situation, the unspeakable horror that hung over the fate of my companions, unnerved me. With a little respite, I regained my self-possession. Reflecting that I might have more assailants than one, and that the most exposed place which I could occupy was the boat, I seized the fowling-piece, rifle, and ammunition, and clambering up the bank, took shelter behind a tree, and commenced to reload the rifle. If, thought I, the captain or George, or both, escape, I will have the boat ready. If they have been massacred, and the Indians approach, I can see them coming. I can jump into the boat, row across the stream, take refuge in the woods, and try to make my way to the post at the mouth. My hope of the safety of the captain and George was indeed faint, when I recollected that the report I had heard was that of a rifle, and the captain had taken one of the fowling-pieces.

I had scarcely had time to think and do what I have just described, when I heard a sound, and looking through the trees, I saw a flitting appearance, such as a man at a distance presents, as he runs through the uncertain light amidst the trunks of trees in a dense forest. My gaze concentrated on the shifting object. Instantaneous resolve and execution must follow the discovery of whether the approaching form was friend or foe. All at once, a little opening in the trees emitted a white flash, and I knew that the captain had escaped. Before leaving the boat, he had disencumbered himself of his coat, and I knew that no Indian wore any garment so white as a shirt. A minute later, the captain broke his way through the bushes, and stood at my side. His face was deathly pale, scratched and bloody, and his clothes were nearly torn from his body, in his desperate progress through the bushes.

"Not a word!" said he to me, glancing at the dead Indian, picking up the guns, and hurrying into the boat, which we shoved off and commenced to pull down stream. "Listen, and be cool. I see what you can be by what you have done. George is captured. He was in advance, carrying my gun. Two Indians leaped out of the bushes, seized, and bound him. Pull Fred! For God's sake, pull! O my son, my son! Listen again. There is work to be done. They seized him, I say. I was unarmed, and a hundred yards distant. I could do nothing. Jack rushed to his rescue. I saw the knife of one Indian flash, as he plunged it into the faithful beast. The other Indian fired at me as I escaped in this direction. You know the rest. We are armed. You are a boy, but equal to a man's part. The canoe in the bushes must belong to the Indians. They started in that direction."

"Captain," said I resolutely, "you can depend on me."

"I believe you," muttered the captain through his clenched teeth. "When the time comes, be prompt, for everything depends on that."

We entered a reach in the river, above the place where we had seen the concealed canoe. The captain backed water with his oars, unshipped them, and made me a sign to do the same with mine. He then unshipped the rudder, and taking one of the oars, commenced to scull the boat noiselessly along the very edge of the trees that overhung the bank. The expression of the captain's face was frightful. It was as rigid as if hewn in marble, and well-nigh as white; and his gaze had an intensity that was terrible to behold. Such a blended expression of woe and dread and fierce determination, it would seem impossible for the human countenance to express.

At last, after we had rowed some distance, a penetrating whisper came from his lips.

"This is the place," said he. "One hope remains. We have distanced them. If we approach nearer to the canoe, we shall be discovered, and they will take to the woods."

He sculled the boat in towards shore, on the up-river side of a projecting tree, whose lowest branches, almost dipping into the water, afforded concealment.

Again the thrilling whisper pierced my ear; (everything now seemed like a horrid dream.)

"Fred," said the whisper, "they cannot be far off. Ship a pair of sculls. They will shove the canoe into the stream. The rifle;—is carefully loaded?—the ball rammed home?

"I am sure of it," I replied.

"The rifle," again whispered the captain, "is the gun. Buckshot scatters, and might kill George. The moment they are clear of the bank, I shall fire. No matter what happens, pull out into the stream, and give chase. I will take the other pair of sculls. But until I fire, be still in the bottom of the boat. George's life may hang on the movement of your hand. God grant steadiness to mine!"

After this neither of us spoke. I placed a pair of sculls gently in the rowlocks, glanced around, and coiled myself up in the bottom of the boat. I restrained even the heaving of my chest, so that when the critical moment arrived, I might communicate no more motion to the boat, than if I had been a corpse. The suspense became dreadful. I strained to catch a sound. The ticking of my watch was distinctly audible, and I commenced to count the minutes. Three, four, five, passed. Six, seven—I thought I heard a faint, distant sound, like muffled voices. It must be, I thought. Again, but muffled still, I heard something like the accents of the human voice. A distant splash. The captain moved. A report!

"Up Fred," I heard him cry.

But I was up and in my seat and straining at the oars. The captain seized his, and pulled furiously. The water boiled around the bow of the little skiff.

I looked over my shoulder, and a glance showed the situation. The captain's shot had taken effect. The body of one Indian hung lifelessly over the side of the canoe, putting it entirely out of trim. The other Indian was attempting to right the canoe by shifting the body of his companion. George, apparently pinioned, was seated about amidships.

I again glanced over my shoulder. The Indian had not succeeded in budging his companion from the position into which he had fallen, and had relinquished the attempt. He was paddling with all his might.

Another glance showed me that we were gaining rapidly on the canoe. The effort of the Indian to make speed was entirely frustrated by the canoe's position in the water, and he dared not stop paddling, lest we should lessen our distance from him.

When I looked again, I saw the canoe heading towards shore.

"Give way," shouted the captain, who had observed the same thing; "he may land and drag the boy off into the woods."

The elastic oars bent as we plied them with all the strength with which we were endowed. A single misstroke, and all might have been lost. The canoe came within ten yards of shore. Its bow touched the bank. The Indian leaped from it, and pulled it towards him, as if he was about to take hold of George, and lift him out of it. At that moment, the captain dropped his oars, seized a fowling-piece, and levelled it at the Indian, who hesitated, then turning, sprang up the bank and fled. The captain who, for fear of wounding George, had not intended to fire, except as a forlorn hope, discharged his gun at the Indian, as his form was disappearing amongst the bushes.

In a few moments, we were alongside of the canoe. I jumped out, gun in hand, and ran up the bank, to guard against a surprise; while the captain cut the thongs by which George's wrists had been so tightly bound that they were lacerated. I soon discovered, by the marks in the bushes, that the Indian had made good his escape. The one left in the canoe was mortally wounded, and almost expiring.

On scanning him closely, I recognized him as the Indian who had represented himself to be a chief, and with whom Brady had had the difficulty on the Key on which some of the goods from the wreck had been landed.

When I descended from the bank, and ascertained this, I mentioned it to the captain. He scarcely seemed to hear what I said. After releasing George, whom he tenderly embraced, he had fervently lifted up his eyes, and then seating himself in the boat, he had buried his face in his hands, and remained in that posture.

At length, he raised his head and said to us: "I was overcome. I hope that I am duly grateful for the favor which has been vouchsafed to me. George come here, and let me kiss you again, my child."

"There is much to be done yet," resumed the captain, suddenly starting to his feet. "The commandant of the post must be notified. And boys, let us not forget our faithful friend, even if he is a dog."

OR, FRED RANSOM.

CHAPTER XXXVII

THE CAPTAIN GIVES THE ALARM—THE COMMANDANT'S SUSPICIONS—
HIS REQUEST TO THE CAPTAIN—THE INDIAN'S CONFESSION—JACK'S
DEATH AND BURIAL.

*T*HE captain arose, and approaching the canoe, and bending low over the Indian, listened to ascertain whether he still breathed. Satisfied of the fact, he felt the Indian's pulse, and then raising the almost lifeless body, placed it in an easy position. Unbending our painter, he fastened one end to the bow of the canoe, and the other to the stern of the dinghy. Then telling us to get aboard of our boat, he and I put out the sails, while George took the tiller. The captain told George to steer for the post at the mouth of the river, and we started with the canoe in tow. George was extremely quiet. He had passed through a scene of wild excitement. The roughness of his savage captors, the altercations of hope and fear, the sudden joy of deliverance, had followed with transition so rapid, that they had left him subdued and speechless.

We soon reached the post, and the captain briefly explained to the commandant all that had happened.

The commandant, after glancing at the wounded Indian, said to the captain:

"I need not tell you, Captain Bowers, that trouble is brewing. This Indian's dress, paint, and weapons indicate that he was on the war-path."

"I knew it, when I saw the Indian who was shot by this boy," replied Captain Bowers, indicating me with a gesture.

"This preparation is not for the attack of the post," said the commandant, "but for that of some unprotected settlement, probably Indian Key. These Indians were probably on

207

their way to join their comrades. There will be no danger in acceding to your request. I will send a squad of men with you, and when you have recovered your noble dog, you must instantly return to your vessel. You have a duty to perform. You must immediately get underway, sail for Indian Key, and warn the settlement of its danger."

The captain assented without a moment's hesitation. The Indian was removed to the quarters of the soldiers. We left our boat, and getting into the boat belonging to the post, a squad of four soldiers escorted us up the river. George was left at the post to await our return.

We landed at the the same point from which the captain and George had started, and two soldiers stayed near the boat, to guard it, and bury the dead Indian. The other two set out with us towards the place where the Indians had lain in ambush.

The mystery of their presence in that place was very easily solved. The previous day, they must have come across the dead panthers, and concluded that we would return to the place to procure the skin of the female one. They there awaited our coming, after having detached one of the party to capture the boat and cut off our retreat.

We proceeded cautiously through the woods, for fear that we might be waylaid by some lurking Indian, and our advance was necessarily slow. In a quarter of an hour, we arrived at the place. There, in a pool of his own blood, lay poor Jack. The captain gently placed his hand on the region of the animal's heart, and felt a slight fluttering pulsation. The soldiers, with the aid of their knives, cut some boughs, and constructed a litter, on which Jack was carefully deposited, and borne along towards the river. When we reached the shore, the captain took off his coat, placed it in the bottom of the boat, and Jack was laid upon it. The captain then proceeded to staunch the blood, which was still ebbing from Jack's wound.

By the time that he had accomplished this, and adjusted a bandage made of our handkerchiefs knotted together, the corpse of the Indian had been buried in a shallow grave. We then started down the river, and again landed at the post.

The commandant was on the shore, awaiting our arrival, and at once said to the captain:

"It is as I thought. The Indian died a few minutes ago; but, before expiring, he answered a question of mine. Indian Key is on the eve of being attacked. You must hasten to get your vessel underway."

We immediately transferred Jack to our own boat, and bidding the commandant farewell, set sail across Key Biscayne Bay.

As soon as the boat was fairly underway, the captain renewed his attentions to Jack, who showed increasing signs of life. At last, he opened his eyes, moaned slightly, and then raising his head, licked the captain's hand. After awhile, he was seized with frequent and intense twitching of the limbs, and moaned more frequently, as if suffering acute pain. Oh, how George and I watched him and cried over him! for we loved the dog. The captain, with one hand on the tiller, reached out the other, and constantly patted the head of his faithful friend. Once more, Jack raised his head, licked the captain's hand, and turned his head to lick George's and mine, as we placed them near his mouth, to gratify the affectionate yearning of his nature. He closed his eyes, as if satisfied, and then quivered all over. His limbs twitched and struck out spasmodically, and he uttered a sharp bark, ending with a howl. He became rigid; his eyes opened and glazed; his lower jaw dropped; and his tongue protruded.

"Boys," said the captain, mildly, "he is dead."

I look back through the vista of many years, and see in that stiffening form, what men call a dog, but I, one of the dearest friends I ever had!

We landed on the first large Key that we reached, and lifting Jack out of the boat, laid him on the shore. The captain dispatched me to the vessel to fetch two of the crew with spades. As I set sail, I saw him and George lift the body of Jack, and carry it towards the high ground on the Key.

Before an hour had passed, I had returned with the men and the implements for which the captain had sent me.

In a densely wooded spot, far removed from the beach, we dug a little grave. The captain folded his coat more closely around the dog, and buttoned it over his chest. We laid him carefully in the grave, and took one look at him. The captain made a mark on a neighboring tree, and we turned sadly away, and walked towards the beach.

When we reached the boat, the captain, turning to us boys, who could not restrain our tears, said:

"He was worthy of our love, proving his by yielding up his life in our defense."

We were soon underway, bound for Indian Key.

CHAPTER XXXVIII

THE FLYING CLOUD SAILS FOR INDIAN KEY—THE MESSAGE FROM CAPTAIN BOWERS TO DR. CLUZEL—NO ATTACK EXPECTED THAT NIGHT—THE SURPRISE—THE MASSACRE—THE MURDER OF THE DOCTOR—THE ESCAPE OF HIS FAMILY AND OF FRED RANSOM.

IT was three o'clock in the afternoon. The schooner had a fair but moderate breeze. The captain set every rag of canvas on her, and we glided slowly along the line of Keys. Our mission was fraught with life and death. Would we be in time to give warning? Why not? The Indians, if they purposed an attack, would make it at night; and as we passed a wrecker, towards the southward, she made no signal, as she would assuredly have done, had she possessed any tidings. But then, on the other hand, the attack might have taken place during the preceding night, and the wrecker might not have sighted any vessel towards the southward. True, the attack might have been made during the preceding night. I felt as if the fickle wind and sluggish waves clogged the sails and once-swift keel.

The captain, standing near the helm, had apparently been pursuing the same train of thought, for he turned towards me, and said:

"The Indians may have attacked the Key last night. If not, we shall be in time, even with this breeze, for they will not attack before the dead of night. I knew that, or I would not have spent even an hour in burying Jack."

"Oh, captain!" exclaimed I, "I am so glad to hear you say that! I feared that we should be too late."

"So we may be," replied the captain, "but not if the attack hasn't already taken place. Go down into the cabin, and sit with George. Perhaps you had better try to take some

rest, to recover after the fatigue of the day. You may be needed in a few hours. George is too much overcome to be of any
use in an emergency. I shall be obliged to depend upon you
alone."

I found George as I had left him. He lay in his berth,
with his eyes open; perfectly calm, but unable to compose
himself to sleep. I sat down beside him, took his hand, and
talked to him. Being thus diverted from the thoughts which
had engrossed him, the fatigue which he had undergone
exercised uncontrolled influence, and he soon fell fast
asleep. Then I slipped off my coat, and threw myself into my
own berth, knowing that the next few hours might tax my
utmost energies, and determined to brace my nerves by the
refreshment of slumber. Blessed, indeed, as Sancho Panza
says, be the man who invented sleep!

When I awakened, I was in darkness, and I felt a cool
breeze rushing through the cabin. I called to George, in a
low voice, but receiving no answer, got out of my berth, put
on my coat, and ran up the companionway.

The captain was seated near the helm. Apparently, he
had not relinquished his post. The breeze had increased. It
was quite fresh, and the schooner was scudding along, with
her sails bellied out, and lee-scuppers almost under water.

"I hope that you have had a good rest," observed the
captain. "It is ten o'clock. We shall reach the Key in an
hour's time. I'll leave you in charge of the deck. Call me the
moment we come in sight of the Key."

The captain left me, and, a few minutes afterwards, on
putting my head down the companionway, I knew, by the
loud snoring, that he had not been long in obtaining the
slumber which the seafaring man, tutored by the experience
of surprises, dangers, and fatigues, seldom woos in vain.

In a little over an hour, a distant light apprised me that
we were approaching our destination. After confirming
myself in this opinion, by appealing to the helmsman, I
awoke the captain. He instantly came on deck. We were soon
abreast of Indian Key.

"We are in time, Fred," said the captain, as the schooner rounded to and let go her anchor. "Ashore, all appears too orderly for anything to have happened. There is no noise, and the lights in the windows of the houses near the water show as usual. I have got some service for you to perform. My duty keeps me here. Take a man or two, and row ashore. Go to Doctor Cluzel's house, and give him the intelligence. In case he should consider the schooner a safer refuge than his house, let him come off with his family."

"Certainly, sir," I replied; "but I don't need anyone. I can pull ashore without any help; and, as the boat is small, and the doctor may accept your offer, I had better dispense with even one of the crew. There is a pretty stiff breeze rising, but I can manage the boat."

The dinghy was lowered, I jumped into her, put out my sculls, and rowed for the Key.

On landing, I ran hastily to the doctor's house and up the steps leading to the piazza, and pounded at the front-door for some minutes before I could make myself heard. At length, the doctor put his head out of the window, and asked who was there. I announced my name, and said, in a low tone, that I had something of importance to communicate. The doctor withdrew his head, and soon opened the front-door.

In a very few words, I told him the news, and gave him the captain's invitation. The doctor looked grave, but after a short silence, said:

"I must confess, that the suspicions of the commandant of the post, and of Captain Bowers, are not unwarranted. Of course, I don't doubt after what you have told me, that the Indians contemplate some outrage; but I do doubt that they intend to attack this settlement. No signs of them have been seen about here. It is many miles from this place to the mainland. The residents here, being wreckers and fisher-men, are daily in the habit of visiting the neighboring Keys; and if any Indians had been lurking there, they would have been discovered. At any rate, no attack will be made tonight.

Look over the water in this direction, and in that. everything is as silent as the grave. Hold! let us go into the cupola. Thence we can command a view in every direction."

Saying this, the doctor left the piazza, on which we had been standing, and led the way into the house, and upstairs to the cupola.

Nothing could be more peaceful than the scene which presented itself from the cupola. The waters surrounding us lay calmly shimmering in the light of the setting moon. The shores of the adjacent Keys showed quite distinctly, and the only sounds that we heard were those of the gentle waves splashing against the piles of the neighboring jetty, and the sighing of the increasing breeze, as it struck the crannies in the roof, and the open casement of the cupola.

"It is past twelve o'clock," said the doctor, examining his watch. "Surely, if danger is brewing, it will not overtake us tonight. I like to act with caution; at the same time, I wish to avoid giving a needless alarm to the settlement. I cannot think that there is danger tonight; and, by daylight, the people will be less alarmed at the news. However, I will be on the safe side, and communicate it to the two most reliable men here, obtain their opinion, and let them use their own judgment."

We descended the stairs, and Doctor Cluzel, after donning his coat, left me standing on the lower piazza, while he went on the errand which he had mentioned. After an absence of half an hour, he returned, and stated that he had seen both of the persons to whom he had alluded. They agreed with him in thinking that the lateness of the hour indicated, that if an attack had been in contemplation, it would be postponed until another night. The doctor and they had concluded to divulge the news on the following morning, and preparations could then be made for repelling an attempt upon the settlement.

"It is within five minutes of one o'clock," said the doctor, again consulting his watch. "Everything is perfectly quiet, and likely, in my opinion, to continue so. You must not think of returning to the vessel. Your late fatigue must have nearly exhausted you. Come into the sitting-room. I have a shakedown there, always ready for the use of a friend."

I was worn out, and seeing no reason which should urge a return to the vessel, I gladly accepted the doctor's offer. He soon left me, and retired to his own chamber, continuing carefully to guard against making any noise which might disturb the family, and, by the unwonted circumstance, arouse their apprehensions.

When I was left alone, I partially undressed, and threw myself on the couch. For a long time, I lay with my eyes closed, with an abstracted gaze, on the face of an old clock which stood in the corner of the room. The scenes of the last few hours vividly presented themselves to my imagination. But the curtain of sleep fell not before my hot and weary eyes, and the drama closed with my present situation, only to be again repeated. How long I had lain thus absorbed, I knew not, until my gaze, which had rested on the face of the clock, without my being conscious of the object upon which it centred, resuming its function, showed me the hands indicating two o'clock in the morning. I sprang up, and was in the act of divesting myself of my remaining clothes, when a horrid yell smote my ears. Almost simultaneously came a volley of bullets, and the sound of crashing glass showed me that the musketry had been levelled at the upper windows of the house.

At that yell, heard by me for the second time, but now vociferated by many discordant voices, I needed not the accompanying discharge of bullets to tell me that the Indians were upon us.

Fatal error, reflected I, that lapped us in fancied security! But there was no time for reflection. I seized my lamp, and hurried with it to the corner of the room, where I set it down, and screened it with a chair and a cloth hastily snatched from a table.

Voices and footsteps sounded upstairs. I had hardly time to clothe myself decently, when the doctor, Mrs. Cluzel, and

215

their three children, poured into the room.

The doctor was cool and collected; but Mrs. Cluzel was speechless with alarm, and her son James, in maddened terror, clung to her night dress. The doctor hurried us all to a trapdoor leading to the cellar, already described as being used for a bathing room. The doctor raised the trapdoor, but Mrs. Cluzel hesitated to descend. Her daughters threw their arms about her, and besought her to seek refuge there. But the thought of leaving the doctor seemed to be more than she could bear. In the midst of this distressing scene, came the crashing blows of axes, as the Indians commenced to force their way into the opposite dwelling. At the sound, Mrs. Cluzel's agony of terror so prevailed, that she hurried with us all into the dark opening, down the narrow stairs, and into the water of the bathing room. As we descended, the doctor ran hastily towards the interior of the house. We passed through the bathing room, and made our way to an oblong place which communicated with it. This place was separated from the wharf by posts driven into the marl. We had hardly concealed ourselves there, when we distinctly heard the doctor's voice speaking to the Indians from the upper piazza. He addressed them in Spanish, telling them that he was a physician. When he said that, they gave a shout, and, from the sound of their voices, we judged that they were retiring, having resolved on abstaining from further molestation of the house. As the murmur of voices gradually became more and more vague, as the Indians retired, we heard the doctor's footsteps near the trapdoor, which we had left open in our hasty descent.

"We are safe," whispered he, putting his head through the trapdoor. "The Indians have gone. I told them that I was a medicine man and they respect that title. Remain where you are for a while longer."

Saying this, Doctor Cluzel eased the trapdoor, and, judging by the sound, I think that he must have dragged over it a heavy chest which I had observed in the room.

Who can depict, save one who has been a witness of

216

such a scene, the slow torture of the minutes and hours that ensued! With clothes saturated with water, and bedraggled with mud; worn out with suspense; half-crazed with horror; what must have been the feelings of that poor mother, with her children clinging around her? From a distance, now and then came the noise of resounding blows, as the Indians broke into house after house, dismantling it, and heightening their demoniac instincts by swilling the spiritous liquors which they found upon the premises. Sometimes, the crashing sound of axes and the murmur of voices seemed to be approaching, and we felt sure that the savages, maddened with drink, were returning, to imbrue in our blood, hands reeking with that of many already ruthlessly slaughtered. The hoarse, drunken shouts came borne in fitful blasts from a distance, or startled us by their proximity, as they were bellowed by a swiftly passing throng of infuriate wretches. And utter darkness shut in our retreat, and what we could not hear, the imagination divined with a vividness that reality could scarcely exceed.

I could not ascertain the time of night, or rather morning, for my watch, being immersed in the water, had stopped. Otherwise, I might have discovered the time by feeling the hands.

After hours, seemingly years, of weary watching, we thought that we perceived, through the chinks between the piles, the gray light of morning stealing through the air. We cautiously whispered the news to each other, and, for the first time, hope seemed to revive in every breast.

Scarcely had this feeling commenced to resume its sway, when our hearts sank within us, for again, and close to the house, we heard the yell of the Indians. Then came a terrific battering at the front door, and at that renewed sound, I gave up all for lost. Scarcely a minute had elapsed, when by the noise of hurrying feet above, we knew that the Indians had forced an entrance. The sound of footsteps rushing up the stairs, showed that the Indians were searching for the family. Again, the battering on a distant door apprised us that the doctor had retreated to the cupola—the place to which he had taken me but a few hours before, to show me the peaceful scene that lay spread out for miles beyond! Foiled in their first attempt to enter the cupola, the yells of the savages became frightful, and the inmost recesses of our retreat seemed to vibrate with the horrid clamor. Then came a crash of planks, and one general yell, louder than all the rest, revealed the fearful truth. The Indians had broken down the door. A few wild yells and trampling sounds ensued, and the noise of numerous and rapidly approaching footsteps rumbled down the staircase. It was clear. The doctor had been murdered in cold blood. I heard a groan at my side, and a lifeless form fell on my breast. I encircled it in my arms, and kept it from dropping into the water. Mrs. Cluzel's long agony had overcome her, and she had fainted. I cautiously whispered the fact to the girls, who approached and aided me in supporting their mother above the surface of the water. We threw some of the fluid in her face, chafed her hands and wrists, and in a few minutes she was sufficiently restored to consciousness to enable her to raise her head. Then, the horror of our situation seemed so suddenly to burst upon her, that, judging by the convulsive rising of her shoulders and inflation of her chest, that she was about to give vent to a scream, I clapped my hand over her mouth, saying, "For Heaven's sake, we are lost if you raise your voice."

"It was involuntary," replied she, with a groan. "I bore accumulating horrors, but the memory of it all, in one second, distracted me. The doctor—"

I thought that she was about to faint again, but the girls supported her, pleading with her to be calm. And then came a scene!—what a strange mourning scene! The mother, daughters, and son, interlaced in each other's arms, shivering and benumbed, mourned and wept together, for they knew that above lay the body of the husband and father.

They seemed to be stupefied by the danger and grief that encompassed them. I was, as I should have been, the one who best preserved his senses. The last blow had overwhelmed them so completely, that the mere instinct of self-preservation, alone, seemed to control them. The noises above now appeared to fall all unheeded on their ears. The sound of heavy objects, dragged along the floor, indicated that the pillage of the house had begun; and I knew by the frequent crashing of glass, that the Indians were engaged in wantonly destroying what they could not carry away. Hope that they would speedily depart then took possession of me; for I said to myself, "After they have pillaged or destroyed all the valuables upon which they can lay their hands, what can detain them? They have gratified their love of drink, with bestial intoxication, and glutted their thirst for blood, by the murder of many besides the doctor."

Discovery, at times, seemed imminent; for some of the Indians were immediately overhead, and once an Indian lifted the plank by which the turtle crawl could be entered, and peered down into the darkness. Had there been much light, no doubt our presence in the oblong passage, which lay between the bathing room and the turtle crawl, would have been discovered. I shuddered when I saw the plank replaced, and realized how narrowly we had escaped.

I then felt as if our last trial of fortitude had passed. But I was mistaken. Another was in store for us. Hardly had the sun risen, when, by the light which penetrated our retreat, I perceived wreathing lines of smoke coming from the floor above. The house was on fire. Soon the smoke descended in volumes so stifling, that we were obliged to keep our faces close to the water, to avoid being suffocated. The roar of the flames grew louder and louder. All hope vanished. The alternatives seemed to be death by suffocation, or by the hands of the Indians. The house soon fell into the cellar, and even now, when I recall the ensuing scene, it seems impossible that human nature could withstand what we endured. We could not see each other. The planking, which covered the long, narrow space in which we were ensconced, took fire, and we were constantly obliged to dash water upon it. At the same time, we were obliged to cover our heads with marl, and throw water over them, to diminish the intense heat, and disperse the smoke, so that we could breathe. James could endure no more. He began to scream. His mother forcibly held him, and gagged him with her hand; while one of his sisters held his arms. But, frantic with terror, he broke from them, and displacing one of the palmetto posts, which separated our place of concealment from the turtle crawl, made his escape.

We now thought our fate sealed, and desperately awaited the arrival of the Indians. Blank despair settled upon us. I confess that I had not a ray of hope that we would not be discovered and murdered. We waited for some time, in dreadful suspense, but heard no noise. Mrs. Cluzel, feeling that we could not exist much longer there, approached the line of palmetto posts, and, with her hands, dug up the marl at the bottom of some of them, until she removed it sufficiently to withdraw them. We all passed out under the adjoining wharf, on which was some blazing cord-wood, dropping its cinders into the water below. As we emerged from the wharf, we perceived James standing on the shore, gazing distractedly in every direction. Near the wharf beyond, we espied a large launch, to which we waded, beckoning to James to follow us. We dragged the boat into deep water, jumped into it, and commenced poling and rowing with all our might, to get clear of the Key. Fortunately, James know how to manage a boat, and we made good speed. We once ran aground, but soon succeeded in getting the launch afloat. Some of the Indians happening to discover us, as we got clear of the shore, ran down to the water's edge, yelling with rage. But we were beyond rifle-shot before they could recover from their surprise. We then saw a boat from the *Flying Cloud* pulling to our assistance.

We were saved. The presence of the launch seemed providential. Laden with goods stowed in it by the Indians, in a brief interval of their absence, it changed from the means of pillage to the instrument of our safety.

It was afternoon when we got aboard of the schooner. A few residents of the Key had already reached her. Others, who had secreted themselves in various places on the Key, were discovered when the Indians had retired. Mrs. Cluzel and her children were led into the cabin, and the captain begged them to take anything with which they could cover themselves. They had nothing on but their night-clothes.

After the Indians had left, some scattered dresses were found, and they were distributed among the sufferers. The situation of Mrs. Cluzel and her children was deplorable in the extreme. Bereft of the head of their family, destitute of clothing; devoured by restless fear of a renewed attack by the Indians; they needed, and, I must say, received our fullest sympathy and aid. All that the captain could do, he did, to alleviate their sufferings, physical and mental. On the night of the second day after their arrival on the schooner, they heard the report of two rifles, which was understood to be a signal agreed upon in case the Indians attacked Tea-Table Key. So unnerved were they by the ordeal through which they had passed, that, although a storm was raging, the idea of the proximity of the Indians put them in so great a paroxysm of terror, that they implored the captain to let them have a boat to leave the vessel. The captain, in a kind but firm manner, refused to accede to their request. If he had done so, they would inevitably have perished in the storm.

Towards evening, there arrived a United States schooner, commanded by an officer of the Navy. He at once surrendered his stateroom to the Cluzel family, and, the next day but one, sailed for Cape Florida, to await the passing of a steamer in which the family could reach St. Augustine.

Some of those who had taken refuge on the *Flying Cloud*, as well as those who, by hiding themselves on shore, had escaped the massacre, returned to their dwellings.

I learned, afterwards, that the Cluzels were safely put aboard of the steamer. On transferring the party to the naval vessel, on the evening preceding her departure, the commanding officer requested Captain Bowers to sail for Key

West, to carry the news of the massacre. We got underway at once and stood down the coast.

CHAPTER XXXIX

FRED RANSOM'S REFLECTIONS—A SHIP ON FIRE—THE RESCUE OF THE CREW—MUTUAL RECOGNITION.

HE sun had set, but twilight still lingered, as we spread sail and glided swiftly along the shadowy line of Keys. The storm which had raged nearly without intermission, since the fatal night of the 6th of August, subsided, and a double calm ensued, after the strife of the elements, and the more fearful violence of man. We had reason to look back with satisfaction at the part which we had acted in the events of the last few hours; yet to the retrospection belonged so much that was painful, that I rejoiced in a change of scene which might disturb the memory of the late pillage and ruthless massacre. I had had enough adventure to satisfy the craving of the most romantic youth. As a consequence, I experienced a longing to return home; and it was with a joyful feeling that the thought flashed across me, that it was in my present frame of mind, and in no other, that I could honorably do so. By dint of pondering came the idea of leaving the vessel when she arrived at Key West.

Then, for the first time, I realized the strength of the tie which bound me to the captain and his son. On that account, I felt reluctant to go. Yet my father had said that when I could state that I was cured of my spirit for adventure, I might return home. I was sure that I could say so now. I asked myself whether I ought not to return when I could say this with truth. I had no right to give my father the pain of a prolonged and indefinite separation. The accomplishment of my desire, and his injunction, were reconcilable, and all that opposed them was the anticipated pang of separation

223

from my wrecker friends. I resolved to leave the vessel at Key West.

Ever since the morning after the massacre, my thoughts had taken this turn; but my final determination was not made until the evening upon which we weighed anchor. About nine o'clock, I was alone, reclining on the trunk-cabin, gazing at the stars, and listening to the purling sound of low waves sweeping past the schooner. The calm influence of night and solitude inspired a thoughtful mood, and I resolved to encourage it until I had reached a solution of the question which had engaged my mind.

As I ceased communing with myself, my spirits rose. Doubt had vanished. My desire and my duty were in accord. I felt supremely happy. I sprang to my feet, and walked towards the cabin with the intention of telling my friends of my determination; but, on second thoughts, I concluded to defer telling the news until we reached Key West, for I felt sure that it would grieve them both to know that we must part.

Passing the companionway, I heard a murmur of conversation. One of the survivors of the massacre was recounting to the captain some of the details of his escape with his family. The children, with their mothers, were retiring to rest, as I judged from the glow of a light behind a blanket which had been hung across the cabin, in order to afford privacy to the female passengers.

Brady was at the helm. I sat down near him, under the lee of the bulwarks. The loquacious fellow instantly took the opportunity to ask me some questions about the killing of the "chafe," and about the events of the night of the 6th of August, although he knew that the captain allowed no conversation at the helm.

"I will not talk to you, Brady," said I. "It is against orders."

"Did you hear that," said Brady, quickly.

"I tell you, Brady," returned I, "that I will not talk to you. If you go on, I'll be obliged to report you."

"It's a gun, I mane," said Brady. "I heerd a gun."

"Nonsense," said I, thinking that his imagination was running upon the Indians. "We are miles away from Indian Key."

"It's a cannon, I mane," said Brady. "There! Do you hear that?"

"I did not," said I, rising. "And, moreover, I think that the cannon is in your imagination. But perhaps I couldn't hear so well where I was, as you can by the helm."

A short time elapsed, and I was on the point of resuming my seat, when I heard the report of a distant cannon.

"Don't you hear that?" exclaimed Brady.

"You're right," said I. "Captain!" shouted I, calling down the companionway. "Please come on deck. I hear signal-guns."

The captain sprang up the steps, followed by one of the passengers, and stood beside us.

The sound of the guns came at regular and frequent intervals, as fast as a single piece of ordnance can be loaded and fired.

"I should judge by the sound," said the captain, "that the vessel must be well off shore,—fifteen miles at least."

Two or three of the male passengers now joined the party, and one of them, who was a sea captain, agreed with Captain Bowers in his estimate of the distance from our vessel to the vessel in distress.

"It seems to me," he added, "that she must bear about south-southeast from where we are."

Captain Bowers assented.

"She is to the southward, certainly," remarked one of the passengers; "for don't you observe that the reports have become much louder?"

"She bears about south-southeast," said Captain Bowers, in a confident tone. "I shall keep the schooner on her present course, for awhile; and then try to cross the Reef, through a channel I know. In four or five miles we'll be abreast of her."

225

When we had sailed about that distance, the correctness of the view expressed, as to the vessel's first hearing from our position, was confirmed, for the sound of the reports came from the eastward.

"All hands stand by to haul in the fore and main sheets," shouted the captain. "Here, you three men, come aft. Luff her up, Brady. Haul away now. Give a pull at the main-peak halliards, men. Trim the jib sheet. Steady at that, Brady."

The schooner was now close-hauled, and running directly towards the Reef. Before long we passed through the channel, and the reports of the cannon became more and more distinct. Suddenly, near the horizon, a bright light glowed, encompassing a large ship with a momentary halo.

"She's on fire!" shouted everyone on deck. The noise brought up all the crew who were below, as well as those occupants of the cabin who had not retired to rest, and our forward deck was filled with eager gazers.

The glow quickly reappeared, and as suddenly vanished. Again it commenced, shone flickeringly, and died away into utter darkness.

With a quick leap, the light arose once more, increasing in intensity, until the ship became a great bonfire, lighting up the horizon with a dazzling glare.

The darting blaze, amid her masts, devoured her sails, as powder is consumed in the quick breath of its explosion. The sails gone, the blazing hull then lighted the masts, which soon showed like pillars of fire, until, charred to the core, just before they fell, quick streaks of light coursed up and down them, like the darting of electric sparks. The whole of the forward part of the ship, even to the mizzen-mast, was in flames. It was very evident from the character of the conflagration, that the ship had been for a long time afire in her hold; the hatches had been battened down to exclude the air, and smother the flames, which, although pent up, imperceptibly gained the mastery, and suddenly bursting their bonds, had wrapped the ship in a tornado of flame.

The deck of the *Flying Cloud* was a scene of bustle and preparation. The boats were prepared, so that we could lower them at a moment's notice. The two quarter-boats, with close stowing, could hold a dozen persons besides the oarsmen. The dinghy we had lost at Indian Key. We had nothing upon which to depend, except the quarter-boats.

"I've got just two crews of four men each, for the boats," said Captain Bowers to the sea captain. "You take command of one of the boats, and Fred Ransom will take charge of the other. I'll run as close as I dare. Hannibal and I can manage the vessel, with the aid of one or two of the passengers. Take your stations by the boats, men," shouted the captain. "Hannibal, take the helm."

The men ran up the companion ladders, and reached the quarterdeck. One of them got into each boat, to unhook the falls as soon as she was lowered, and the others stood by the davits.

The light of the fire was now so vivid, that on our decks, the face of everyone shone brightly in the glare. We were ploughing rapidly through the sea, and objects on the ship became at every moment more distinguishable. She drifted, an unmanageable mass, with the flames sweeping from her stem almost to her stern. Near the stern, we could see dark clusters, which we recognized as human beings, trying to escape, on the verge of the taffrail, the blast of the fiery furnace.

The excited shout and rush to the forward deck, with which all on the deck of the schooner had involuntarily greeted the discovery that the mysterious vessel in distress was a ship on fire, had at once given place to brief command, disciplined and prompt obedience. In a minute afterwards, we were standing motionless at our posts. The passengers who had retired commenced to emerge from the cabin, their scanty dress and excited gestures betokening that the sudden noise had, owing to the scenes through which they had lately passed, produced in them an alarm little short of a panic.

We were nearing the ship so rapidly, that we could sometimes see a figure separate itself from one of the little knots of human beings, run quickly to and fro, and then again become merged in the dark mass that hung, like swarming bees, close to the taffrail.

The captain luffed the schooner slightly, so as to run to windward of the ship. As we held on our new course, and the ship drifted slowly to leeward, from our new point of view the figures in the groups on the ship's poop began to appear detached. Just after we had changed our course, we thought that the ship's passengers must for the first time have seen our vessel; for a fluctuating movement was perceptible amongst them, and then a shrill sound, like a cry of distress, was faintly borne to our ears.

We were soon within hearing of the agonizing cries of the ship's passengers. The progress of the flames was depriving them of the little space in which they had huddled, cowering on the deck to escape the scorching heat. Objects of various sorts were being hastily thrown overboard, and human forms were seen leaping into the water. Some rushed wildly to and fro, wringing their hands, stopping abruptly, and then precipitating themselves into the sea.

"Oh, if we could only have arrived a few minutes earlier!" exclaimed I to the sea captain, who was standing at his post on the other side of the deck. "I am afraid that they will all be lost."

"Never fear," he replied, "the ship must have been afire for a long time, and those things that were thrown overboard, before anyone leaped, were prepared for that purpose. The sea is pretty smooth. We may pick most of the people up."

We were now so near that the crackling and roar of the flames were distinctly audible. Only two figures were visible on the ship's poop. They showed like silhouettes against the background of flame.

The two female figures (for they were in female costume) showed so distinctively, that I could recognize by their respective height and size, that one was a woman, and the other a young and slender girl. They stood poised on the taffrail, clasped each other in a momentary embrace, and then, hard in hand, sprang into the sea.

I heard the captain's voice shout, "Down with your helm, Hannibal!"

The schooner shot up into the wind's eye, and slowly lost her way, and as soon as the captain dared, he said, "Lower away the boats."

To lower the boats, unhook the falls, shove off from the schooner, point and let fall the oars, and pull in the direction of the place where most of the ship's passengers had leaped into the sea, required but a few seconds. A few more brought us to the place where, clinging to spars, boxes, barrels, and other articles, so numerous that it was evident that they had been prepared, we found some drowning wretches tossing amid the waves. We dragged them into the boats, working with desperate eagerness, so as to avail ourselves of the bright light of the burning ship, which was rapidly drifting away to leeward. Sometimes, when we had almost given over further search, a faint cry led us to the rescue of someone yet struggling in the water. All at once, I thought of the two female figures that I had seen precipitate themselves from the ship. Neither was in my boat. After taking aboard seven people, I had been for five minutes vainly pulling around in every direction. I bethought me of pulling towards the other boat, to see if they were there. They were not. There was not a woman nor a girl in either boat. I recollected that they had remained last on the ship. If they were to be found, they were nearer to the ship. I steered along the fiery track of the ship drifting to leeward. I soon heard a shrill cry. Then a louder one came. The light from the burning ship showed a dark object on the crest of a wave. I steered in that direction. I distinguished cries for help. We reached the place, found and dragged into the boat two female figures. One was that of a woman of mature age, the other that of a mere slip of a girl. They were clinging to a spar, and were almost exhausted by their efforts to retain their hold. They must be the persons of whom I was in search, thought I.

I saw the other boat approaching mine, and heard the hail of the sea captain who was in charge of her. I rowed to meet him, and as we neared each other, he hallooed:

"I have the captain of the ship aboard my boat. He wants to make a count, to see who are missing."

The boats ranged up alongside of each other, and the captain of the ship, as soon as he came near, recognizing, some of the people in my boat, asked the names of others whom, at the first glance, he could not distinguish. "Are Mrs. and Miss Brenton aboard?" said he.

"There are a woman and a girl in the bottom of the boat," said I. "I don't know their names. They are too much exhausted to speak."

"Then," said the captain of the ship, "all that can be saved, are saved. One man, when the fire was first discovered, became panic-stricken, jumped overboard, and was drowned."

We steered for the schooner, and aided the passengers to reach the deck. I jumped out of my boat, and taking Miss Brenton by the hands, lifted her up to the deck, while one of the men assisted her mother.

Miss Brenton was so exhausted that she tottered. To keep her from falling, I was obliged to encircle her waist with my arm. As I turned, in the act, to address some words of encouragement to her, I for the first time obtained a full view of her face. I was seized with astonishment so great, that I nearly let her fall to the deck.

"Julia!" exclaimed I.

She glanced at me with a startled look, and murmured, "Fred!"

"Fred Ransom!" echoed Mrs. Brenton.

"This is no time for explanations," said I, addressing them. "You are both exhausted. You had better go down, at once, into the cabin."

Saying this, I escorted Julia and her mother to the companionway, where they were received by two of the lady passengers.

Some of the ship's crew were accommodated forward. Some remained on deck. The captain of the ship, his three officers, and two of the male passengers, finding how crowded the cabin was, declined to accept a place there. Captain Bowers gave them a change of clothes, and some light bedding which they spread on deck.

The captain did not attempt to return through the channel across the Reef. When, an hour before, he had passed through it, the urgency of the case admitted of no debate. We were forced to keep on a course along the outside edge of the Reef, breasting the current of the Gulf Stream.

The ship burned, until, owing to our increasing distance and the waste of material for combustion, she showed like a great live-coal upon the surface of the sea. When day dawned, she was out of sight. At that time we were still far from Key West. During the latter part of the night, the wind had been extremely fickle, and as the schooner had had to contend with the current of the Gulf Stream, she had not made much way.

It was late in the morning before Mrs. Brenton and Julia were able to come on deck, owing to the fact that their clothes were in process of drying. The other lady-passengers were not able to replenish their wardrobe, for they themselves were destitute even of a change.

I anxiously looked for the Brentons, and was gratified when, about ten o'clock, they emerged from the cabin. They were both pale and weak, and Mrs. Brenton leaned on her daughter for support.

"Take my arm, Mrs. Brenton," said I, advancing. "The fresh air on deck will revive you."

"It is like a dream," said Mrs. Brenton, half soliloquizing, and half addressing me. "It was only a fortnight ago," added she, in a weak voice, "that I saw your father, and we were talking of the prospect of your return. Julia and I were on our way to join my husband in Valparaiso. What will

231

become of us! I was not able to save even the money which I had in my trunk. For the sake of your father's friendship for my husband, you must stay with us, Fred."

"I will, indeed," I replied. "And I would have done so under any circumstances. I shall not appear to have so much merit now, when I confess that, before I met you, I intended to return home when this vessel reached Key West. It seems providential that she, of all the wreckers, should have been so fortunate as to save you. The captain and his family are strong friends of mine. I have a little sum of money saved up in Key West, and the moment that we arrive there, you will be provided with what is necessary, and my remaining funds will be sufficient to pay our passage to New York."

"I have, indeed, reason to be grateful," replied Mrs. Brenton.

Julia timidly smiled her thanks.

For half an hour, they walked the deck, and then, being fatigued, returned to the cabin. I seized the opportunity to communicate to the captain my intention of departure, assigning the reason which I have already given the reader, adding the additional one, of the necessity of my becoming protector of the Brentons, who were friends of our family.

A shade passed over the captain's face. George said that I could not go; that the Brentons could take passage from Key West for New York, just as well without me as with me.

But the captain checked his son, and turning to me, said:

"I approve of your intention, Fred. The reason that you first gave me was sufficient. Never forget your wrecker friends, my boy."

"Never!" said I, walking away to conceal my emotion. And I never shall forget them.

CHAPTER XL

ARRIVAL AT KEY WEST—FRED RANSOM AND PARTY SAIL FOR NEW YORK—THE VOYAGE HOME—THE OLD BACHELOR'S ADIEU.

BUT little remains to be told. My story draws to its close.

When the *Flying Cloud* reached her wharf in Key West, the news of the massacre quickly spread through the town. During the whole day after our arrival, the citizens poured down to the schooner to learn the particulars of the catastrophe.

The doors of the hospitable residents of the Key flew open to welcome the distressed people whom we had brought with us. Mrs. Bowers received the Brentons in her house, and her sympathy and aid soon restored the two agitated sufferers to comfort and equanimity.

I may as well mention here what I afterwards learned in relation to the doings of the Indians near our wrecking station off Cape Florida. The mill on the Miami was burned to the ground. The keeper of the lighthouse at Cape Florida was attacked by the Indians, and driven into the tower. He took refuge in the lantern, from which position he made so stubborn a defense, that the Indians desisted from their attempt to dislodge him, and after setting fire to the staircase, retreated. The keeper, unable to descend, remained for hours on top of the tower, whence he was finally rescued by an armed party of whites.

An opportunity to reach New York soon presented itself, in the arrival of a ship which put into Key West for repairs, after having been subjected to stress of weather in the Gulf of Mexico.

I drew all the money remaining to my credit on the

233

books of the owners of the *Flying Cloud*. It amounted to a considerable sum; for in addition to what was due for salvage, my monthly allowance had always been remitted by my father, although, after the award to me of a share in the salvage, I had released him from his promise to make me an allowance.

The time of parting came at last. It was with a heavy heart, although I was going home, that I bade the captain, George, and the men, good-bye. The captain's whole family came to the wharf to see us off in the boat which carried us to the ship. I promised the captain and George that I would often write to them, and assured them of how gladly, at some future time, I would seize an opportunity to visit them in our old haunts. I went through the final shaking of hands, jumped into the boat, and waved my handkerchief from the ship, as long as my friends were within sight.

Soon we were on the broad ocean. Nearly one year before, I had left home, an unwilling voyager, sailing away into that unknown, mysterious world which I had longed to see, and which, when the opportunity offered, was by circumstances divested of all the charms with which to my fancy it had been endowed. Through what strange vicissitudes of fortune had I not passed!

Not a cloud now obscured the serenity of my mind. The breeze all day seemed to whisper the word, Home. The crests of the swiftly-gliding waves seemed to peer at me over the bulwarks, and murmur, Home.

Mrs. Brenton was terribly prostrated by sea-sickness. Julia, after a slight attack, recovered, and was not again affected by it during the voyage. At night, we two paced the deck, arm in arm, conversing in tones subdued by the influence of the mighty deep.

One moonlight night, just before we reached New York, we were thus pacing up and down the deck. The slight figure of my companion moved gracefully at my side. I was so enthralled by the loveliness of the scene, and the discourse of Julia, that I wished that the spell might endure forever.

"Julia," said I suddenly. "I must give you some memento by which you can recall my connection with the strange adventure through which you have just passed."

"I can never forget your connection with it," she replied, "for you saved our lives. I need no other."

"But I wish to make you a present of something which I have, that will be safer in your possession, and more appropriate too, than in mine. Wait and you shall see it."

I went to the cabin, and brought back the box containing my shell basket. Carefully lifting out the basket, I deposited it on a seat, that it might be seen to the best advantage. The moonbeams shone brightly on the clusters of pearly flowers, and on the delicate trembling tendrils.

"Is it not beautiful!" said we both at once, stooping, at the same time, to examine it more closely.

Julia's curls grazed my check. As she raised her head, blushingly conscious of the accident, I said:

"All that I ask in return is the least bit for a locket."

Reader, you think that this was the beginning of a love affair, the sequel to which, after some years, was that Julia and I were married. You forget that I said I was an old bachelor. I am. Therefore, I did not marry Julia, although I did save her from drowning. We parted. You and I must also part.

As I write these words, which are some of a very few yet to be written, I feel a sadness steal over me. The gaslight in my room seems to grow dim, and, as I glance around, I feel as if I were about to be more solitary than I have been of late.

Over the arm of yonder sofa hangs the skin of the male panther (we never got the other one), and, on the mantlepiece, are a few branching corals that serve for decoration, and to recall the past. For your amusement, and mine, I have written the story that I promised, but as yours commences, my own must cease. For a brief space, I have been a boy, but as I lay down my pen, I am again a lonely old bachelor.

THE END